By Sabrina A. Eubanks

PO Box 247378
Columbus, OH 43224
www.TripleCrownPublications.com

Library of Congress Control Number: 2011920067
ISBN: 978-0-9825888-4-0

Author: Sabrina Eubanks
Photography and Design: Treagen Kier
Editor-in-Chief: Vickie Stringer
Editorial Team: Marian Nealy, Christopher Means
Editorial Assistant: Caitlin McLellan

First Trade Paperback Edition Printing 2011

10 9 8 7 6 5 4 3 2 1

Printed in the United States of America

To my brother Julius James Eubanks Jr. My first best friend.
We’re still here. Much love.

Acknowledgements

Dear Heavenly Father:

It goes without saying that my deepest thanks go to God. Through Him all things are possible. My faith in Him is endless and sincere. I'm nothing without Him.

My parents Mary and Julius Sr. Thank you for providing the framework. I miss you guys so much. You are both gone too soon. I love you still.

Thanks to my brother, Julius Jr. for always holding me down. You've been my biggest supporter and my harshest critic. Thanks for the love, Bro. Thanks to my wonderful little son, Derrick Jr. You are the light of my life and the joy in my world. You'll never know how much I love you. Love to my niece and nephew, Jayson and Joli.

To my family. Aunt Kadie you are priceless. Aunt Elias, who loves so hard behind the scenes. Uncle June, I don't have to tell you, you already know. All the rest of my uncles and aunts and cousins, you all know who you are and what you mean to me. Love you all.

Shout outs to very special friends. Vera, thanks for everything. I love you very much and you know why. Brenda, keep smiling and laughing. It will carry you through the roughest times. Mad love. Desiree, remember … when you're a Jet, you're a Jet all the way. To my oldest friends, Vickie, Barbara, and all the rest of y'all, love you my forever friends. Shout out to Dr. B. Lewin. Thanks for always being there- I told you before you're one of my favorite people. Craig, you're my homie for life. Thanks Mrs. Davis for being so cool.

To all my TA people, y'all know who you are, thanks for holding me down! Mad love crazy respect!

Thanks, Brian, for some zingy one-liners.

Thanks to NYPD officers Ian Knight and Christopher Dent for helping me with the technical stuff.

Rest in peace to those who were lost. Bernice and Felicia. We'll cherish the memories and love you always. A special shout to one of my biggest fans and sweetest friends, whom I lost tragically. My friend Mohammed. I love you Mo. Rest in peace.

To everyone on my fan page. Love y'all for real. Thank you so much for your faith and support.

To my editors, Caitlin McLellan and Marian Nealy. Thanks for the valuable insight, and thanks for making my editing such an easy process. You both are a joy.

Finally, to Ms. Vickie Stringer for seeing something special in me and giving me a chance. Thanks for the faith, Vickie. God bless you.

If I didn't mention you by name, know that you're in my heart.

Time for the huge shout out to the Readers. GOD BLESS THE READERS!!!

Did you hear me?

Chapter One

Night Terrors

Lucas Cain was stuck in a nightmare that made no sense. He was caught in a funhouse that was full of twists and turns, but no discernable exits. There were dogs chasing him. He could hear their low growls and their pattering feet. Worst of all, he could smell them. Lucas hated dogs. No … that really wasn't true. He was terrified of them. He had been since he was a little kid.

He was winding his way through a contorted hallway, holding a TEC-9, with his detective's badge hanging from his neck. A door popped open on his left — a door that hadn't been there a second earlier — and Simone Bainbridge stepped out. She was naked, sultry and beautiful. Simone smiled at him and beckoned to him with her finger.

"C'mon, Lucas. You know you want it," she said, enticingly licking her lips.

Lucas frowned at her and pulled the trigger. Lucas probably hated the memory of Simone more than he hated dogs. She disappeared with a puff of smoke instead of a splash of blood and gore. Lucas wasn't surprised. He was a rational man, and he was dreaming, after all.

Oscar Tirado, one of the dirtiest cops in NYPD history — and the bastard who'd blown their cover — staggered across Lucas's field of vision, holding his own head in his hands. The Trinidad brothers, Tate and Troy, had decapitated him when he gave them up to the feds. Oscar was a ghastly apparition, with his bloody stump of a neck glowing eerily in the strange light of this bad dream.

Lucas raised his gun to send him on his way. The head in Oscar's hands looked at him with dead and doleful eyes.

"I didn't mean for things to go this far," the lifeless mouth said, and then smiled a gruesome smile. "Guess I lost my head."

"Blast him, Luke," Noah said from somewhere behind him. Lucas pulled the trigger of his gun and sent Oscar to meet Simone in the hell they shared.

"Nice shot. Keep movin', Luke. Hurry up and get us outta this place. I can't stay here," Noah said, from just over his shoulder — like he was right behind him. Lucas turned quickly to check for him … but Noah wasn't there. There was nothing behind him but pitch blackness.

Lucas turned a buckling corner and was faced with two sets of short, weird stairs. One way went up, the other went down. He hesitated for a moment.

"Up, Luke. We gotta go up. Down's no good," Noah's disembodied voice said, urgently. "Hurry up, bro. You're wastin' time. Move, Luke."

Lucas trotted up the stairs. There was an open doorway at the top, just as dark as the blackness behind him. Troy Trinidad popped out of it, unexpectedly, like he was spring-loaded, wielding that fucking machete he used to scalp people. The same machete he'd tried to attack Noah with after he'd shot him three times.

Lucas blew his ass away without a second thought. Again, he wasn't surprised when whatever Troy's ghost was made of dissipated in a funky curl of green vapor. He was what he was, Lucas guessed.

Lucas kept moving. He walked up a rickety, spiraling staircase. The boards didn't seem quite solid. They threatened to give way with each step he took. He faltered at the top as his foot sunk three inches into the riser. He grabbed the railing and pulled his foot out of the soft, unrealistic wood. It made a small sucking sound that gave him the creeps.

"That's nothin', bro. Can you deal with the shit at the top of the stairs?" No sooner than that scary, bodiless Noah-voice asked the question, a door at the top of the stairs was thrown open. A light shone out of it, so bright it almost blinded him.

Justine stepped out of the light. She was smiling at him and holding something in her hand. Lucas took a step back and tucked his lips in. He ran his hand over his beard and stared at her. He hadn't seen her in a long time, not even in his dreams. Lucas figured this wasn't the day for surprises — because he wasn't surprised to find he still loved her. He probably always would.

"Justine." Her name felt strange on his lips. He hadn't said it in so long. Nicole was his love now. Why wasn't she here? Where was she?

"She's hurt, but she's alive, Luke. All these people here are dead. Can't you see that?" Noah's voice spoke plainly.

The hair stood up at the nape of Lucas's neck. "Yeah? Then where are you, Noah? How come I can't see you?"

"I ain't really here, Luke," Noah replied. Irritation was edging into his voice. "Stay focused, bro. She's got somethin' I need. Get it away from her. Don't let her keep it, or I'm stuck here. Hurry up, Luke!"

Lucas looked back at Justine. She was beautiful. She always was. But her smile abruptly turned into a frown, and suddenly she wasn't so pretty.

"I hate what you did to us, Lucas. It was all your fault. Look what you did to me." Her face changed in an instant, from lovely to decaying like paper. Her beautiful eyes shrank back into her skull and her lips stretched grotesquely over her teeth.

"Oh, God," Lucas said in horror. He took another step back, but someone who wasn't there pushed him forward like a strong phantom.

"Fuck that! Don't let her keep it. I ain't stayin' here. Go get it! It's mine!" Noah yelled at him.

Justine held the object in her hand high over her head. It swung on its chain and glittered in the bright light, snug in its leather case. Lucas knew what it was immediately. It started to beep like a small gold bomb.

Lucas reached for it. "What are you doing with that? It's not yours. Give it back!"

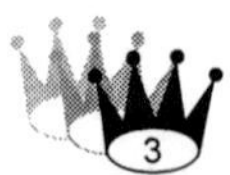

Justine laughed, and it was like nails dragging across a chalkboard. "Come get it, Lucas!"

She flung it over the railing of the stairway into nothingness. Lucas dropped his gun and leapt after it instinctively. His fingers closed around it, and now it was beeping louder. He fell into the void, falling fast, clutching Noah's badge in his hand.

Lucas came awake with a disoriented jolt. The first thing he felt was the tendrils of agony in his forearms and the crisp pain in his neck. It took him a moment to remember that he was hurt. His mind wasn't as sharp as it should have been, because they'd given him something for the pain.

Leah Wheeler was standing over him, still pretty in her heartbreak. Her hand was on his shoulder. "You okay, Lucas?"

Lucas sat up in the chair he'd been sleeping in and looked around. He got up and sat at the foot of the bed that held Nicole. She was asleep with an IV drip in her right hand. A machine that monitored her heart rate beeped sharply in the corner. That's where the sound from the dream had come from.

Everything came crashing back all at once. Oscar Tirado had blown their cover with the Trinidads. He'd paid with his life, but it had cost them plenty. Nicole and Tony Colletti had gotten shot up pretty badly in Tate Trinidad's last-ditch effort not to be defeated. They'd set their dogs on Lucas, and Nick had shot him in the forearm trying to get them off. He also had a graze on his neck from an errant bullet.

Noah. Noah had gotten the worst of it. Troy had shot him three times: once, point blank in the chest. Lucas vividly remembered Noah crashing right before his eyes, and him feeling utterly helpless. He stood up and realized he was holding Noah's badge in his hand.

"Lucas?" Leah was looking at him, her brow creased with worry.

Lucas looked down at Noah's badge. He'd gotten it away from her, he thought, with a certain knowledge he was being irrational. Maybe Noah would be okay. He slipped Noah's badge around his neck and it laid there with its little dots of Noah's blood next to his own.

"I'm okay," he said, looking at Leah. "Any word?"

"They're bringing him up from surgery."

Lucas sighed deeply and looked at Nicole, who seemed to be holding her own. He put his arm around Leah's shoulders and led her out of the room. It was time to go check for Noah. Lucas was scared for his old friend. Scared to death.

Chapter Two

Who's That Girl

Nadine knew she was going to die. She felt her knees buckling even as she tried to run. Her heart was pounding toward what seemed an ultimate explosion, and she was trying desperately to catch her breath. She knew she was having a full-fledged panic attack. Captain Myers himself had her by the arm. He'd come and rung her doorbell, personally, to tell her the news she prayed everyday not to hear. Just hours ago she'd begged Noah to be careful and he'd made some stupid joke. Now he was.

She stepped into the elevator with Captain Myers and the DEA Agent — *Griffin,* she thought his name was — and rode silently up to ICU. The elevator opened onto a sea of cops with sad faces. They were *everywhere,* lining the walls in tragic clusters. They were keeping vigil for their own, praying, and trying to send them their strength. Nadine didn't recognize any of them, but they stopped talking amongst themselves in their hushed voices, and nodded respectfully as they passed — like they recognized *her*.

Nadine had Myers in a death clutch as she leaned against him heavily. Griffin had her by the other arm. She thought of her children. When Myers rang the doorbell, Nadine passed out cold at the news. When she came to, Noah and Raine had been hysterical. They were with her sister now. Noah Jr. wanted to come with her, but she didn't want him to see Noah like this. Hell, *she* didn't want to see Noah like this.

They neared the end of the hallway, and she saw Lucas standing just outside Noah's door like a sentry. Lucas was like a life preserver in that sea of blue. He walked toward her, looking exhausted, with his lips tucked in, frowning with worry. One arm was in a sling while the other was heavily bandaged. There was another small dressing on his neck. His face, arms, and hands were covered with scattered scrapes and contusions.

Lucas wasn't his usual, quietly expensive dapper self. There were no tastefully tailored threads today. Instead, Lucas was wearing a black heavy metal T-shirt that was a size too small. That would have been funny under a different set of circumstances, but at the moment it horrified Nadine. She vaguely wondered what had been on his shirt that made him want to take it off. Despite their tumultuous history, his presence was the one she was most thankful for. Lucas reached her and looked down at her with enormously sad eyes that looked like they'd been crying.

Nadine's breath hitched in her throat. "Lucas."

She collapsed into his arms and he held her tight. Nadine cried into his chest without shame until she could pull herself together. Until she had enough to go on. She pulled away from him slowly, careful of his arm that wore the sling. Myers had his hand on Lucas' shoulder, his eyes full of sympathy. Griffin had his hands clasped in front of him, studying his shoes.

A doctor came out of Noah's room and Nadine was suddenly nauseous. She had absolutely no desire to hear what he had to say.

Lucas looked down at her and took her arm. "Nadine, are you ready?" he asked in a quiet voice.

Hell no! She wanted to scream back at him, but she couldn't seem to get her mouth to work. She nodded against her will and turned to face the doctor, a tall, toffee-colored man, with salt-and-pepper hair and kind brown eyes.

"Mrs. Ramsey?"

Nadine nodded and he extended his hand. She took it like she was sleepwalking.

"I'm Dr. Garrett. I performed your husband's surgery."

Nadine felt like there was no moisture left in her mouth at all. She couldn't answer him if she tried. Nadine leaned into Lucas and nodded.

"I have to be honest with you, Mrs. Ramsey. When your husband got here, he was an absolute mess. He was shot twice in the torso. One bullet fractured his left collarbone, travelled downward a bit and exited through his shoulder blade. It looked messy, but it was fairly clean. The second went through his sternum. It ricocheted through his left lung and collapsed it ... then it moved upward and nicked his aorta."

Nadine gasped and put her hand over her mouth. The doctor put a calming hand on her arm as he finished what he was saying. "Mrs. Ramsey, I'm one of the best heart surgeons you can get, and I performed the surgery myself. Your husband is tough. He's a fighter. The nick in his aorta had him bleeding out internally — and the collapsed lung wasn't helping. He crashed twice on his way here, then he went into shock ... but he held on long enough to get to me. I closed the hole immediately. Right now, we're trying to wait and see how everything goes. The heart should no longer be a problem, unless something unforeseeable happens. We don't want him developing any fluid on his lungs."

"Is he going to be okay?" Nadine asked shakily.

Dr. Garrett put his hands on his hips and sighed. "Well ... barring he doesn't develop fluid on his lungs — or any other adverse situations," he said, nodding slowly, "I think eventually he'll be fine, but it will take a while."

"How have you graded his condition?" Lucas asked.

Dr. Garrett gave Lucas a cursory look, his eyes lingering on the arm not in a sling. "No longer grave. Critical and guarded. You his partner?"

Lucas nodded. "Yes, I am."

Dr. Garrett nodded and turned back to Nadine. "He's in rough shape and he doesn't look very much like you're probably used to seeing him. He has some facial wounds, which we cleaned and dressed. They should heal well. He was shot in the left hand and it chipped the bone in his knuckle. That's in a soft cast. His left arm is in a sling because of the collarbone break. Oh, and his left leg is in a cast and traction. He was shot in that leg, as well, and he's got a fracture in his femur and a dislocated kneecap."

"Oh, my God," Nadine whispered.

He nodded. "I agree. Your husband looks like he was in a war, Mrs.

Ramsey." He cast a disgusted glance at Captain Myers.

Myers looked at him. "He was, Doctor."

They stared at each other for a moment, then Dr. Garrett turned back to Nadine. "You can see him, if you're ready." He put his hand on Lucas's unslung arm. "You need to get that looked at. You're not supposed to be bleeding. How did that happen?"

Lucas shrugged. "Doesn't matter. I wasn't very cooperative."

Dr. Garrett smiled, then looked at Nadine. "You guys got kids?"

"Yes. A boy and a girl."

"Don't worry, Mrs. Ramsey. He's in extremely good hands. I'm on call until he's out of the woods."

Nadine managed a smile of her own. "Thank you, Dr. Garrett."

"You're welcome. Go on in and see your husband." He touched Lucas' shoulder and gave Myers that same glowering look. "This man looks like he's been in a war, too. Don't forget about your arm, sir." He turned on his heel and walked down the hall.

Nadine looked at Lucas. "Have you been in yet?"

Lucas passed his free hand over his beard. "No. They just brought him up, not too long ago. You want me to go with you?"

"I think I need you to."

"All right." Lucas put his arm around her and shouldered the door open slowly.

The first thing they saw was a perfectly nice little table, with a perfectly lovely vase of tulips sitting on its surface. Lucas ducked his head around the door and Nadine watched his face change.

His eyebrows went up, just a little. He blinked, then closed his eyes … like he wanted to erase what he'd just seen. Lucas opened his eyes and took a step further into the room. The look on his face was alarming because Nadine had never seen it before. He looked like he was trying hard not to cry. Nadine stepped around him and looked at Noah. She put her hands on the bed railing and started to weep.

Noah was on his back with four different machines monitoring him. He had a tube in his mouth and an oxygen tube under his nose. Noah had stitches over his eyebrow and his cheek was lightly bandaged. There was a smattering of lesser abrasions scattered across his face. The left side suffered the worst damage: the skin was bruised

and swollen, to a shade that was almost purple. That eye was shut. The other eye didn't appear to be completely closed; Nadine could almost swear she saw a whisper of gray. His lashes were damp like he'd been crying.

There was a huge and ugly bruise flowering up from the bandages that covered his chest and shoulder. It seemed to be five different colors. One arm was in a sling and covered in a soft cast. His leg was also in a cast and in traction.

Nadine looked down at his other hand laying limply on the bed, with an IV drip inserted into it. She frowned as she began to notice the little things. There was blood between his fingers, under his nails, and in his hair. Noah's lips were terribly chapped and there was an unnerving bluish tinge under his eyes. Nadine let out a shaky breath and looked over at Lucas. He was staring at Noah, arms across his chest, his head lowered.

"Lucas ... he looks ... ." Nadine couldn't bring herself to say it, but Lucas did.

"Dead," he said, flatly.

There it was. He wasn't though. She thanked God for that. Yes, he was alive, and even though he looked like he wasn't, he was in there somewhere. Nadine wiped at her tears and gently took Noah's hand. She leaned over and spoke in his ear.

"Noah? Sweetheart, it's Nadine. I'm here, and I love you very much. Can you hear me, baby?"

Lucas moved closer and stood just behind her. "Nadine, look at him. I don't think he can hear you." Nadine concentrated on Noah's face, ignoring Lucas, even though he could have been right.

"Noah ..." She kissed his forehead. "It's me, baby ..."

"Nadine ..."

Nadine whipped her head around angrily. "No, Lucas! Stop it! Don't act like that. Look ... he's right here." She ran her fingers through Noah's hair and gingerly gripped his hand. "Noah, how worried should I be, sweetie?"

Lucas put a hand on her back. "C'mon, Nadine ..."

Nadine shrugged him off. She was terrified for Noah. "No! I'm scared ... Noah ... do you know how much I love you?"

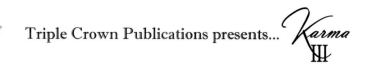

Lucas put a hand on her arm and started to move her away, gently. "Stop, Nadine. Don't do that."

She turned on him, eyes flashing, tears falling. Nadine pulled away from Lucas, slapping at his hand. "Shut up, Lucas! You don't know …"

"Let him be, Nadine." She thought that had come from Lucas, but it didn't. She looked over her shoulder and Big John was standing there looking very much like a brown-eyed older version of his son. Noah's mother, Anita, was at his side, looking like she was ready to catch Nadine if she fell.

"Come, Nadine," Anita said. Nadine wanted to, but she couldn't. She wanted Noah to wake up and look at her. Maybe squeeze her hand. She wanted him to do *something*. Just lying there like that was scaring the shit out of her. She didn't budge.

John turned to Lucas and hugged him. "Lucas, how you doin', son? You all right?" he twanged at him in his New Orleans drawl.

"A little banged up, John. But I'm all right."

John sighed. "I think it's about time for you boys to quit bein' heroes." He turned to Nadine and put his hand on her arm. "Come on, baby. Go sit down, now. I ain't toleratin' no hysterics in here over my boy. It ain't what he needs. Go on. Sit down, now."

Nadine was not about to argue with John. She'd never win. She touched Noah's face and was dismayed by how cold it felt. She sat like she was told.

John stuck his thumbs in the back pockets of his jeans and stared down at his son. Anita disappeared into the bathroom and came out with a basin of water and a towel. She sat on the side of the bed and started to wash the blood off her boy. Lucas's eyes watered up. He tucked his lips in and turned away, looking out the window.

"Look at my child. Lord have mercy," John said mournfully, shaking his head.

"He will, John," Anita said over her shoulder. Dr. Garrett walked into the room then, greeted Noah's parents, and gave them the rundown.

Nadine stood and joined them. "Why won't he wake up?"

Dr. Garrett looked down at her and smiled. "Don't look so worried. He will."

Nadine shook her head. "It's like he's not even here."

Dr. Garrett laughed softly. "He's not. I sent him to Dreamland. When he wakes up, he's going to be in a great deal of pain and I might have to send him back." He checked Noah's vital signs and seemed satisfied. "I know this is pretty heavy stuff. Why don't you all take a break? I'll make sure Noah's here when you get back."

They reluctantly started to disperse, but Dr. Garrett put his hand on Lucas' shoulder. "Not you, Noah's partner. You come with me. I'm going to change your dressing myself, before you find yourself in a lot of trouble."

They took a break. Nadine checked on the kids, bought some flowers, and begged off dinner with John and Anita. Nadine and Noah had gone through a bitter divorce four years ago because Noah, as cherished as he was by Nadine, refused to keep his pants up. Now Nadine was getting some long and strange looks from Noah's folks, and rightfully so. Since the divorce, Nadine had treated Noah like she hated him. She couldn't sit through dinner with his parents and suffer through those looks, because now she was behaving like she was still in love with him. Which she was.

Nadine had never stopped loving Noah. She didn't think it was possible. Sure, she'd felt a genuine hate for him when she first divorced him. Noah's constant infidelity was an insurmountable issue at the time. She'd let him know in every way possible that having her husband sleep with any pretty woman that caught his eye was unacceptable behavior. But Noah, who'd been a handsome chick magnet all his life, refused to change. He acted like it was his God-given right to fuck as many women as he pleased. After all, he came home to *her*. Nadine had divorced Noah to punish him. *Fuck you, then*, she had thought back then. *Screw whoever you want, Noah, but you won't be screwing me, too.*

The divorce had hurt Noah as much as she'd hoped it would. She'd wanted him to be in the worst pain of his life for humiliating and disregarding her for so long, like it was all right. Nadine had succeeded, too. She'd filed the papers silently, without a word to Noah. Then she'd caught him totally off guard by having him served at work — in front of everybody. She'd threatened his whorish ass before and he'd kept on doing what he was doing like he thought hell would freeze over before she'd leave him.

She'd fixed him, though. Nadine had brought Noah to his knees like she'd given him a swift kick to the balls. To say he hadn't taken it well would have been the understatement of the decade. She'd had his shit packed up and waiting for him at the front door when he got home.

Noah was hardly ever highly emotional. When things bothered him he usually brooded or acted unaffected. It was a rare thing for him to put his emotions on display, but he did *that* day. He'd screamed, he pleaded, and he'd begged. He'd cursed and thrown things ... and in the end, he'd cried like a little baby — and she'd laughed in his face. *Fuck you, Noah. I hope all those bitches were worth your marriage*. It had almost killed her to do it, but she'd done it.

Noah hadn't stayed stuck on begging her. Noah Ramsey didn't beg women. After all that screaming and crying, the next time she saw him, he was so cold to her she expected an ice cube to fall out of his mouth. Nadine had been shocked at his level of frigidity. After she'd slapped him with those papers and Nadine hadn't given in when he broke down, talking to Noah became like talking to him through a sheet of ice. He wouldn't even look at her.

That coldness from Noah had hurt Nadine almost as much as his infidelity. Noah didn't even want to see her. When he came for the kids, he wouldn't even come inside. He wanted no parts of Nadine... and it hurt. The divorce was an ultimatum to make him change. To make him want to. The only thing Nadine had achieved by divorcing Noah was driving him away.

She'd already hurt his pride and damaged his humongous ego. She couldn't possibly stay in that much pain alone. Noah didn't seem affected enough to her. She wanted him on his knees like she was.

Nadine thought she'd get a rise out of Noah by going for his pockets. She got a lawyer and asked for what she knew was an unreasonable amount of alimony and child support. She knew she wouldn't get what she wanted when she filed the papers. Nadine pulled her fair share of financial weight around the house. She was a successful photographer with her own studio. As a matter of fact, that was how she'd met Noah. She'd seen him one day and asked if she could take his picture.

Noah had shown up to that hearing with his own slick lawyer. The judge dropped the petition for alimony, and awarded her reasonable child support. Noah hadn't even looked at her during the entire hearing, but when he stood to leave, he looked over at her and smirked, his beautiful gray eyes dark and stormy. He let her know he knew she'd tried to fuck him and he was thumbing his nose at her.

Nadine didn't appreciate the gesture. She wanted to wipe that cute crooked smile off his handsome face once and for all, and she knew just how to do it. She went back to court and filed a petition for sole custody of their kids, with restricted and supervised visitation. She knew she probably wouldn't win that one either. Noah, if he was anything, was an outstanding father.

She'd gotten a rise out of him all right. She'd finally really hurt him. Their kids meant the world to Noah. He'd called her in the middle of the night, upset, and more than a little drunk. She still remembered exactly what he'd said, *"Nadine, please. I'm sorry a thousand times. Please don't take my kids from me. Please don't do that."* Nadine also remembered exactly what she'd said to him. *"Fuck you, Noah. See you in court."*

Nadine looked over at Noah now, heart her full of regret. She should never have divorced Noah. They should have tried to work it out. She wished she could take back that nasty custody hearing. She'd stabbed him in the heart with that one, and though it was long and drawn out, they'd ended up getting joint custody anyway because he'd fought her so hard.

It had taken them almost a year to get back on speaking terms after that. Noah was slow to thaw and so was she. Eventually, they'd reached the point of polite conversation, though it was mostly tinged with acid and sarcasm on both sides. Too much hurt had gone on. Too many things they couldn't forgive each other for. Still, they were talking.

Nadine started dating Walter as filler. Filler for Noah. Walter was a good and decent man, but he couldn't hold a candle to Noah. Nobody could. Nadine lost count long ago how many times Walter made love to her in his decently average way and she'd imagined in her heart it was Noah — unbridled, raw, and completely satisfying. Poor Walter fell short every time. Nadine had been trying to figure out a way to get her husband back, when the kids started coming home from weekends spent with their father talking about some bitch named Lissette.

Noah was a womanizer, but he didn't bring those women around his kids. If they were starting to talk about this bitch, then she was important. Nadine held her tongue and bided her time. She figured this whore, Lissette, would eventually get as tired of Noah's need to fuck other people as she'd gotten herself. No such luck. That slut had dug her heels in and gotten Noah to get her pregnant. She was pregnant *now*.

Lissette's pregnancy had gotten Nadine's ass in gear. Sure Noah had fucked around on her with an inestimable number of women, but Lissette was real competition because she was carrying his child. That bitch could actually take Noah away from her! Nadine had to stop her.

There was one sure way of doing that. Granted, it was the oldest trick in the book. It hadn't been hard to get Noah to sleep with her. After all, she was — at least up until now — the love of his life. Now Nadine finally knew how it felt to be the other woman. Noah was cheating on Lissette with his ex-wife. He'd found out Nadine was pregnant, too, the day before this horrible thing had happened to him. Now he had no choice but to choose. Nadine had no doubt that she'd win.

Nadine thought of all these things as she watched Noah's heart beat blip across the monitor. She loved Noah, and she didn't want to lose him. Nadine lost her train of thought as the door opened and someone walked in.

It was a woman, a little less than average height, with a nice curvy figure. She was very pretty, with stylishly short hair. Nadine frowned, but relaxed some when she saw the 9mm clipped next to the detective badge on her belt. People had been in and out of Noah's room all day. She was just another cop looking in on him.

Nadine still didn't think anything of it when she saw that she was crying — she'd seen a lot of that today, but when she ran her fingers through Noah's curly hair and bent to kiss his face, Nadine sat straight up in her chair. She watched as the woman picked up Noah's hand, kissed it, and held it to her face. It was one hell of an intimate gesture. Nadine stood and quietly walked up on her.

"Excuse me, but who the hell are you?" Nadine asked, one hand on her hip, her eyes sizing her up. The woman took her time answering her. She gently returned Noah's hand to the bed and turned to face Nadine, wiping her tears with her fingers. A small smile curved her lips.

"You must be his ex-wife ... Naomi."

Nadine's eyebrows went up. *No, this bitch didn't!* Nadine folded her arms over her chest and shifted her weight to one foot. "That's *exactly* who I am. Mrs. Nadine Ramsey. I'll ask my question again. Who the hell are you?"

That small smile was still on her face. Nadine bit her bottom lip. She wanted to scratch that smile off with her fingernails. She felt herself starting to sink. She wanted to dig her heels in to keep from going there, but her downward slide to a lower level had already begun and to come back would be like trying to climb out of quicksand.

"You're holding on to an old title a little too hard, Nadine. It's a lot like Miss America trying to keep the tiara from the new girl."

Nadine narrowed her eyes. "What new girl? *You?*"

The woman kept her sweet smile and shrugged. "You never know."

Nadine had to tuck her hands under her arms to keep from hitting her. "I'm not going to ask you again. Who *are* you?"

Her smile became derisive. "You just did." She gave Nadine the same once-over she'd given her. "I'm wondering if I should take that as a threat."

"Maybe you should."

She laughed and it infuriated Nadine. "You're funny. You want to beat my ass because I won't tell you my name. What difference does it make?"

Nadine wanted to rip her hair out by the roots. "Are you fucking my husband?"

Another chuckle. "You're divorced. Noah's not your husband. Does it matter?"

"Oh, it matters. Noah married *me*."

She scoffed at her. "You're delusional. He's a single man. He can do whatever he wants."

Nadine frowned. "Noah wants to come home."

She looked back at Nadine, slyly. "He doesn't know what he wants. That, plus the fact that he's single, makes it fair."

"What are you, his girlfriend?"

The more upset Nadine got, the cooler this woman seemed. "Well … I'm a girl … and I *am* his friend. You'd have to ask *him* about the extent of his feelings." She looked Nadine in the eye. "Look, I'm a realist, Nadine. I might have started out as a side piece, but you're a little peculiar. I think I may be about to get bumped up."

Nadine smiled. "Noah's not bumping up a side piece. You're just a hoe to him. Just something he was doing."

"You really want that to be true, don't you?"

"It is true, and while you're so busy telling me things I need to ask him, why don't you ask him about his baby?"

She dismissed Nadine with a wave of her hand. "Please. I know that girl is pregnant."

"I'm sure you do, but I doubt he had enough time to tell you about *our* baby." Nadine patted her belly in triumph. *Top that, bitch!* Nadine finally ruffled her feathers. She looked down at Noah sharply and Nadine knew she'd drawn first blood. She took a moment to come back at her. Nadine watched with satisfaction as she gripped the rail of the bed, stared down at Noah and pursed her lips — obviously having an internal debate. Nadine didn't like who won.

"You know something?" she asked, turning her head to face Nadine. "I don't give a rat's ass if you are. That's one of the oldest tricks in the book. Don't you think he knows that? You lack confidence, Nadine. The move you made is an ultimate show of desperation."

Nadine stared at her with her mouth open. She couldn't believe her audacity! Talking to her like she was stupid, and like she had Noah's affections sewn up and in the bag. Where had this heifer come from?

Nadine clenched her teeth and fisted her hands. "I think you need to leave."

She smiled at Nadine. "Guess I struck a nerve. Okay. I'll go, but not for you. Noah doesn't need to wake up to this." She walked to the door, opened it, and turned back to Nadine. "Oh, since you wanted to know so bad, my name is Leah Wheeler. Now that you know my name, I should tell you something else about me. I am very tenacious … so you might want to keep your dukes up."

Nadine watched the door close and walked over to Noah. She reached into her pocket and took out a new tube of Cherry ChapStick and broke the seal. Nadine put it on Noah's lips, careful not to disturb the tube going down his throat. She returned it to her pocket and pulled his covers up. Nadine touched his hand. If it was a fight that bitch wanted, then it was a fight she'd get.

"I love you, Noah. Always have, always will."

The door opened and Noah's parents re-entered the room. John pulled up a chair and sat close to his son as Anita reached for Nadine. "You look tired, honey. Why don't you check on the children and get some rest. If there's any change, we'll call you."

Nadine resigned herself to lifting her leg all the way up to mark her territory. She rubbed her still flat belly. "You're right. I *am* tired. This baby is taking a lot out of me."

John put his face in his hands and shook his head. Anita didn't seem thrilled. "Does Noah know?"

Nadine nodded. "Yes, he does."

Anita's mouth turned down at the corners. "I see."

Nadine sighed. "The baby's Noah's, Anita. It's his baby."

Anita looked shocked, and John stretched his legs out and laced his hands over his stomach, still shaking his head. "If that boy wasn't already unconscious, I'd knock his dumb ass out."

"John ... " Anita started.

"I told him. Boy never did listen." He looked at Nadine hard, his brown eyes glowering. "'Night, Nadine."

Nadine slipped out quietly after wishing them both a good night. John and Anita didn't bother her. Their disapproval of the way she intended to keep her man was a small thing. They'd come around in time. In the meantime, her plate was more than full. Now she had to find a way to keep not one, but two, bitches's claws out of Noah.

Chapter Three

Pleading the Fifth

Leah had never in her life wanted to slap the taste out of someone's mouth as badly as she wanted to slap Nadine. She wasn't privy to the inner workings of their failed marriage, but if what Nadine had shown her was any indication of her true personality, she couldn't blame Noah if he'd chosen to stray. She sighed and got out of her car. If Nadine said anything greasy to her today, she was going to let her ass have it; she didn't care if Noah had just started to come around, whose parents were there, or how pregnant her ass was. She was gettin' it. Little condescending, stuck-up, crazy bitch.

Leah walked into the Starbucks across the street from the hospital and picked up some snacks. She had a feeling Lucas hadn't thought ahead to feeding himself. He was too busy dividing his time between Nick, Noah, and Tony. The last time she'd seen him, he'd been asleep with his head on Nick's bed, using his hurt arms for a pillow. Nick had been asleep, too, with her fingers in his hair. Leah smiled to herself. It had been an especially sweet and touching moment in the midst of so much sadness.

Leah paid for her stuff and was starting to shift her mood out of the funk Nadine had put her in, when someone touched her arm.

"You need some help with that?"

Startled, Leah turned and found herself looking into the pudgy, fatherly face of Butch Harper. Leah was surprised to see him, but she gave him the bag of goodies and pushed the door open. "Sure, thanks Butch. Should I say it's nice to see you, or should I not be sure yet?"

Butch was I.A. Not everybody in Internal Affairs was an asshole or a robot with a busted attitude. Some people had compassion and weren't willing to get your ass with no grease — guilty or not. Butch was pretty much one of those people. Still, to see him at all was enough cause to make you queasy. He was a nice man, but he rarely made social calls. *Someone* was about to get reamed out.

Butch laughed jovially as he crossed the street with her. "I'm not *that* bad, am I?"

Leah smiled at him. "No, you're a sweet guy, Butch. You make things a little easier."

He laughed and his eyes twinkled as he held the door for her. "Well, you know what they say, 'a spoonful of sugar helps the medicine go down.'"

"Yeah, so they say."

Butch followed her down the hall to the bank of elevators, making small talk. When Leah reached out to push the button, Butch stepped in front of her. "You know, Leah, I really gotta tell you how sorry I am that so many of the people you're close to got hurt. I truly am. Thank God everybody's got the chance to recover." He paused and offered her a regretful smile. "Unfortunately, something has come to my attention that I have to talk to you about."

Leah's eyes got big and she pointed to herself. "*Me?* What did I do?"

"You're not the only one I need to talk to. I need to have a word with Ramsey, Cain, and Hardaway, too. *Especially* Hardaway." What the hell was he talking about?

Leah frowned. "What do you mean, 'especially Hardaway?' Why do you want to talk to the four of us? What do you think we've done?"

Butch rang for the elevator himself and smiled. "I thought I was the one who asked too many questions. What floor?"

"Five," Leah said. Why on earth were they sending I.A. down on them? Shit, they'd risked their lives to bring Draco down. What kind of bullshit was this?

Butch smiled serenely as the doors slid closed. "It always happens this way. Now you're not so pleased to see me."

"If it bothers you, maybe you should change departments."

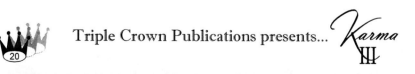

Butch raised an eyebrow at the barb, then he chuckled. "I would, Leah, but it gives me indescribable pleasure to witness a truly bad cop come to the end of the road."

Leah dropped her head. Nick had been her partner for eight years. She didn't believe it was Nick. It *damned sure* wasn't her. Noah? Lucas? That just couldn't be. Noah and Lucas were highly decorated First Grade Detectives. They didn't do bullshit detail. They were reserved for the most dangerous jobs, because they got the job done. Rookies aspired to be like them. Everybody wanted to work with them. They were the goddamn Rock Stars, for Christ's sake! Leah's stomach lurched in her singular moment of doubt that one, or both of them might be dirty. They stepped out of the elevator and she shook it off. *No way that shit was true.*

"I gotta tell you, Leah, I'm gonna do my best to get the hell outta your hair as soon as possible. I'm gonna talk to you guys all at once. I've already requested a wheelchair for Detective Hardaway. We'll meet in Ramsey's room, since he can't be moved. I got Cain on his cell phone. He was en route. I asked if he'd meet us there."

So Lucas had gone home. Leah was quietly relieved. Butch didn't necessarily need to know Nick was his woman.

"Yeah, okay."

He smiled at her. "Relax, Wheeler. This isn't really about what maybe you think it is."

She frowned. "I'm not into cryptic messages, Butch. What's it about, then?"

Butch took his cell phone off his belt and made a 'be patient' gesture at her with his hand. "I got a couple of calls to make, then I'll meet you in Ramsey's room. Relax." He handed her bag back to her and started off toward Nick's room with the phone to his ear.

"Relax. Right." Leah mumbled to herself. She turned the corner and walked down the hall to Noah's room.

It had been a week since their shoot 'em up with the Trinidad brothers. It had taken six days for Dr. Garrett to let Noah out of the twilight he'd kept him in. Leah hadn't seen him since he woke up. She'd left early when that screwball, Nadine, started tripping and Noah's father told them both to get the hell out of Noah's room with that mess.

Leah hadn't done anything, just watched peaceably, as Nadine ranted and raved about her presence and made a gigantic fool of herself.

Leah had deferred to Big John and done what she was told, without argument. She didn't mind. She liked him and it had only made Nadine's ass look crazier. Besides, she was pretty sure John was used to having his way.

Leah paused when she got to Noah's room. The door was unexpectedly open and she heard a woman laughing. Leah walked in as the nurse was pulling the privacy curtain. "Good morning!" she said brightly. She was a full-figured, cocoa colored woman, somewhere in her thirties. She had sparkly brown eyes and pearly white teeth. Her hair was swept up into a swingy ponytail.

"Good morning." Leah smiled at her.

"Just give us a second. I'm trying to get a pair of shorts on Mr. Ramsey. We're almost there."

"Sure thing." Leah set her bag on the little table that swung across the bed, and put her purse down.

Leah listened to Noah's banter with the nurse. His voice sounded low and raspy, but he sounded like himself — he was flirting outrageously. Leah smiled, not even mad at him. She was ecstatic that he was okay. She felt more for that man than she'd ever admit to anybody, herself included.

The nurse threw back the curtain and raised Noah into a sitting position with the remote. Leah stepped around the curtain as the nurse was fussing with a pillow behind his head. When Noah saw her, his eyes twinkled and he smiled at her. "Hey, Leah."

She smiled, too. "Welcome back."

They'd taken the big bandage off his face, leaving a smaller one on his cheek. Though his face was still bruised, it was no longer swollen, and that scary bluish tinge was gone from beneath his eyes. Noah had his color back. He looked like himself again, despite all the remaining broken bones and bruises.

The nurse disappeared discreetly and Leah heard the door snick closed behind her. Noah's left arm was still in a sling, but he reached for her with his right. Leah took his hand and sat on the bed next to him. Noah brought her hand to his lips and kissed her knuckles.

He smiled at her warmly. "Did you miss me?"

Leah tried to smile back, but she choked up. "Oh man, Noah. I was so scared for you." Tears bubbled up from nowhere and spilled over.

Noah pulled her to him with his good arm. He kissed her lips and rubbed her back. "It's okay. It takes a lot more than that to break me." Noah held her until she pulled herself together.

Leah sat up and wiped her tears away, finally smiling. "I met Nadine."

Noah's eyebrows went up. "Yeah? What was that like?"

"It was an experience. She didn't seem to care for me too much."

Noah rubbed his hand along her thigh and her heartbeat picked up. He smirked. "Yeah? Imagine that."

Leah touched his curly hair. Ran her fingers through it. "She seems to think you're still her husband."

Noah didn't look at her. He seemed absorbed in watching his hand rub her thigh. "I'm not. What else did she say?"

"She said you wanted to come home."

"She did, huh? What else did she say?" Noah kept rubbing her thigh but he raised his eyes to meet hers.

"She says she's pregnant. Is that true, Noah?"

He sighed and his hand stopped moving. "I'm pretty sure she is. What did you have to say about that?" Noah stared at her and she stared back. Leah took her hand out of his hair and kissed him hard on the mouth. Noah's hand moved to hold her face as he returned the kiss, sweet and slow, like he kissed her the day they removed Tamiko.

"What did you say, Leah?" He didn't really break the kiss, just spoke around her lips.

Leah giggled, kissed him indulgently, and sat back. "I said … well, what I said doesn't matter. What matters is the way you feel about me. So let me ask you, Noah, do you want me to be the average chick and walk away from you because Nadine behaves the way she does and plays by her own rules? Or do you want me to stick around and see what's going to happen between me and you? It's your call."

Noah looked at her for a long while, as his hand returned to her thigh. "Leah, I'm real sorry," he said quietly. Leah's heart sank. Noah saw the look on her face and his lips went up at one corner. He squeezed her thigh.

"I'm sorry about *Nadine*. I got caught up in old feelings ... I got kids with Nadine, you know? I mean ... I married her."

Leah looked at him sadly. "You still love her."

Noah frowned. "Leah, I'll always love Nadine. We got history ... but people change. Nadine changed. I probably made her change. Hell, I know what I put her through."

"Have *you* changed, Noah?"

"I always said, 'Noah don't change,' but Luke told me once, everyone has the capacity to change. I know for a fact, his ass did. I watched him do it, and I couldn't believe my eyes ... but he did."

Leah put her hand on his. "We're not talking about Lucas. We're talking about you. Have you changed?"

Noah leaned back into his pillow and looked at her. "I don't know."

Leah knew that pressing Noah wasn't always a good idea, but she did. "Do you want to?"

He looked at her with some remorse in his eyes. Noah closed his fingers around hers and opened his mouth to say something, but Lucas walked in, looking and smelling like a million bucks, and the moment was lost. Noah untwined his fingers, but didn't let go of her hand.

Lucas touched Leah's shoulder in greeting, but his attention was on Noah. "Noah! What's good, baby?" Lucas looked extremely happy to see Noah so far improved. Leah couldn't recall ever seeing him smile like that.

Noah mirrored his smile. "Shit, Luke, everything." They dapped each other slow and held each other's eyes for a moment. That look spoke volumes. You could tell how much they felt for each other.

"Did you get 'em?" Noah asked, looking at him seriously. Lucas sat down, leaning forward with his elbows on his knees.

"I got 'em both," he replied, just as serious.

Noah nodded and seemed satisfied. "Thanks, Luke. I can live with that. Can you?"

Lucas nodded. "Most definitely. Don't mention it. You would have done the same for me."

Noah smiled. "Without a doubt and no hesitation."

Lucas smiled back. "I'm real glad you're okay, No."

Noah laughed. "Shit, me too. Now, somebody tell me why I.A. is tryin' to bust chops over this way."

"Harper thinks somebody's dirty," Leah said.

Noah was instantly indignant. "*What?* Who? It damn sure ain't nobody here. Butch Harper can kiss my ass for that line of bullshit he's dishin' out. Fuck his fat ass and his goddamn I.A.B." Leah looked at Lucas.

Lucas shrugged. "Don't look at me. I don't appreciate the shit, either. I say fuck him twice."

Butch walked in, pushing Nick in a wheelchair. She was frowned up with her chin in her hand. "I heard what you said, fellas. I gotta tell you, it wasn't very flattering. You're hurtin' my feelings."

Noah looked at him sideways. "Yeah? Well, you're breakin' our balls, Butch. State your business."

"Just a sec, Ramsey." Butch parked Nick next to Lucas on purpose and put the brake on her chair. He rubbed his hands together, surveying the room. "Hail, hail, the gang's all here."

Butch patted Noah on his good shoulder and looked at him fondly. "Glad to see you're doin' better, Ramsey. I said a prayer."

Noah smiled sarcastically. "Gee, thanks Butch." Leah hadn't realized she was still sitting on Noah's bed. She moved to get up, but Noah returned his hand to her thigh. "So, why are you here, Butch? Spit it out."

Butch took a seat. "We got a dirty cop to catch."

"Stop stalling, Butch. Who is it? Because it's none of us," Lucas said.

Butch looked Lucas in the eye, then turned his head to include Nick. "It's Keith Childs."

Lucas sat back in his seat like somebody pushed him. He glanced at Nick, then quickly turned his face away. "I don't believe this shit," he said under his breath. Lucas passed a hand over his beard and then fell silent, staring at the floor.

Leah looked at Nick. Nick was frowning at Lucas with her mouth open, like she didn't know what to make of his reaction. She turned her head to Butch, her eyes narrowed and her teeth clenched. Leah stood up. Nick was about to blow.

"What the fuck are you talking about, Butch?" Her voice was low and shaky, like she was barely controlling not screaming on him.

Butch was unruffled. His eyes moved from Lucas, slowly back to Nick. "What I'm sayin', Detective Hardaway, is that your ex-lover has close ties with just about every drug gang in this freakin' city, except for the goddamned mafia. I also gotta tell you that we believe the man you used to live with was riding shotgun with Tirado when he alerted the Trinidads about the sting. Now ... I'm thinkin' maybe he had knowledge of you guys involvement with the sting from the meeting on the Promenade. The boys in the Ivory Tower ... not so much. A bunch of people lost their lives when this thing went down. Five cops and three agents. Look, Hardaway, I don't have to tell you how cops react when we lose one of our own. We want blood and retribution ... and we especially want it when it's a dirty cop sullying the badge. Do you understand what I'm saying to you?"

Nick leaned forward, gripping the arms of the wheelchair. The look of anger had been replaced with one of complete and total disbelief. She looked mortified. "Butch, please don't tell me you're sitting there accusing me of ... Jesus, Butch, what are you accusing me of?"

Her voice wavered and Lucas, who was having a hard time holding on to his usual poker face — got up and walked to the window. He stood with his back to them and his hand rubbing away at his beard. Butch's eyes followed him, scrutinizing his body language. Leah put her hand on Nick's shoulder. This was fucked up. She looked at Noah. Noah's eyes bounced from Lucas to Nick to her.

Butch sighed. "Listen, Hardaway, I'm not personally accusing you of diddley, but the fact remains, you and Keith Childs had a relationship that lasted at least two years. You were close enough to live together. It goes without sayin' the guys at One Police Plaza are findin' it hard to believe you had no clue as to how this guy operates. Now even though I hate to do it, I gotta ask you point blank, Hardaway. At any time, during the course of your relationship with Keith Childs, were you consciously aware of Detective Childs using his badge to commit heinous acts and conduct illegal activity?"

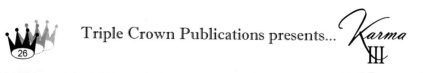

Lucas looked down at her over his shoulder to see how she answered. Nick looked at Butch like he'd struck her, then her beautiful face turned into a mask of rage. Nick had never been a woman who cried easily, but angry tears filled her eyes and spilled over.

She banged her fist so hard on the arm of the wheelchair, it sounded like a shot. "I was not, Inspector Harper."

Butch watched her with sympathy. "Look, I know you hate my guts right now, but I gotta ask you another fucked up question. I'm sorry for this, Nick. Have you, yourself, ever used your badge to commit unlawful acts, or were you ever coerced by Detective Childs to do so?"

Nick was so mad, she was shaking. She moved forward like she meant to get up, but Leah pulled her back before she could hurt herself. "I have *never* compromised my badge for anyone or anything. Have you questioned *him*?"

Butch shrugged. "Can't find him just yet. He's AWOL and he hasn't been at his last address. We're working on smoking him out. We'll get him. I.A.B. has eyes and ears everywhere." He looked toward the window. "You okay, Cain?"

Lucas answered him without turning around. "Uh-huh. I'm good."

Butch got up and stood just behind him. Butch was usually a nice guy, but he was also one of the best men in I.A. He did his job. "You know, Lucas, I believe you got every right to be angry. I come in here accusing your girlfriend of co-conspiracy, corruption, and possibly being an accessory. Guess it seems like no matter how many times you put your foot in Keith Childs's ass, he seems determined to pay you back for stealing his girl, huh?"

Lucas smiled a little, but it held no humor. "I would ask you how you know all that, Butch, but it's obvious you keep your sticky little feelers out."

Butch smiled, too, but his smile was real. "It's a small world, Cain, and I like to know what makes it turn. Forgive me for bein' nosy like that. People talk, and everybody knows I've got my spies … and they're every where."

Noah sat up a little. "Do tell? Who are they?"

Butch chuckled. "That's information you'll never get outta me, Ramsey."

Lucas looked down at him. "You can't make charges like that stick, Butch."

"I don't want to make 'em stick. What I want is to send Keith Childs away for a long time. I came here for two reasons: to get a formal statement from Nick and to see if I can get anything from you guys that would be helpful in my investigation."

Leah blinked and sucked her teeth. "You want us to help you with the investigation? I can't believe you, Butch, after you came in here slinging accusations and collecting formal statements. You must have lost your damn mind."

Butch shrugged. "Not really, Wheeler. Look, I gotta tell you guys, with the amount of animosity on both sides, it will be a lot easier to smoke him out with your help than to waste time and let him get further away from us, just plain searching for him. Doing it the hard way, we'll probably have to extradite him. With your help, we'll have his ass in a heartbeat."

Noah looked in Lucas's direction, holding his tongue. Lucas was looking at Nick. She looked back at him apprehensively as he walked over to her and touched her hair.

"Don't you see what's going on? They want to use you as bait," he said quietly.

Nick took his hand out of her hair and held it in her own. She held onto Lucas but she looked at Butch. "I'm not risking my badge, or my reputation for that asshole, and I'm not going for the guilt by association, okie–doke?" She took a deep breath, closed her eyes and opened them. "My official statement for the record, Inspector Harper: I, Detective Second Grade Nicole Dana Hardaway, was involved in an intimate relationship with accused Detective Second Grade, Keith Alexander Childs, for almost three years. During that time, I was unaware of any illicit activity on his part or abuse of his badge. If the department needs my assistance leading to his apprehension, I will comply immediately."

Butch nodded. "Okay, Nick. Good enough. Thank you."

Leah sucked her teeth. Even though Butch Harper was better than most, she hated the bullshit of his job.

Butch looked at her and shrugged, but not with indifference. "You know how it goes, Leah. Regardless of personal feelings, I still got a job to do."

"Yeah, and right now your job is to railroad Nick into helpin' you catch this scumbag!" Noah started angrily.

Butch cut him off. "Whoa, wait a minute," he said, frowning and putting his hands up defensively. "Railroad? What are you sayin'?"

Noah looked at him accusingly and actually pointed a finger at him. "You I.A. guys are all alike. Nick might not have a lot of experience dealin' with you sharks, but me and Luke have. You strolled your fat ass up in this hospital like you were on her side, shuckin' and jivin' and doin' your little tap dance to lull her into a false sense of security. Then you did the swoop down, right Butch? You sugarcoated everything, then you showed her your teeth and let her know you were lookin' at her for co-conspiracy and corruption charges. You delivered that shit like a wolf lookin' at a sheep and lickin' his chops."

Butch was still frowning in offense. He attempted to cut Noah off again. "Wait a minute, Ramsey —"

Noah moved forward like he forgot he was hurt and his leg was in traction. He closed his eyes and gritted his teeth against the sudden pain. Noah opened his clear gray eyes and gave Butch an extremely hostile look. "You got one more time to cut me off when I'm talkin'. You better be glad I can't get outta this bed and put my foot in your ass."

Leah was startled by Noah's vehemence. He shouldn't be working himself up like this. He was going to hurt himself.

She went to him in an attempt to smooth him out. "Noah, you need to calm down. Why are you going off on Butch like this?"

"'Cause he ain't bein' straight with Nick. You see it, don't you, Luke?"

Lucas shrugged. "I gotta tell you, Butch, it stinks like a deal to me. A lousy deal." Nick frowned and stared at Butch with anxious eyes. "What's he talking about?"

Butch looked coolly from Lucas to Noah, then back at Nick. "I really can't say."

"That's bullshit. You can," Noah said.

"Yeah, why don't you tell her the only option she really has is to do whatever you want her to do, because if she doesn't, you people are gonna trump up charges on her and either suspend her or relieve her of her badge. Does that sound about right, Butch?" Lucas said, eyeing him like he wouldn't mind kicking his ass, and looking like he'd be able to do it — despite his injuries.

"What?" The word squeaked out of Nick's throat.

"They're puttin' the squeeze on you, Nick, and if you ask me, that's pretty damn dirty, too," Noah said, trying to get comfortable. He glanced at Leah and she shifted his pillow.

"But why? Why are you putting these kinds of conditions on me? What did I do to deserve this? I could've gotten killed, and you treat me like this?" Nick said, angrily.

"It's simple. They can't find him by ordinary methods, they need you to flush him out, and they're not givin' you room to say no," Lucas said, staring a hole through Butch.

Nick frowned. "I guess I never really had a choice." She looked at Butch like he'd grown up out of the ground. "You tricked me into making a statement. You tricked me, Butch. I thought you were different than that."

Noah snickered. "He's not. He's a fuckin' goblin from the goddamn I.A.B. No offense, Butch. You're a nice enough guy on your own, but when you got on your I.A. costume, you ain't got no reflection."

Butch chuckled and put his hands in his pockets. He looked back at Noah with eyes much harder than Leah remembered. "See ... I know how you feel about I.A., Ramsey. Your fights with us are legendary you and Cain. If you two weren't so busy firing your weapons every chance you got, you'd never hear from us."

"We don't fire our weapons without just cause. You people stick us in life threatening situations and you don't expect us to protect ourselves? Fuck you on that one, Inspector Harper," Lucas said, and paused. "With all due respect."

Butch spread his hands. "I'm not gonna stand here and take shit off you guys."

"Then don't. Get outta my sickroom. You got what you came here for. You hoodwinked Nick and you know we won't let her do this shit alone. So get a sandwich or somethin', fatso, and we'll get back to you with the plan."

Butch shook his head. "You got a big mouth on you, Ramsey, I gotta tell you."

Noah smirked. "Don't worry about me and my big mouth, and

don't worry about this Keith Childs bullshit, either. 'Cause with or without Nick, me and Luke are just like the pizza man. We deliver. See you around, chubby."

Butch moved to the door. "You know, Nick — for what it's worth — it is my job."

If Butch could have died from the look she gave him, he would have hit the floor with no heartbeat. "Yeah, and mine is to be your puppet. You could have waited until I was a hundred percent."

Butch looked apologetic as he pushed the door open. "Unfortunately, there's no time. We have to move as soon as possible. I'm sorry for that but you won't be unprotected. That's a promise. We've got men to give you 'round the clock."

"I've already got men to give me 'round the clock."

"Your men are hurt," Butch pointed out.

"Ain't nothin' happenin' until we get outta here. I don't give two shits about your time frame," Noah said.

"You'll be on crutches, Ramsey."

"Noah on crutches and us working together is better than anyone you can send us," Leah said, not really caring all that much for Butch any more.

"We'll keep your protection for backup, if it's necessary. I got a feeling it won't be," Lucas said. The look in his eyes suggested Keith's imminent demise if he rose up. Leah looked at him standing there all crisp and clean and handsome. She smiled to herself. She'd learned a lot about these guys. Noah was loud, where Lucas was quiet. Noah would talk shit to you and let you know where you stood with him, while Lucas would watch you like a hawk and wait for you to fuck yourself.

Noah was quick to pull his weapon out and shoot you, but unless it was a dire situation, like the one they'd just come out of — you'd probably end up with a permanent disability, but you'd still be breathing. When Lucas took the safety off his weapon, he was looking to kill you. End of story. If Keith was willing to play himself with Lucas, he might as well fold himself into a morbid contortion — bend over and kiss his ass goodbye.

Butch nodded. "We'll work it out. Rest up. I'll be in touch soon." He stepped out the door.

"Bye, Fatty," Noah called after him. "Thanks again."

"You're welcome, Asshole," Butch called back. "See you soon." Noah leaned back into his pillow and grimaced.

"Are you okay?" Leah asked. She looked at him carefully. He seemed paler than when she'd come in.

Noah sighed. "I'm alright. That bastard just left a few of my nerve endings standing up." Leah picked up the call button and rang for the nurse. "What are you doin' that for?" Noah asked, reaching for the button.

Leah stepped out of his way. "Time for her to give you something for the pain. You're gonna take it, too. It's not debatable."

Noah thought it over for a moment, seemed to decide he wouldn't win, and turned his attention to Lucas. Lucas was still standing near Nick, but he was looking out the window. He seemed to be a million miles away.

Noah cleared his throat. "Hey, Luke?"

"Yeah?"

"Don't even think about it. Get it out of your mind."

Lucas's eyes stayed on whatever he was looking at beyond that window. He ran his hand over his beard, slowly. "I ain't thinkin' about nothing, Noah."

"That's bullshit, Luke. I know you better than I know myself, bro. I know what's on your mind. Forget that shit before you let it grow into an idea."

Lucas turned away from the window and looked at him. Leah didn't like the look in his eye. It was unsettling.

"What idea is that?" Lucas asked.

Noah shook his head. "You can't go after Keith yourself, Luke."

"Says who?"

Noah struggled to sit up. Leah could see the pain in his face and gently put her hand on his shoulder to keep him from hurting himself. He just as gently took it off. "Lucas! You hear me talkin' to you? I said don't do it. *Please*. Okay? Do you hear me, or are you settin' the wheels in motion? I can see your mind workin'. Luke, don't make it personal."

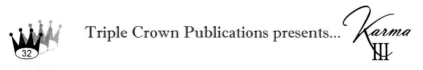

Lucas looked at Noah and his eyes were like fire, but he kept his voice quiet. "Keith made this shit personal a long time ago. Don't you see, Noah? *This* is what happens when you leave a lunatic alone, and you don't nip their shit in the bud at the first sign of disturbing behavior. Look at us, Noah. When you don't check somebody like that, people get hurt and people die. You'd think I would've learned that by now."

Nick was looking at her lap. She would have been wringing her hands if there wasn't an IV drip in the back of one. Leah was startled. She'd never, ever, seen Lucas this mad before. Not even when he was throwing Keith's ass out of their office.

Noah was watching him close. "Luke, um … I think …"

Everybody flinched when Lucas actually started hollering at him. "I *know* what you think, Noah! *I know, okay?* You're fuckin' right, too! Right as fuckin' rain! *I'm tired, Noah!* I'm tired of crazy people fuckin' my life up. Do *you* hear *me*?"

The nurse walked in with her syringe. She took one look around the room and stopped in her tracks. "Is everything okay in here?"

Noah looked at the nurse apologetically. "Could you give us a moment? You can come back in a minute with your needle full of pixie dust." The nurse exited with a wary look.

"Lucas. Could you do me the courtesy of comin' over here, seein' as how I can't get up?" Noah said, quietly.

Lucas took three steps toward him. That was it. "Say what you gotta say, Noah."

They stared at each other hard. "Alright, Luke, listen to me. I see blood in your eye, bro. *Wait for us.* If you go out there by yourself, it's only gonna end one way for Keith — with his ass kicked unmercifully and a bullet in his forehead. Fuck Keith. It's what he deserves, but I ain't gonna sit here and be quiet and watch you cross the line between police work and murder. Let's face it. That's what it would be. Who knows, walk the line the way you're supposed to and you might get the same results. At least then it would be a righteous kill. Believe me, I'm prayin' for it … but in the meantime — I won't see you throw away everything you have and everything you are, just to rid the world of one more asshole who offended you, Lucas. *I won't.* Calm down and take a walk." Lucas seemed to deflate as Noah talked to him. Some of that scary fire left his eyes. He closed the distance between him and Noah.

Noah smiled his charming smile and held his fist out to him. "We cool, Luke?"

Lucas gave him a very small smile of his own as he touched his fist to Noah's. "Like ice, No."

Noah put his head back on his pillow and put his hand on the small of Leah's back. "Good, then take your woman back to her room and whisper sweet nothin's in her ear, while I still got time to rub on Leah's ass before the nurse comes back and puts my head out."

Lucas smiled. "You got it."

Noah smiled. "I got a lot. Come by before you leave."

"I'll be here," Lucas said and rolled Nick out with one hand.

Leah looked down at Noah. "I'm worried about Nick."

"She'll be fine. She's got us." His hand slipped down and cupped her ass. Noah looked up at her with a wicked grin. "What color are your panties?" Leah smiled as she undid the button on her jeans and pulled the privacy curtain.

Chapter Four

One Down

Keith couldn't quite believe his recent run of pure unadulterated luck. Everything he'd envisioned since he first met Oscar Tirado had finally come to pass. They'd worked hard, he and Oscar, to get to the point Keith ended up reaching alone. He was vaguely rueful that Oscar hadn't made it with him, but not very. After all, Keith never intended for him to. That's why he gave him up to Tate and Troy Trinidad.

Oscar Tirado had been one of the dirtiest cops the NYPD had ever seen. Just like Cain and Ramsey, he'd been a highly decorated First Grade Detective, but he'd lived a double life for a long time. Oscar had also been a drug dealing, money laundering, cop killer in his spare time. Cain and Ramsey had been instrumental in ending Oscar's reign of terror, and Oscar hadn't appreciated it when they'd brought him down. Keith hadn't given Cain and Ramsey much thought. He'd dismissed them as minor, but important, figures in the cast of Oscar's downfall. Mostly he'd just been glad that when the shit hit the fan, none of it was slung on him.

Keith might not have given Cain and Ramsey a second thought, but Oscar had obviously let revenge fester in his mind like a wound that wouldn't get well. Oscar had gone into the joint looking for ways to get out. He'd been adamant that he'd never serve his full sentence, and he'd kept his lawyer very busy. Oscar sent his lawyer to the Feds to make a deal. Let him out and he'd hand them the Trinidad brothers on a silver platter. The Feds went for the deal. The fact

that Cain and Ramsey were heading the sting was gravy for Oscar. He'd finally get those assholes back for cutting his fun short.

Oscar decided to give the Trinidads a heads up about the sting to exact revenge on Cain and Ramsey. He called a meeting with them on the night he died. Keith had known the Trinidads *and* Oscar long enough to know that it would be fairly easy to gum up the works of that covert pow-wow by going against Oscar. Keith had taken his life in his hands by having the balls to fuck Oscar right in his face, but the hell with it. Keith could admit to himself that he was a greedy opportunist, who ultimately wanted everything for himself. That was the nature of the game, after all. To the victor goes the spoils, and he was going to make sure he was the last man standing.

It would be a long time before he forgot the look Oscar gave him when Keith informed Tate and Troy that Oscar had been solely responsible for bringing the heat down on them. That Oscar had his lawyer contact the Feds to get them to cut him a deal.

After cursing Keith to eternal damnation for his Judas kiss, Oscar started groveling. He knew Tate and Troy would never let him leave there alive. Tate had stood up at his desk and told Oscar, if he got on his knees, he'd think about it. Keith had never in his life seen a look as black as the one Tate got from Oscar.

Keith had to give Oscar credit. He was a tough bastard to the very end. He lifted his chin and spit right in Tate's eye. *"Fuck you, Tate. You're gonna have to kill me, you son of a bitch!"* he'd said, defiantly. Tate had used his handkerchief to wipe Oscar's spit out of his eye, laughing with real humor, almost tickled. *"I'd be delighted,"* he'd said with a chuckle, *"Oh Troy!"*

Troy had leapt across Tate's desk with his machete in his hand and taken Oscar's head off before he could turn around. Also some shit Keith had never seen before. Oscar's head hit the ground with a surprised look on its face and rolled between his feet. His body stood a little longer — jetting blood — then collapsed on the floor next to his severed head. Tate had tucked his handkerchief back into his pocket and looked at Keith. *"Run if you want to live, before I change my mind,"* he'd said — and he didn't have to say it twice. Keith had hightailed it out of there, but he was almost sure things would continue to work in his favor.

The sting was set to go down the following day. Keith knew the Trinidad brothers wouldn't just lie down, give up, and go to jail. He also knew if Cain and Ramsey were the undercovers, Tate and Troy weren't getting away. He personally might hate their guts, but their track record spoke for itself. *Draco was going down.* Keith had been certain that when the sun set the next day, Tate and Troy would no longer be among the living.

That was the way it turned out, of course. Both Tate and Troy were dead, but they hadn't gone without a fight. They'd put a world of hurt on the opposition. Killed a bunch of cops and agents. They'd put the hurt on Ramsey's big-mouthed ass, too. Keith heard they'd lost him a couple of times before he stabilized. Too bad. Before it was all over, Keith intended to make sure his slick ass wished he was dead — and he could blame arrogant-ass Lucas Cain for all his future trouble. He and Nicky.

Keith had been mildly upset to hear Nicky had gotten hurt. He did still care for her, but perhaps she'd gotten what she deserved. She still had to pay for tossing his ass aside for the perfect Mr. Cain. Keith clenched his teeth and swallowed like he tasted something awful. *Lucas Cain*. Keith's hand curled into a fist and his lips went up in an unconscious sneer. *Lucas Cain*.

He'd hated that motherfucker since the academy. Hated his ass on sight. Conceited, swaggering, bastard. He thought he was the shit. Thought he was the motherfucking man. Living in his goddamned fly-ass brownstone, pushing a fucking 500. He stole his woman. *Nicky*.

No matter how he turned it over in his mind, Keith *could not* deal with that particular pile of bullshit. He couldn't take it. It was like an atom bomb to his manhood. He frowned. Oscar had laughed at him — tried to say he should be *glad* it was Cain who'd taken his woman. Like that shit was supposed to make him feel better. Well, fuck Oscar's dumb ass. He should have given more thought to what fell out of his mouth. That was one of the reasons his ass was dead. Keith was not the one for taking shorts. Sooner or later he'd get your ass back.

Keith had more to get Cain back for than losing Nicky. He'd shamed him. *Twice*. He'd manhandled him once. Cain had thrown him out of that office on his ass so hard he'd skidded across the floor, everybody snickering and laughing. He'd embarrassed him in front of everybody. Then Cain had the balls to come to the place Keith was staying and kick his ass in his own hallway, like Keith wasn't shit. Keith had never been in a fight where his feet actually left the ground. Nigga had tossed him like he was 5 years old.

Cain broke Keith's nose ... broke his finger ... *shattered his ego*. Ramsey provided the background music of humiliating laughter. Cain moved so fast, he didn't even give Keith the chance to fight back. Cain's fists were like steel. He'd smashed his nose with one punch. Beat his ass ... embarrassed him ... stole his woman.

Keith wanted to hurt him bad. Needed to. *Had to*. He wasn't trying to fight him, because he knew he would most likely lose. There were other ways to hurt Cain. Sometimes it was more fun to hit people where they lived. Keith was going to hit him low and where he could do the most damage. Right in the heart.

It had been six weeks since the sting had gone down. Ramsey — as far as he knew — was still using a crutch, with his arm in a sling, and Nicky was using a cane for her shot leg. Both almost well, but still a bit incapacitated. Cain himself still had bandages on his arms. Keith knew all this because he'd seen them. More than once. All congregated in Cain's great room, having a real swell time. Nigga should keep his curtains closed.

Ramsey seemed to be doing his convalescing there, which made things easier for Keith. He could literally kill two birds with one stone. The easiest way to get to Cain was to hurt the people he cared the most about. That was the plan, but first Keith was going to serve Ramsey a heaping plate of tragedy and grief — with a side of guilt and humility. Keith cracked his knuckles. He'd teach that hyena to laugh at him. Fucking curly head pretty boy.

He turned his head and looked down the block. Keith started to watch the corner in earnest now. It was almost time for him to make his move. He watched the children pour out of the school and start to board the buses that were idling at the curb. Some were met by parents, others walked away in small groups, laughing and talking. Keith stayed where he was and kept his vigil. Soon enough she came out. Keith looked at her intently and smiled to himself in appreciation. He had to give Ramsey one thing. He sure didn't mess around with ugly women.

His eyes followed her as she crossed the street and walked toward her car. Wow. She was beautiful. Medium height with dusky brown skin, and a head full of long, silky, dark hair that hung lushly down her back. She was wearing a white skirt and flat white sandals, with a gauzy summer blouse that draped modestly over the round curve of her expectant belly. It was an interesting shade of orange. Tangerine, maybe. It made her skin look like it glowed. She carried two black canvas tote bags. One over her left shoulder and one in her right hand. She carried a small plant with pink flowers in her left – probably all the stuff she'd acquired over the course of the school year, taking it home since this was one of the last days of school.

Keith walked discreetly to his car and started it up. He smiled. It was funny to him that people never knew when something like this was about to happen. He watched her take her time putting things in her car, pausing in a picture worthy moment of maternal bliss to pat her belly in protective indulgence and calm Ramsey's kicking child. She opened the door and got in, primly holding her skirt around her knees, then pulled off. Keith stuck a stick of gum in his mouth and followed her.

Yes, his luck had definitely been good as of late. Lissette Maldonado had practically fallen into his lap. He'd found out about her when the sting had first gone down and Ramsey and the rest of them were still in such fragile condition. This had been before Keith had gone AWOL and his character had started carrying a question mark.

He'd seen her come out of Ramsey's room on more than one occasion Keith had asked around, looking to find out who she was. Keith had been impressed with the amount of women who'd left Ramsey's room with tears rolling down their faces, but Ms. Maldonado had been the only pregnant one. A few well-placed questions left him privy to the fact that she was, indeed, Ramsey's girlfriend. He'd played his hand and tried to dig a little deeper with a woman who turned out to be his ex-wife, but she'd given him a lukewarm greeting, accepted his sympathies and effectively frosted him out. She was pretty, but that broad was so cold, she probably pissed ice cubes.

He didn't need her anyway; after all, he had the lovely Lissette to exact his revenge on. Cain was the ultimate target of Keith's retribution, but he owed Ramsey his share of humble pie. Keith had a one-way ticket to Costa Rica and a brand new life of luxury, but he was determined to take the shine off those rock stars and pay Nicky's ass back before he left. He refused to leave until he took care of them. His ego wouldn't let him.

Keith trailed Lissette to her apartment in Williamsburg. He watched her get out and begin to laden herself down with all her stuff. Nothing looked really heavy, just awkward. Keith got out of his car and started toward her.

The thought crossed his mind that maybe he should just take his flight and get the fuck out of New York. Somewhere in the deep recesses of his mind that were still sane, something flickered and tried to find a voice. *Maybe he should leave it alone. Maybe he was about to fuck with the wrong people.* His lunatic ego stomped that small spark of clarity out with big boots. Fuck them niggas. They weren't shit. Besides, they were both hurt, and a hurt nigga could only do so much. Tate and Troy had tried, but it was time for somebody to put a real dent in their swagger. Keith wasn't about to just dent Ramsey's. He was about to shatter it into a million pieces.

Keith had taken his time to decide the best approach, and he thought he'd come up with a good idea. He was dressed like he was just out for a jog — sweat shorts and a tank top. An iPod and a fanny pack for good measure. He jogged up to her just as he took the plant out of the car. It was a geranium.

"You've sure got a lot of stuff for a lady in your condition," Keith said, jovially. Lissette turned and looked at him sharply. Keith spread his hands in a nonthreatening manner and flashed a winning smile. "Do you need any help?"

Lissette smiled at him with some hesitation. "Thank you, but I'm okay."

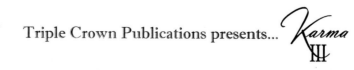

Fine. Time to gain her trust and put her at ease. He laughed and produced his badge and ID; Keith smiled when she actually took the time to read his name.

This time her smile was more genuine. "Okay, Detective Childs. I guess I could use a little help."

People were so stupid. He'd sedated her rational, city dwelling, case of distrustful nerves, brought on by a stranger offering unrequested assistance, just by showing her proof that he was a bona-fide officer of the law.

He was sure she also felt her safety was guaranteed because she now knew his name — and possibly his shield number — in the off chance something jumped off that shouldn't. Stupid. Just plain stupid.

Meanwhile, Keith kept smiling. "No problem. Glad I was able to put your mind at ease long enough to be of some service."

She laughed musically. Keith was very impressed with how pretty she was. What looked good from far away, was beautiful up close. She was that startle your heart pretty, like Nicky. He had goose bumps.

"Nothing like a cop to make you feel safe," she said, handing her bags to him. She held onto the geranium, and walked up the steps of the well-maintained brownstone. She took out her key and opened the door.

"Then you must feel safe a lot. I saw you at the hospital after the sting went down."

She raised an eyebrow. "Really? Were you involved in that?"

He nodded. "I guess you can say I did some work out of the loop. A lot of people I know got hurt. I noticed you coming out of Ramsey's room."

She started up the stairs and he followed. Lissette smiled at him over her shoulder. "Oh, you noticed me, huh?"

He smiled back. "Forgetting your face is highly unlikely. What's your name?"

She stopped halfway up and turned around, looking slightly amused. "Are you coming on to me?"

Keith smiled and shook his head. "No. I just asked for your

name. That's all."

She looked at him funny. "So … you know Noah?"

He nodded. "Yeah. We went to the academy together."

"Oh. Well, my name's Lissette. I'm his girlfriend."

He wanted to ask her if she was sure about that, but he kept his mouth shut. "Really? When are you guys due?"

"In September," she said, proudly patting her belly.

"Congratulations."

She smiled. "Thank you."

Lissette started back up the stairs. She probably felt she'd just put him in his place, nicely. Let him know not to come barking up the pregnant lady tree. She'd laid *her* claim *and* Ramsey's. She was his *girlfriend*. Women were so into titles. None of it meant shit to him. That wasn't what he was here for.

Lissette stopped at an apartment on the second floor. "This is me. Thanks again, I really appreciate it," she said, with a smile and with finality. This was as far as she was willing to accept his charity. She wasn't letting him in. Not so stupid after all, but stupid enough.

Keith slipped the bags off his shoulder and sat them by her door. "You're welcome. How's Noah doing? He was hurt pretty bad. We did a lot of praying for him."

"We appreciate it. It must have worked. He's doing much better, but he's still got to take it easy."

Keith nodded. "Yeah, I'd imagine … well, nice meeting you, Lissette. Give Noah my regards." He turned to walk away.

"I sure will. I'll make sure to tell him I met you."

Keith smiled. *No, you won't, but he'll know I was here.* Keith moved fast, putting his foot between both of hers and forcing her body against the door with his own. He had his hand over her mouth before she could scream.

"Open the door and I'll take it easy on you."

The hand covering her mouth was suddenly wet with tears. She was making a scared moaning sound behind his hand. Keith reached into his fanny pack and pulled out a short knife with a sharp blade. He held it to her stomach just hard enough for her to know what it was. She froze. Even seemed to stop breathing.

Keith leaned forward and spoke in her ear. "I said, *open the fucking door*. Don't make me hurt you in this hallway."

Lissette whimpered, but she opened the door. Keith pushed her inside and nudged the door closed with his shoulder. Lissette stood staring at him with huge eyes, one hand over her mouth, the other on her belly. Keith put the knife back in the fanny pack and took out a length of cord. The realization of how dire her situation was showed on her face. She watched with desperate fear as Keith wrapped the cord around both of his fists.

Instead of cowering and mewling, she took off in a mad dash for the bedroom. Keith was right behind her, his instincts telling him she was going for a gun. She sprinted into the room and jumped across the bed, reaching for the drawer in the farthest nightstand. She reached in and came out with a silver .32, rolling over on her back, and taking aim.

She would have gotten him pretty good if the weapon had fired. Instead, when she pulled the trigger, nothing happened. If that pistol had come from Ramsey, Keith was certain of two things — it worked, and it was loaded. He jumped on the bed, one knee on either side of her and wrenched the gun out of her hand so hard, he heard the bone in her finger snap. Lissette cried out in pain.

Keith glanced at the gun, looking down at her in mock annoyance. "Next time take the safety off. Oh, wait ... you don't get a next time."

Lissette started fighting, but he subdued her long enough to get the cord around her neck. "Please!" That was all she managed to get out before Keith started choking the life out of her.

He looked at her with eyes just as sorrowful as the ones looking back at him. "I'm sorry, Lissette. I regret this more than you know. You should have been more discerning about the company you kept. Thank your lover for this. *Go to sleep*."

He made sure she was gone, then he looked at her beautiful face. Her features were puffy and her skin had an unnatural color from the violence of the act he'd just committed. It wasn't as easy as it looked like it was in the movies, to strangle a person who didn't want to die to death. It was violent and it took strength and determination.

Keith looked down into her sightless eyes. He hadn't really wanted to do what he'd just done, but he believed it had been necessary. He also realized that he'd better do whatever other dirt he planned to do and get the fuck out of Dodge. Keith put his hands down and closed her eyes. There was no going back now. He'd started a war. He might not be able to swing this alone. He took out his cell and called a couple of old friends.

Chapter Five

At Last

Although she knew she probably shouldn't, Nick was enjoying this quiet interlude in her life. It had been almost six weeks since the sting had gone down, and everything was slowly getting back to normal. Normal in a strange way.

Lucas, she'd come to learn, had an enormous protective streak. Nick thought his reaction to her when Keith punched her had been because he was already sweet on her, and maybe he was. After they'd all gotten hurt in the sting, Lucas had gathered all his chicks in his large and spacious home to get well. Leah was there so much it was almost like she was staying there, too. Noah had protested at first, but he'd given in because it made sense.

Nick turned her head and looked over at Lucas, sleeping peacefully on his back. She was sure Lucas's nurturing tendencies had a lot to do with his childhood, or his lack of it. It was a quality she found endearing, rather than annoying. She thought Noah probably felt the same. She watched Lucas frown in his sleep and wondered what he was dreaming about. He wouldn't talk to her about it, but she knew for a fact, he'd had more than a few nightmares after the sting.

Since he wouldn't talk to her, Nick asked Noah if he had any idea what they could be about — other than the obvious. Lucas *had* killed more than a few people that day. Even though they were cops and sanctioned by law to do it legally, it affected people in different ways.

Noah had looked at her and laughed, then he'd made a joke

about Nick shooting Lucas in his smartass way. Nick's knee-jerk reaction was to be horrified. Shooting Lucas was the last thing on earth she'd meant to do. She hadn't meant to hurt him, she'd only been trying to get those pit bulls off of him. Noah saw the look on her face and stopped his friendly fire jokes and put a lid on his smile. He'd told her Lucas had a lot of things to have nightmares about, but maybe this time it was the dogs. Maybe.

Lucas turned onto his side and reached for her. His hand slipped around her waist, and Nick felt the familiar thrill in the pit of her stomach that always accompanied Lucas touching her. Nick smiled and stretched her body against his, luxuriously. Lucas surprised her by gently turning her over on her back and planting a very passionate kiss on her.

Nick kissed him back, meeting his passion with her own. He was kissing her teasingly with his wonderfully skillful tongue. Lucas was curling her toes. His hand pushed her camisole up and over her breasts. He paused to lick his thumb and used it on her nipple to create a sweet, barely there friction that sent warmth coursing through her body, and had her breath hitching in her chest. Nick moaned and her body quivered. Lucas laughed softly, breaking the kiss.

Nick frowned and smiled. "What's so funny?" she asked.

Her body was aching for him. Lucas hadn't touched her like this in six weeks. He hadn't wanted to hurt her. She may still be healing, but she wasn't *that* hurt anymore. Nick wanted him bad. She was dying for him. Lucas's hand left her breast, skimmed over her stomach, and parted her thighs.

Nick held her breath, but it burst through her lips in a little puff as Lucas touched her very precisely and circled his finger tantalizingly slow. Lucas laughed that soft, smug, little laugh again as her hips rose automatically to meet his hand.

He kissed the tip of her nose. "Good morning, Nicole."

The ball of his finger slid over her deftly and she shuddered and squealed. "I thought you were asleep, Lucas."

That laugh again. "Every closed eye ain't sleep," he said, and kissed her neck.

Nick closed her eyes. "Who told you that? Noah?"

His tongue slid along her collarbone. Lucas moved, positioning himself, but his hand never stopped its magic. "Maybe. Might have heard it when I was a kid." He tasted her navel.

Nick shivered hard and clenched her teeth. "If you put your mouth on me, I think I'm gonna faint," she breathed.

Lucas raised an eyebrow and smiled. "Yeah? Let's find out."

Nick raised up on one elbow, a trembling smile on her lips. She shook her head. "Oh, Lucas, no you don't. I'll make too much noise."

Lucas put her hurt leg gently over his shoulder. The dimple appeared in his right cheek. "I love the sound of your voice. Scream all you want. It's my house." He kissed the inside of her thigh and she put her hand in his hair.

"No, Lucas, every time you do that I —"

He shut her up by putting his mouth on her, licking her into submission with his very talented tongue. She surrendered to him, powerlessly. Nick didn't think she was capable of putting up any real fight to keep him from having his way with her. She didn't want to. Nick wanted Lucas too bad to try and play games with him. Her hip was still sore and her leg still hurt, but Nick didn't care. What Lucas was doing to her made her oblivious.

His tongue swirled over her with a hot and deliberate finesse. He was relentless. Nick's eyes snapped open as she felt the shock of the first sublime pulsation beat through her body. Nick screamed an agonized song of pleasure as she trembled uncontrollably. Lucas was kissing her there like he was kissing her mouth — a sensation so highly erotic, her hips left the bed and she rubbed herself against his mouth until she sent the climax she was already in into overdrive. She went over the edge whimpering and quivering.

Lucas' slide into her caught her off guard. He stroked her deep and slow. All the way in … all the way out. Nick gasped and grabbed his ass. He moved inside her with that long stroke until he felt her start to throb and twitch. Lucas thrust himself into her all the way, rocking his body against hers, not pulling back. The pleasure was excruciating. He subjected her to a delectable torture as he found what he was looking for, and glided across that soft, sensitive, pillow of flesh that was still a mystery to most men, but not to Lucas. He

seemed to find it every time, at just the right moment, like he had a divining rod.

His lips found hers and he kissed her deep and slow. Nick twined her legs around his, ignoring the small flashes of pain that zipped through her leg and hip, and moved her hips to meet his with each long thrust. She felt a warm wave of satisfaction when Lucas put his cheek next to hers, tickling her skin with his soft low beard. His breath came in a rush as he slammed into her. It seemed he couldn't quite help himself. Lucas couldn't stifle it — it took him over and he dipped into her powerfully, hammering hard and filling her up. His hands were on her hips, holding her there so she couldn't get away ... not that she wanted to. They were both half screaming, rocking with each other until the last spasm was over. Lucas kissed her again, even though they were both out of breath. He turned onto his back and pulled her with him.

Nick put her head on his shoulder and smiled at him. "My leg hurts."

Lucas laughed. "I'm sorry, baby. I tried to go easy on you."

Nick giggled and snuggled into him. "You *never* go easy on me, Lucas, but you *always* leave me happy and satisfied. You're the man."

"I don't know about *that*, but I'm *your* man, so that makes it my job to make sure you're happy."

Nick rose up on one elbow and looked down at him. "You have no idea how much I love you, Lucas."

He smiled and sat up. "I do have some idea. You did ask me to marry you. Remember?"

Nick sat up, too, and threw the sheet off. She rolled her eyes at him. "Of course I remember. I also remember the fact that you never answered me."

He got up and offered her a hand. Lucas pulled her to her feet and let her lean on him as they walked to the bathroom. They stepped into the shower and Lucas turned the water on. He looked down at her, mild worry on his face.

"You still in a lot of pain?"

Nick shrugged. "It's getting a lot better. It could always be worse."

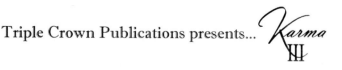

She'd been lucky. A lot luckier than Noah or Tony. She'd been shot three times. In the thigh, the hip and the arm. All three had passed through the muscle with no major damage. The shot in the arm was really nothing more than a bad graze.

Tony lost his spleen, but he was doing much better. Noah had gotten the worst of it, but Nick had to give it to him — Noah was made of some pretty strong stuff. He'd taken his arm out of the sling himself last week. The bandage was off his face and the skin had healed nicely. Lucas had gone with him just yesterday to get the cast off his leg. The soft cast had come off a few days ago.

He was still limping because it wasn't a hundred percent, but he said his dislocated kneecap bothered him more than the bullet breaking his thighbone. Noah had a cane to use when it really bothered him, but it wasn't a standard hospital issue like Nick's. His father had dropped by and brought him a cherry wood walking stick with a silver tip. *"Can't have you lookin' busted just because you're crippled, boy,"* he'd said, in his lazy N'Orleans drawl. It wasn't a cane. It was a pimp stick, plain and simple.

They took their shower and went back into the bedroom to get dressed. Nick watched Lucas as he put his clothes on, jeans and a black T-shirt. She kept watching as he combed his hair and used a small brush on his beard.

He looked at her watching him in the mirror and smiled. "Stop staring at me."

Nick stood and pulled on her shorts. It was hard as hell not to stare at him and he knew it. Lucas was handsome as hell, with his beautiful dark skin and those big chocolate eyes with those long-ass eyelashes. She picked up her brush and started to pull her hair into a ponytail. Nick looked over at him again. He was putting his watch on.

Lucas looked at her suddenly, with that direct, penetrating stare. "Something on your mind?"

Hell yeah, something was on her mind — and she hadn't brought it up. He did. She'd purposely left it alone because there was so much going on, but now that he'd spoken on it, she wanted an answer. Nick knew she'd have to choose her approach carefully. She didn't want Lucas shutting down on her. She didn't want him to feel pressured.

"Nothing. It's nothing," she said, and busied herself with her hair.

Lucas sighed and threw his hands up. "It's always something with you, Nicole. I know what this is about."

She frowned and turned around to face him. Her hand went instantly to her hip, and she couldn't keep the swivel out of her neck if she tried. "Who are you talking to, Lucas? I *know* you're not talking to me like that."

He walked toward her. "I'm talkin' to *you*. I know what you're doing. You were trying to figure out how to come at me about marrying you."

Her mouth dropped open for two reasons. Number one, he was right, number two, why was he talking to her like this? Lucas was almost yelling. It was totally out of character. "Don't you talk to me like this. What's the matter with you, Lucas?"

He rolled up on her and put his hands on her hips. "What's the matter with *me*? I'm tired of seeing that look on your face, *Nicole*. I'm tired of you walkin' on egg shells, actin' like you don't know how to talk to me. This is *me* … Lucas."

He paused and kissed her on the corner of her mouth. Nick sucked her cheeks in to keep from smiling.

"Ask the question, Nicole. Ask me," Lucas said, quietly.

Nick tilted her head coyly. She loved this man. She lived to breathe his air. Nick never thought she could feel like this about anybody. She knew what he was doing and could barely contain herself, but she played along.

"Alright, honeybunch. Do you want to marry me or what?"

Lucas's head went back and he looked offended. "*Excuse me?* Is that all you got?"

Nick smiled and made a big deal out of looking at her fingernails. "'Fraid so. What have *you* got?"

Lucas shrugged and lifted her hand, pausing to plant a kiss on her knuckles, melting her with his chocolate eyes. "Not a lot. Just me."

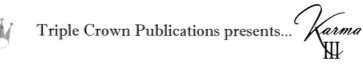

Nick grinned. "That's a hell of a deal. I'll take it."

"Good. Maybe you'll take this, too." Lucas put his hand in his pocket and pulled out the very thing Nick had been dreaming about since the night he'd come to her rescue from Keith. Lucas held the ring between his thumb and forefinger by the band.

It was a beautiful brilliant diamond in a unique setting. Although it was what she wanted, Nick was stunned that Lucas was standing there with a ring in his hand. She felt like she was dreaming. Realizing her mouth was open, she covered it with her shaking hand. Lucas picked up her equally shaky left hand and slid the ring on her finger.

"I've had enough time, Nicole. I'm where you need me to be. I love you."

Nick looked at the ring, then back at him. "Jesus, Lucas!"

He laughed. "Is that a yes?"

Nick threw her arms around his neck and kissed him hard. She couldn't believe how her life had changed in such a short time. She couldn't believe she'd found Lucas. Nick felt lucky. Blessed. Loved. She came up for air.

"You better believe it's a yes. I'd marry you right here, right now, right in this room. I love you, Lucas." She smiled and looked at her ring again.

"Do you like it?"

"I love it, honeybunch. It's beautiful."

Lucas kissed her. "Good. If you make me breakfast, I'll give you a ride downstairs."

Nick flashed her new ring, waving it dramatically. "Sweetheart, you're now entitled to whatever you want from me for the rest of your life ... but I'll take the ride."

Lucas raised an eyebrow. "Anything?"

She nodded and smiled. "Yep. You're entitled, but that doesn't mean you'll definitely get it."

He smiled back. "Guess I'll have to keep my demands within reason."

Nick looked at him sincerely and touched his face. "Lucas, you know there's nothing in this world I wouldn't do for you."

Lucas smiled at her devilishly. "I know," he said and put her over his shoulder in a fireman's carry. Lucas grabbed the cane she was using from its spot by the door and took her downstairs, depositing her in the kitchen.

"I want waffles," Lucas said, looking like he was daring her to change the menu. Nick wrinkled her nose. Waffles were not her favorite food and he knew it. She hated making them. They were work.

"Waffles," he said again, looking amused. Nick made a small show of sucking her teeth and pouting, but he'd get his waffles. Lucas could have waffles every morning for the rest of his life if he wanted them. He was marrying her and she was ecstatic.

Nick looked him in the eye. "Waffles it is."

"I know," Lucas said with exaggerated smugness.

Noah came through the door with his pimp stick, talking on his cell phone. He wasn't favoring his bad leg too much today. He made his way to the kitchen and ended his call.

Noah looked at Lucas expectantly. "Well?"

Lucas took a long swig from the bottle of water he'd taken from the fridge. "Well what?"

Noah looked at him like he didn't appreciate him being a smartass. "Don't make me pop you in the head with this cane, Negro. What did she say?"

Lucas smiled. "She said what I thought she'd say."

Noah smirked. "Turned you down, huh?"

Lucas laughed. "Fuck you, Noah."

Noah smiled, giving him dap and a one-shouldered hug. "Fuck you back, Luke. Congrats, man."

"What's the matter, Noah? You got no love for me?" Nick asked with a smile, as she turned on the waffle iron.

"Got plenty." He kissed her cheek and gave her a warm hug. "What does that make you now? Like my sister-in-law or something?"

Nick smiled at Noah with great affection. "Yeah, you know, I think it does. You smell like smoke, by the way. Didn't Dr. Garrett say stopping might be a good idea?"

Noah looked annoyed. "Who's good idea? *All* doctors say that crap. I *like* to smoke and I'll make my own decisions. I'm a grown-ass man."

Nick looked at Lucas. Lucas shrugged. "He's a grown-ass man."

Noah nodded and sat down. "That's right, so you can stop with the naggin'. What's for breakfast?"

Lucas looked at him with a smile. "Waffles."

Noah laughed. "That's cold, Luke."

Lucas's cell phone rang. He frowned when he looked at the number. "What the hell?" he said, but answered it anyway. Nick and Noah stopped talking and turned their attention his way.

"Cain. Uh-huh. Now? But it's —" Lucas turned away from them and spoke in low tones. Nick glanced at Noah. He looked at her and they both turned back to Lucas.

"We'll be right there. Don't worry, we're leavin' now." Lucas ended the call.

Nick was frowning because she saw that Lucas was trying very hard not to. She saw that he was struggling to keep his face impassive, but Nick could see in his eyes that something was terribly wrong. Noah felt it, too, because he was frowning the same as she was. Lucas ran a hand over his beard and looked in Noah's direction, but didn't meet his eyes.

That got Noah to his feet. "Who was that?"

Lucas glanced at him and his eyes darted to Nick, then nothing in particular. Very bad sign. "That was Myers."

Noah took a step toward him. "Myers? What happened?"

Lucas looked at the floor and shook his head. His hand retraced its path over his beard. Lucas took a deep breath and let it out slowly, when his eyes finally met Noah's they were full of terrible news. "You remember Sal Vestri?"

Noah nodded, still frowning. "You know I do, Luke. He's a lieutenant over in homicide."

"Yeah, Noah, he is."

The frown slid off Noah's face and both his eyebrows went up. "Luke?"

"He called Myers to tell him … um … Noah, Myers is at Liz's

place with Sal Vestri right now."

"What?" Noah said the word like he'd been punched in the chest.

"He says he wants us over there. Says there's somethin' that …" Lucas trailed off, and Nick's heart went out to both of them. *Oh God.*

"What?" Noah repeated. Horror was creeping into his eyes.

"Liz is dead, No. Sal says, according to the condition of the … um … of the condition that Liz is in, they're estimating she was murdered some time Friday. We have to get over there."

Noah's mouth opened. He closed it and shook his head. Lucas took a step toward him and Noah took a step back. Noah's hands went to his head like he'd been hit with a bad headache.

Noah closed his eyes like he was in sharp and sudden pain. "Friday, you said? *It's fuckin' Monday mornin'!* Alright. Okay. Liz is … *murdered,* you said?"

Lucas was watching him hard. "Yeah, Noah. Yeah."

Noah opened his eyes and looked at Lucas. His eyes had turned a deep and stormy gray. "*Murdered*?" he said the word like it was rancid.

"Yeah, Noah. We gotta go … okay?" Lucas replied, looking at him warily.

Noah tested his weight on his bad leg and winced. He seemed frustrated that he needed his cane. Noah ran his hand over his face and spoke to Lucas. "Could you do me a favor and go get my gun?"

Lucas looked at him steadily. "And your badge?"

"Right … my badge, too."

Lucas disappeared to get Noah's things and Nick stood there waiting for Noah to pop. She thought he'd be screaming and throwing things in a rage by now, but he was silent and eerily still.

Nick put a tentative hand on his shoulder. "Noah?"

Noah patted her hand, gave it a squeeze, and removed it. "I'm okay, sweetie. Thanks."

Nick didn't believe him for a second. Lucas came back with Noah's badge and service weapon. He had his own already clipped to his belt.

Lucas handed Noah his stuff. "You ready?"

Noah slid the clip of his gun over his belt and hung his badge around his neck. He narrowed his eyes and looked at Lucas. *"Who the fuck would want to kill Liz?"*

Lucas stared at him for a moment, then headed for the door. "I don't know, but we're gonna find out."

Nick watched them leave, looking very grim. She had no doubt they'd find out who had taken Liz's life. A very tiny part of her felt a little sorry for the poor bastard. May God have mercy on his ass.

Chapter Six

Contrition

By the time they got to the crime scene, Noah was so angry he felt like he was on fire. Lucas hadn't said one word to him since they'd gotten in the car and Noah appreciated it. The silence stoked the fire of his rage. Whoever killed Liz had sealed his own fate. Her killer couldn't possibly be allowed to live after committing such an atrocious act. He had to leave this world. Noah refused to let him live in it.

They got out of the car and walked through the small throng of police and curiosity seekers and into the brownstone. Lucas paused and looked at him without speaking.

"I'm good, Luke," Noah said, gamely.

Lucas's eyes were filled with concern. "You sure?"

Noah had a lump in his throat that was hard to talk around. He was afraid to open his mouth because he had no idea what might come out. Noah nodded and tried to swallow that lump down. It wouldn't budge.

Lucas looked at him like he knew he was lying. "Okay, No. I got you."

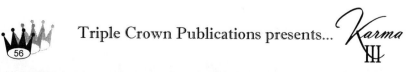

Noah nodded again and started up the stairs behind Lucas. He grimaced and was pissed by the springy pain in his knee, but grateful that it wasn't as jarringly painful as it had been. They reached the second landing and Noah almost couldn't stop himself from screaming. His nose had caught the scent. You could barely discern it. If you didn't know what it was, you'd probably miss it altogether, or think it was something else.

Noah knew it for what it was. It was Liz. Liz and his baby. The reality of it was abominably offensive to his heart and his soul. *It was intensely personal.* His gut instinct — his cop instinct — told him this was no random act. It *was* personal. Someone killed Liz to get to him. Killed his baby.

Myers was waiting outside Liz's apartment with Sal, talking low. They looked over at the stairs with somber eyes and fell silent when they saw them approach. They greeted each other all around and Myers looked at Noah with deep sadness.

"Ramsey, I can't begin to tell you how sorry I am. *Truly.*" Myers put his hand on Noah's shoulder in a well-meaning show of affection and compassion.

Noah didn't look at Lucas, but he could feel his eyes on him. He knew Lucas was waiting for him to flip out like he always did.

Sal Vestri was also watching him carefully. He shook his hand solemnly and sighed. "It's good to see you, Noah. I just wish it wasn't like this."

Noah nodded and found his voice. "Did they ... is she still here?"

Sal sighed and nodded gravely. "Yeah, Noah. We didn't move her yet. We haven't been here too long. Nobody's touched her. Off the record, I called Myers before I followed standard operating procedure. We put our heads together and decided it might be a good idea to give you a call as a courtesy, off the record. I sent my partner on a short run. You guys were never here."

Lucas shifted his gaze from Noah to Myers. "What's going on, Boss?"

Myers shook his head. "Something pretty shitty."

Sal looked as if he found the entire situation distasteful. "Amen to that. Looks like I ain't got much work. The killer's known."

Noah blinked. *What?* What the fuck was he talking about?

"Whenever you're ready, Noah, we'll step inside," Myers said.

"I'm ready now." Noah knew it was a false statement, but he said it anyway, because it was what was expected. Sal opened the door and they deferred and let Noah walk in first. Everything was neat and tidy in the familiar space. There were no signs of forced entry.

Noah took a deep breath. "Where is she?"

"The bedroom," Sal replied.

Noah closed his eyes and took a moment before he started walking. He wasn't ready for this. His eyes went to the open bedroom door. Noah could feel the hair stand up at the nape of his neck. He took another deep breath and walked into the room.

Noah knew certain things before he walked into that room. For instance, he knew that it was late June and the weather was very warm, and bodies decayed a lot quicker in the heat. The sickeningly sweet and tainted smell of putrescence never failed to flip Noah's stomach over. He bit his bottom lip and fought the nausea. After all, this was Lissette. His Liz. He loved her very much in his own way. He didn't want to look at her, sprawled across the bed like that, but his eyes couldn't leave her. He took a step closer, then another.

Noah looked down at her. Her glorious dark curls were spilled across the pillow. Her arms were splayed, her legs askew. Liz's skirt was hitched up on her thighs so high, her panties were showing. Noah's eyes moved over the still, round, ball that her belly had become. *It broke his heart.* His child was dead. Liz was gone. Another step. Oh, Jesus. Her face. Liz's skin had grayed out, her closed eyes bulged. Her mouth was slightly open and he could see the tip of her tongue. A huge and horrible purple bruise covered her swollen neck. She'd been garroted. Strangled to death. *Jesus Christ.*

Noah reached out and pulled her skirt down. He placed his hand on her eternally pregnant belly. It was a boy. That much he knew. Liz had told him while he was in the hospital. She'd said, *"It's a boy, if you care enough to know."* Noah cared. He cared a lot — about Liz and his unborn son. He thought of how cavalierly he'd treated her and he was profusely sorry. He wished he could tell her.

Noah made no effort to wipe away the tears that slid silently down his cheeks. Not even when his eyes caught a glimpse of something that had obviously been planted in Liz's left hand. He frowned and used the tail of his T-shirt to remove it, avoiding adding his prints to the crime scene. He knew what it was, because he had one of his own. It was a police photo ID. Noah held it between his thumb and forefinger and felt the first ripple of true rage run through him. There was a message written on the back in black marker. *'Told you I'd get your ass back,'* it read. Noah turned the card over and looked into the face he knew he'd see.

Usually, whenever Noah got angry, he could feel it happening. At the moment, all he felt was a little light-headed. His breath was rushed like he'd been running, and his heart was going a bit faster than normal. He was angry; furious. By now he should have been spitting fire like a dragon. Instead, he felt like he was in a vacuum that was filling up with propane. He knew he probably wouldn't explode until he struck a match on Keith's ass.

Noah turned to Lucas and showed him the ID, message side up. Lucas looked at it for a moment, then back at Noah. A lot was said in the look they shared. A lot of shit they didn't need to say out loud. It was a done deal. The die was cast.

"When you say go, Noah," Lucas said, quietly.

Noah nodded and put the card back in Liz's hand. There had been no need to turn the card over for Lucas to know who it was. Keith had kept his promise. Myers walked up behind him and laid a hand on his shoulder. Noah turned to him and noted Sal was no longer in the room.

"I'm sorry, Ramsey. I mean it." Myers didn't move his hand, but he turned to include Lucas in what he was about to lay down. "I understand Butch in I.A. is leaning on you guys hard about this asshole, wanting to smoke him out to face charges. I'm not a big believer in vigilante justice, but some things you just gotta set right. The way I see it, I.A. was looking for him, anyway."

Noah and Lucas were both staring at him hard. He had their full attention. Myers reached into his shirt pocket and pulled out a small slip of white paper with two fingers. He held it out to Noah. Noah felt like he was in a bit of a trance. Like time was somehow off. Like none of this was real.

"What's this?" Noah asked, turning the paper over in his hand.

Myers looked him directly in the eye so there would be no mistaking his meaning. "I'm not a big believer in crossing the line, either, but I *will* if I believe it in my heart to be just and righteous. I know a lot of people, good and bad. If you lean on anybody the right way, most are liable to fold and give it up." He paused when Noah opened the slip of paper. It was an address. "It's the last known whereabouts of Keith Childs, from an extremely reliable source."

Noah frowned. "South Jamaica? Queens?"

Staten Island and Queens were both unfamiliar territory to Noah. He'd had a few dalliances in both places, but he'd never spent a lot of time in either one.

Lucas nodded. "We'll find it."

Myers continued. "Childs is staying with a cousin of his, some drug head. Neighborhood knows him as Ghost, also a low level drug dealer."

Noah handed the paper to Lucas and looked back at Myers. "Thanks, Boss."

"Don't mention it." Myers sighed and looked resigned. "I just stepped over that line I was talking about. I don't have to tell you guys about the finer points of procedure, you already know. I got both of my big feet on Butch's toes with this one, and he's not gonna appreciate it ... but fuck Butch. He'll get over it because the end result will be the same. I want Childs gone. *Today*. You can lock him up, or you can take him out. Either way will be proven justifiable."

He stopped a moment and looked down at Liz. Myer's eyes rested meaningfully on her pregnant belly. His normally happy face was flushed with anger. "I could kill him myself for this. Do whatever you have to do. If you need me, call. I want this bastard gone before night falls. This never should have happened." He tucked his lips in and gave them both a gruff look of sympathy and affection. Myers patted Noah on the back just as brusquely and walked out.

Noah turned his attention back to Liz. He was sorry in his heart for every bad thing he'd ever done to her. Sorry for every horrible thing he'd ever said. Noah put his hand on her belly and kissed her forehead.

"I love you, Liz." He'd never really straight out said those words to her before, but he said them now, regretting not having done it for her to hear them. Sorrow overtook his heart and fresh tears fell.

Noah tried hard, but he couldn't stop the sob that exploded out of him. He put his face in his hands and wept for Liz and his baby, overcome with an unstoppable onslaught of grief. Noah felt Lucas move closer to him, and although he didn't touch him, Noah was glad he was there.

Noah didn't need compassionate hugs and flowery words of comfort. He needed what Lucas had to give in endless supply. He needed to channel some of Lucas' fortitude so he could go on and do what needed to be done, but he also needed to get this fresh grief out of the way. Noah needed to suck it up and turn it into something else.

Noah's tears subsided, then stopped altogether. They dried by the glow of a white hot rage. This was a feeling he was used to. He knew how to deal with this one. Noah rubbed his eyes dry with the heel of his hands. When he opened his eyes, Lucas was standing at his shoulder with his arms folded across his chest. He was waiting patiently, but his eyes were full of purpose. Noah looked at Liz one last time. The rage was building like a fireball, starting to become a conflagration.

Noah turned to Lucas. "I say go."

Lucas nodded. "Then let's get to Queens."

Chapter Seven

Not Without a Fight

People were creatures of habit. It was sad, but true. Keith mulled this over as he waited. People were prone to do the same things, the same way, every time they did them. Especially mundane things. Routine things. People hardly ever gave things like that hundred percent of their mental effort. Boring things. They did them on autopilot, eager to be done with it; with a dormant arrogance that nothing terrible could happen while they performed the task. Like now. Lucky him.

Keith watched Nadine drive her 4-Runner up the driveway. He smiled. It was Monday and she'd been grocery shopping. Just like she always did. Like clockwork, she walked around to the back of the car and took out two bags. Her cell phone rang. Keith watched her face change. She smiled at first, but the smile dropped off her face almost as soon as it appeared. Her pretty face set into a frown.

"Noah, what's the matter with you? Stop hollering at me!" She walked to the side door leading into the kitchen, opened it and paused. "Noah, are you crazy? There's nobody after me! Have you been drinking?"

Keith smiled. *You should listen to your ex-husband, you pompous bitch.*

He hadn't made a big effort to hide himself. Keith stood behind the house, just out of sight. Nadine went in and dropped the bags she'd been carrying. When she went out for the rest of them, Keith slipped inside. He stood to the right of the door and waited for her to come back.

She did — quicker than he thought she would — carrying her stupid groceries and yapping on her cell phone. "*She's what?* Who the hell is Keith Childs?"

Keith took a step forward and snatched the phone out of her hand as she stepped through the door. "That's me."

Nadine's eyes went wide with terror and Keith put the phone to his own ear. Noah was screaming her name.

"Goodbye, pretty boy," Keith said, and clicked off, ending the call. He threw the phone over his shoulder and reached for her. Nadine's mouth was open and she was breathing hard. Keith thought she'd be easy. He thought she'd be paralyzed with fear. Keith's cockiness cost him a point or two, because he didn't see the grocery bag coming up until it connected with his head.

Keith saw an entire galaxy of stars and heard glass break as his nose was filled with the pungent aroma of olives and marinara sauce. Nadine had hit him so hard, he fought for a moment to keep from passing out. Keith dropped to his knees and Nadine kicked him neatly in the balls with everything she had. The stars he saw exploded into supernovas, but he refused to become immobilized and scrambled to his feet as she darted away from him.

"I'll kill you, you fuckin' bitch!" Keith screamed at her.

Nadine made it to the counter and started throwing things at him. The coffeemaker landed at his feet. A mug hit him in the chest. A plate sailed past his head like a Frisbee.

"You get your ass out of my house, motherfucker!" she screamed back at him, looking for something else to throw.

The pain in Keith's crotch receded to a dull throb. Nadine reached the drawer and pulled it open. Keith stepped in close and grabbed her by the hair. Her hand came out of the drawer clasped around the handle of a paring knife — not very big, but a knife all the same. He pulled her head back and hit her in the face. Nadine cried out in pain and outrage and slashed him across the knuckles, stomping against his shins and insteps with her kitten heeled sandals.

"Help! Somebody! He's trying to kill me! Help!" she screamed.

Keith wasn't having all this noise. He closed his hands around her throat. Nadine reflexively dropped the knife and tried to pry his hands loose. He grinned in victory as he felt the fight going out of her, but was a touch disappointed because he'd wanted to do more than just strangle her to death like Liz. After all, variety was the spice of life.

Nadine started to slump and he went with her, his hands clasped firmly around her neck. Now she was clawing at him. He felt the skin leave the back of his hands. Nadine pitched forward suddenly, in a last ditch effort to save herself. Keith tightened his grip, determined to kill her. Nadine grabbed the dish detergent and squirted it over her shoulder. It went up his nose first, then into his eyes, burning like fire.

"Bitch! You fucking *bitch*!" Keith yelled in unexpected agony. Nadine had blinded him, and to get the soap out of his burning eyes, he had no choice but to let her go. Keith heard her scurry away as he staggered to the sink and splashed cold water on his face in an attempt to flush his eyes. He slung the water away and used a kitchen towel to dry his face. His eyes still stung and felt raw.

Keith didn't have time to do more for himself. He went after her because he had no idea what this crazy bitch was up to. She could be lying in the cut, waiting to ambush him. He took his service weapon out and took the safety off. Keith wasn't taking any more chances with Nadine.

Keith came around the corner, out of the kitchen and into the living room. Nadine was standing there, feet apart, arms straight out in front of her in a fairly good facsimile of a police stance. She was leveling a .38 at him, and she looked like she meant to use it. Keith had his arm extended, weapon in hand. It was a showdown.

One thing Keith could say, was that Ramsey had obviously taken precautions to keep his women safe. Too bad only one of them had taken the time to listen.

"Put the fuckin' gun down, Nadine," Keith said, smoothly.

Nadine was starting to tremble. Her control was deteriorating rapidly. When she spoke, her voice was breathless with fear and anger. "Fuck you! You put *your* goddamned gun down!"

Keith smiled and took a step toward her. Nadine stood her ground and looked down the sight of her gun. "You stop moving! Stop moving or I'll blow your brains out!"

Keith cocked his head as he heard the sudden, unmistakable, wail of police sirens. Goddamn it! Ramsey must've radioed ahead. There was no doubt there'd be an APB out for him now. He looked at Nadine and aimed.

"You put up a good fight. I'll make sure to tell Ramsey how brave you were," Keith fired at her as she turned to run.

Nadine whirled around and fired back blindly. One bullet hit him dead center. Keith dropped to one knee, the wind knocked out of him from the force of impact, and thanked God for Kevlar. He leapt for her, aware that the sirens were closer and his time was short. Keith tackled Nadine like a linebacker and they both fell through the glass coffee table, Nadine taking the brunt of it.

Keith got up quickly and looked down at her. She was unconscious and bleeding in a dozen different places. The sirens were right in front of the house. Maybe she'd bleed out. That was all he could hope for. His time was up. Keith made a mad dash for the bedroom and went out the window. On to his last stop. Nicky.

Chapter Eight

Picking Up The Gauntlet

There was no longer a need to go to Queens. Not at the moment, anyway. They knew exactly where Keith was, unless he'd very recently left. But even if they'd missed him, they had an excellent idea of where he'd turn up.

Lucas was doing 80 with Noah riding shotgun to get to Nadine. He'd never in his career had to put a bubble on his personal car, but there was one on it now. Time was crucial. Keith could be killing her at this very moment. Noah had just gotten off the phone with Myers. Myers had guaranteed there would be a fleet of cars at Nadine's ASAP. Lucas glanced at Noah as he got Leah on speed dial.

He was direct and to the point. "It's Noah. Keith killed Liz. He's got Nadine. I'm assumin' he's gonna try and kill her, too. My guess is this shit will end with Nick. Get your gun and hustle over there and hold down the fort. We'll be there as soon as we can. *Do it now, Leah.* Hurry up."

Lucas made the right turn onto Nadine's street with a loud shriek of rubber. Noah calmly ended the call and took the safety off his gun. "That fuck better hope to God Nadine ain't dead!" Lucas screeched to a stop in front of the house, as Noah checked for his badge. "If she is, he's gonna leave this world screamin' for his fuckin' mother, that's a promise."

Noah threw the door open and got out of the car without the aid of his cane. Lucas put his badge around his neck, too, and followed Noah to the driveway. The wail of police sirens was piercingly loud.

Myers was as good as his word. Five cars pulled up, and the officers poured out ready to shoot anything that moved. Lucas and Noah both held their badges up as a white shirted lieutenant made his way over, a sergeant at his elbow.

"Ramsey and Cain? I'm Lieutenant Forrester." He looked at Lucas.

"Yes, sir. I'm Cain, he's Ramsey."

The lieutenant put his hands on his hips and nodded. "Myers is a personal friend of mine." He paused as an ambulance drove up and double-parked. "He gave me a brief scenario of the situation. I'm gonna send my men around the perimeter. We're gonna go inside with you ourselves. You need a K-9 unit?"

Lucas shook his head and watched Noah eye the open back door of Nadine's truck, then swivel his head to the side door of the house. It stood open five inches out of the frame.

"I don't think he's still here. If not, we're pretty sure where he's headed," Lucas said. His cell phone rang. It was Nicole. "Yeah, baby?"

"I'm outta here, Lucas. I can't run, I can only try to shoot him. He'll get me, stuck in here."

"Where are you going?"

"I'm going to your other brownstone. I don't think he'll look for me there."

It was a damned good idea. "Sounds good. The keys are —"

Nick cut him off, urgently. "I have the keys in my hand, Lucas. I'll tell Leah to meet me there. I love you."

She hung up in his ear and Lucas wasn't mad at her. He knew she was dealing with fight or flight and she was hurt. She'd never beat Keith in a fight. He wanted to call her back, but Noah pushed the open side door with his gun and went into the house. Lucas was right behind him. Noah took high, he took low — locked and loaded — arms extended, prepared for an ambush.

The kitchen was a mess. There was a huge smear of spaghetti sauce, olives, and soap sloshed across the floor like they'd been fighting in it. Broken dishes and small appliances littered the floor. The water was running in the sink. Noah moved cautiously around the debris with a pronounced limp and took the time to shut off the faucet. He looked at Lucas and nodded at the entrance to the living room.

Lucas stayed low and went in first, Noah at his back, and swept the room. There was no one waiting to leap out at them like a homicidal jack-in-the-box. There was only Nadine, lying in the middle of the shattered coffee table.

"Nadine!" Noah seemed to forget everything else. Forgot Keith might still be there, forgot this was a crime scene, forgot he was in pain. He pushed past Lucas and went to her. He dropped to his knees, heedless of his injury, except for an involuntary grunt of pain.

Forrester radioed for the EMTs, then started toward the back of the house with the sergeant. Noah took Nadine's hand, absently putting his gun on the floor. Lucas lowered his weapon. He could see the hysteria building in Noah's eyes as he reached for her throat. Lucas prayed that Noah would find the pulse he was looking for.

Noah waited a beat, then two. Relief washed the hysteria out of his eyes and Lucas let out the breath he'd been holding. Noah started tapping her cheeks lightly with his fingertips. "Nadine! Nadine, wake up, sweetie. It's me, Noah. Come on back."

The EMTs came in and started to work on Nadine. Lucas pulled Noah to his feet and they shared a weighty look. Lucas could not believe this shit. Found it hard to swallow. Was every other person in the world out of their minds? He used to believe lightening never struck twice. Now he knew that particular saying was bullshit. Nadine cried out when the EMTs put her on the gurney.

Noah turned back to her. "Hey, Nadine. I'm here."

"Noah!" Her voice was scared and breathless. "He was here! He was in the house. He tried to kill me, Noah! *Why?*"

Noah stroked her hair and attempted to calm her down. "I know, sweetie. I know. I'm sorry. Everything's gonna be okay, now. We'll take care of it, me and Luke. He won't hurt anybody else," he said, in his most soothing voice.

Nadine looked terrified. "The kids, Noah. Somebody's got to get our kids."

"Shh … it's okay. My folks will get the kids. I'll come check on you as soon as I finish what I have to do. I promise."

"Noah, don't go. What if he kills you?"

"He won't," Lucas said. They would make sure no one else would die at Keith's hands, if they could help it. They looked at each other. Keith was as good as dead.

Noah smiled at her and Lucas wondered how he managed to do it. "See? He won't. I gotta go. You're in good hands. I wouldn't leave you, otherwise."

Forrester came back into the room. "Looks like the perp went out the window in the master. You sure you don't want that K-9 unit? Perimeter search is turning up nothing without it."

Noah nodded. "Yeah, I'm sure. I could use a couple of cars to ride with the ambulance, though. Maybe some boys on the door, once she's in."

"Not a problem. Anything else?"

Noah shook his head and gave him a smile. "That's it. 'Preciate it. You're a prince."

Forrester offered his hand. "You guys get this piece of shit. He's an insult."

Noah shook his hand. "He's as good as got."

Forrester shook Lucas's hand, too, and they nodded at each other respectfully. "Go with God."

Lucas and Noah walked out of the house. Noah was on the phone the minute they stepped outside. He called his folks first, then he checked for Nick and Leah. He was about to call Myers when he hesitated and looked over at Lucas. Lucas was working hard to get across Brooklyn, from Canarsie to his house, in the least amount of time. He was concentrating on the road, but he could feel Noah looking at him. He glanced his way.

"What's on your mind, No?"

Noah put his phone away and fired up a Dunhill. There was really no need for Lucas to have asked that question. He knew exactly what Noah was thinking. He'd known since he'd gotten the call from Myers. It had hung in the air between them, unspoken all morning. It's been said, a good friend will help you move ... your best friend will help you move a body.

"I need you to do me a favor, Luke."

"Name it."

Noah looked as if he wanted to speak on it, but he went a different route. "Could you get off the highway and find me a Rite-Aid?"

Lucas looked over at him with concern. Noah looked a little shadowy under the eyes, but that could be anything. "You in a lot of pain?"

Noah rolled his eyes toward the window, blew smoke out the side of his mouth, then looked back at him. "That would be the understatement of the fuckin' century."

Lucas kept his eyes on the road. Now that they were at a quiet intermission in this one-man horror show Keith was acting out, he started to feel the weight of guilt settle on his shoulders. As a matter of fact, it did more than that. He wasn't a bit shocked when his throat tightened up.

"Hey, Noah?" His voice sounded shaky, even to him.

Noah threw the butt of his Dunhill out of the window. "Yeah?" He said it like he was tired.

"I'm real sorry, No. Maybe if I'd handled things a little different —"

Noah interrupted him, and Lucas was shocked by the indignation in his voice. "Don't you sit there and tell me you're sorry, Lucas! I don't want to hear that shit! Not from you. You ain't got shit to be sorry to me about. You feel guilty? Good, so do I. We can sit here and feel guilty together."

Lucas shook his head. "Yeah, but Noah —"

Noah banged his fist on the dashboard. "Goddamnit, Lucas! Don't put this guilt on you like a brand new suit, bro. You can't. Who would have known this fucker didn't have all his marbles? He's a goddamned *Detective*, Lucas! *Who would have known?*"

"I should have known," Lucas said quietly.

Noah hit the dashboard again. "*Man, fuck that dead bitch!* That's that Simone shit, Luke. Fuck her dead ass. You thought — and rightly so — *one* crazy motherfucker was enough to last any one person a lifetime. Well, you were wrong, bro. Turns out they grow on trees like apples and coconuts."

Lucas held his tongue and pulled into the parking lot of a Rite-Aid. Noah turned to him and put a hand on his shoulder.

"Lucas, listen to me. We both know the truth. Keith is makin' good on his promise to get you back. It's like I said, if you're gonna feel guilty, then we'll do it together. If you're guilty for beatin' Keith's ass, then so am I. I was your front man. I was there eggin' you on every step of the way. I was *dyin'* for you to lay that nigga out. I found out where he was stayin' and I drove you there *myself*. I grabbed his ass off Nick *myself*, okay? So … we'll eat off the guilty plate with two forks. One for you and one for me. Ain't nobody know that asshole would flip out like this. You can't never control a lunatic, Luke. So we move on. We can't take back what he did, but we can make it right."

Lucas knew he was right. Well, if not exactly *right*, Noah's thinking was rational enough for him. Noah got out of the car and limped into the store. Lucas followed him. They didn't talk much as Noah purchased three Ace bandages, a bottle of Tylenol, a bottle of water, and, curiously, a roll of duct tape.

They went back to the car and Noah opened the Tylenol and shook out four of them. He popped them into his mouth and chased them with the water. He waited a second and took another one.

Lucas raised an eyebrow and started the car. "You don't think that was too much?"

Noah laughed. The sound of it was a relief after all the deep shit that had gone down. "Shit, Luke, if those goddamn Trinidads didn't manage to kill my ass, I seriously doubt this shit will."

Lucas couldn't argue. He had a point. Lucas pulled out and got back on the highway. Noah put his seat all the way back and opened the bandages. He took off his sneaker and pulled the fabric of his jeans as close to his skin as he could get it. Noah wound the bandage first around his foot, then around his ankle, working his way up his injured leg, over his jeans, making sure the bandage was tight. He worked methodically. Where one bandage ended, he started another.

Noah kept winding until all three bandages were securely over his knee, then he used the tape and went around his entire leg — foot to thigh — *twice*. When he was finished, he sat back and lit a cigarette.

Lucas glanced down at Noah's duct tape covered leg. He couldn't help but smile and poke a little fun. "So … what are you suppose to be? Robocop?"

Noah laughed grudgingly. "Hey, fuck you, Luke."

"Fuck you back."

They shared a laugh with no real force behind it and fell into one of their silences. Noah finished his smoke and tossed it. He sighed deeply.

"When we find Keith, I'm gonna kill his ass slow. I don't want my kneecap slippin' outta place while I do it."

Lucas smiled without humor. "Not if I see him first."

Noah looked at him, frowning. "Fuck *that*, Luke. I got dibs."

Lucas held his smile. "Not if I see him first," he repeated.

Noah looked at him a moment longer, then settled into his seat and closed his eyes. Lucas glanced at him and returned his attention back to driving. He could totally understand Noah wanting to kill this bastard slow. Keith had done horrible things to Noah.

Lucas didn't favor long drawn out scenes. When he saw Keith Childs, he didn't plan on asking him why, or kicking his ass. He was going to put him in his sights and shoot him until he was dead. Noah would just have to bitch about it later.

Chapter Nine

Just One More Thing

Keith's luck had finally taken a hit, but it was still all good. He'd had to make a few minor adjustments because of that slick bitch, Nadine, and it had thrown him off schedule. He let himself into Ghost's apartment to clean himself up and change his clothes. Keith went into the kitchen first for a bottle of water to get the nasty taste of soap out of his mouth.

Ghost was in there with some nameless flunky, cutting product at the kitchen table. Nameless took one look at Keith and jumped up to run. Ghost glanced, unaffectedly, over his shoulder, then looked back at Mr. Flunky.

"'Sup, Keith? Sit down, man, that's my cousin. He ain't interested in you."

Keith retrieved the water from the fridge, stepping around Nameless, who stood there gaping at him, not sure what to do. Keith laughed at his reaction. "Relax. I got nothing to do with what a man does in the privacy of his own home. I'm not gonna knock you." He returned to his seat, reluctantly, still staring at Keith with distrustful eyes. Keith laughed and shook his head. Fucking mope.

"What you doin' in your uniform, man?" Ghost asked, dropping white powder into a small glassine envelope. He looked up at Keith. "Ain't you a detective? I didn't think y'all had to wear uniforms."

Keith smiled evenly. This fool was sitting here cutting coke in his face and had the balls to ask him some shit like that. To flex on him would have been absurd, though. He'd been AWOL since Oscar lost his head.

"I'm slumming. Carry on," he said, with a fake smile and a dismissive flip of his hand. Keith walked out of the room.

"Guess that means 'mind my fuckin' business,'" Ghost said under his breath.

"That's *exactly* what you should do." Keith said it loud, to let him know he'd heard him.

Keith went into the spare bedroom he'd been crashing in and took off his clothes. He showered quickly and took a few extra moments to shave his moustache off. He peered into the mirror and frowned. Keith had a speed knot just below his right temple from that ho hitting him in the side of the head — catching him out there with her olives and marinara sauce. There was a thin and painful cut sitting right on top of that knot. Keith covered it with a styptic pencil to make sure it wouldn't bleed again.

He looked at the pencil and smirked. Nicky had always wondered what these pencils were for. He couldn't count how many times he'd just wanted to blurt out, *"to hide shit, you silly bitch!"* He looked thoughtful. He'd loved Nicky in his way, but sometimes he'd just wanted to push her beautiful ass through a wall. Nicky was beautiful, a great lay, and she could cook ... but she had too much cop in her. She was constantly asking questions. That alone irritated him to no end. But he wouldn't have to suffer through that anymore. She was no longer his problem.

Still ... sometimes he missed her, but that was mostly physical. His mind's eye conjured up a sudden and brilliant picture of Lucas Cain making vigorous and passionate love to his woman. *His woman. Nicky.* A low growl of fury left his throat like flames and he snapped the pencil in half. Keith hated that bastard, and he hated Nicky for being with his swaggering, imperious, condescending ass. He smiled into the mirror. He hated Noah just as much, with his pretty face and his smirking, ridiculing mouth. He wondered if he'd finally managed to wipe the smiles off their faces and strip them of some of their cockiness.

Keith went into the bedroom and started to get dressed. His underwear, the Kevlar, then one of his old uniforms. He pinned the badge in place. It wasn't his. It belonged to a long dead cop named Calvin Blanchard. Keith and Oscar had snuck him while he was sitting in his patrol car. Keith shot him behind his ear for getting too nosy.

Calvin wasn't the first cop he'd killed. He grinned again. He'd been hanging out with a fellow cadet from the academy … Keith frowned, searching his memory for a name. Jimmy. Jimmy something. Nice guy. They'd been drinking beer on Jimmy's roof on a hot summer evening. Down time. Keith had been telling him how much he disliked Cain and Ramsey, maybe one or two other people. Jimmy implied that maybe, he was jealous. Keith didn't take shorts. He got up and pushed that ass-kissing monkey off the roof.

Keith put on a pair of sunglasses to hide his irritated eyes and distract attention from the knot on the side of his head. He took a couple of Tylenols to keep the pounding in his head to a minimum, and re-packed his luggage. When he was done, he picked that bag up and slung his garment bag over his shoulder. Keith had a 9 o'clock to Costa Rica. His new life started tomorrow. He emerged from the bedroom refreshed and ready for the next leg of his journey. He walked past the kitchen where the two morons had resumed cutting their coke.

Keith poked his head in and smiled at his cousin. "Hey, Ghost? I just wanted to say thanks for the hospitality. Look me up if you ever get to Costa Rica."

Ghost barely looked up from what he was doing. "Will do. Take it easy."

Keith was almost at the door when he heard the other guy's voice. "That's one strange motherfucker."

"I heard. You'd think a nigga would break me off somethin' for my *'hospitality'* since I put him up on such short notice," Ghost snorted laughter, "And seein' as how I won't be goin' to Costa Rica no time soon."

Keith smiled and shook his head. He was right. Ghost was a moron. He stepped back into the kitchen with a .32 in his hand, still smiling. "No, Ghost … *you won't.*"

Ghost turned to him with a look of surprise and Keith blasted him in the bridge of his nose. Ghost fell backward in his chair as his blood and brains created a gruesome backsplash on the wall behind him.

His pal jumped up screaming. "Oh shit! Oh shit! You killed Ghost!"

Keith advanced on him and put his gun in his face. Ghost's fellow cocaine cutter made a strange mewling sound and put his hands up defensively.

"No, man, *please!* I won't say nothin'! I won't say nothin'! Please!"

There was an unexpectedly pungent smell of piss as he voided his bladder. Keith stepped away from the puddle growing at the man's feet with disgust and shot him right in his begging mouth. He wiped his prints off the gun and folded it into the dead man's hand. It was a halfhearted attempt to make it look like a murder/suicide. Whatever. Keith didn't really give a shit. He hadn't planned on killing Ghost or his friend, but Keith really hated a smart-mouthed motherfucker.

Keith pulled on driving gloves to cover the scratches and cuts on the backs of his hands, picked up his bags, and went out to his car. Some kids were standing at the corner across the street, looking back at the house. When people who'd never heard a gunshot in their lives actually heard one, they knew exactly what it was. It didn't sound like a firecracker. It sounded like a goddamned gunshot. Keith could have cared less. He drove to Carroll Gardens to meet Giordano and Rigby — two cops only slightly less crooked than he was.

Giordano and Rigby were fellow miscreants — rogue cops that never should have had the badge — that specialized in wet work. Dom Giordano had *never* walked a straight line. His mother's brother was made and a Cappo in the mob. He had his hands in so many things, it was crazy, and he didn't mind killing your ass. Mark Rigby, on the other hand, had damn near been a choirboy, until he discovered he had a great affection for money. He'd do almost anything for it, to keep himself in the lifestyle he'd grown accustomed to — including killing your ass.

They'd both played integral parts in helping Keith and Oscar in their dirty work, and were recognized members in their felonious band of cops. Dom had guaranteed he'd meet Keith three blocks from Cain's with a cruiser to make it all look legit. How he'd managed to snag a cruiser was beyond Keith. He didn't know and he didn't want to know. After all, Dom and Mark weren't uniforms, they were detectives just like him.

Rigby and Giordano were two of the many "poker buddies" Nicky never managed to meet. Keith parked his car a good distance away, by the park. He walked to where Dom and Mark were parked in their cruiser and got in the back seat.

"What's good, fellas?" Keith asked, cheerily.

"It's all good," Mark replied from the driver's position.

Dom put his elbow over the back of the seat and grinned at him. "Seems like Myers dispatched a plain clothes detail and two cruisers. Cain's block is crawlin' with cops. Virtually impenetrable. A little more, they wouldn't be lettin' people in their houses."

Keith sat back in his seat. "Is Nicky in the house?"

"Negative," Mark said, looking over his shoulder. "She left the residence with another female."

Dom smiled. "Leah Wheeler."

Keith smiled, too. "Very interesting. Any idea where they went?""

Mark added his smile to the mix. "Another brownstone in the next block. Haven't been out since. Also a cruiser on that block with presumed plain clothes detail."

Keith frowned, but Dom held his smile. "Skylar is assigned to that cruiser."

Keith grinned. Another poker buddy. "Now *that's* a beautiful thing."

Dom laughed. "I'll say."

"Cain and Ramsey show up yet?"

"Not a peep, but they're on their way. I guess once they're here, you'll have all you ducks in a row."

Keith laughed. "That's right. All those ducks in a very nicely laid trap. You guys better get your black bands ready for your badges. This is gonna be a big deal. This city's about to lose two of its best cops. The mourning's gonna be deep."

Dom laughed boisterously. "I could give a fuck. I'll be sunnin' myself in Belize."

"Yeah, me too," Mark added.

"And I'll be in Costa Rica. Well, let's get moving. We all got planes to catch," Keith said with a smile.

Rigby drove the four blocks to the other brownstone. They got out and started up the stoop, while Keith stayed in the car. Keith decided to play Nicky's torture by ear. Leah, who'd always thought the worst of him, had bought her cup of heartache just by showing up. He'd always kept one eye on her well-shaped ass. She could definitely get some, too. As for Cain and Ramsey ... he hoped their insurance was paid up, because their cards had just been punched.

Chapter Ten

Brace Yourselves

Nick almost jumped out of her skin when the doorbell rang. They were sequestered in the first floor apartment of Lucas' second brownstone. He'd intended to fix it up for her, but things had taken a different turn, and now it only held her things. For the first time in months she was sitting on her own sofa, in the company of Leah and two other detectives from Midtown South — Saul Adler and Travis Barnes.

No one could have made Nick believe Keith was the person he was turning out to be. She was offended by this dark side he was showing. She felt soiled and used because she'd once been touched all the time by his filthy, bloody, hands.

Beyond that, she found it hard to swallow the fact that she'd been that gullible. Nick couldn't fathom that she'd been that blind to his diabolic alter ego ... to his brutality ... to his complete lack of humanity. It made her shudder and want to vomit.

She couldn't hate Keith more if he were the devil himself. So there she sat ... next to Leah, on her own sofa, hugging herself and shivering — even though it was summer. Because in her heart of hearts she did have an idea about Keith.

She watched Saul get up with his gun in his hand and look through the peephole. Leah and Travis stood, too, weapons drawn. Saul didn't seem alarmed. Nick pushed herself to her feet. Maybe it was Lucas and Noah.

Saul unlocked the door and stepped back. "Hey, buddy, what

gives? Ain't you guys got detail downstairs? If you're up here, who's mindin' the store?"

Two uniforms stepped inside. The black one spoke. "It's covered. Myers wanted to deter Childs with a strong presence, so he put two more cruisers on the block."

The other one smiled. "Yeah, so there's plenty to mind the store. Us? We got lunch detail. You want us to get you somethin'?" he asked, congenially.

Saul grinned and put his gun away. "Now that you mention it, I'll have a corned beef on rye and a diet Coke. Don't forget my pickle."

The smiling, barrel-chested Italian nodded appreciatively. "Sounds good. You?" he asked, looking at Travis.

"I'll have the same, but make mine a Sprite."

"You got it. Ladies?"

"Coffee. Two large. Regular," Leah said. She hadn't put her gun away, but she'd lowered it. It was obvious to Nick, if no one else, that Leah's radar was up and she was suspicious of everyone.

"No food?" the Italian asked, with an inclination of his head.

Leah shook hers. "No. We're good."

He shrugged. "Suit yourself. We'll be right back."

"Hey, don't forget my pickle," Saul repeated and closed the door behind them.

******

Noah's knee was stiffening up on him and he didn't want Lucas to know. That's why he'd taped it up the way he had. Not only was it getting stiff, but there was a dull throb in the center of his knee, like a goddamn heartbeat. He would've loved to have taken a few more Tylenol's, but he didn't want Lucas looking at him funny. Noah stretched his leg out and lifted his foot nonchalantly. It wasn't excruciating, but the shit still hurt.

Noah gave Lucas a sidelong glance and took a sip of his water. They were two blocks away from his house. This shit wasn't going to feel any better any time soon. It would most likely be a lot worse than this at the end of the day — but at least it was the *only* pain he was really having.

His shoulder was zinging a little, but that feeling of being hit in the chest with a fucking sledgehammer was pretty much gone. Noah rotated his foot. Fuck it. *He'd be fine*. He'd worked in a lot more pain than he was currently in. He'd be fine. Had to be.

Like always, Lucas got in his head. "You okay, Noah?"

Noah nodded and put the cap on his water. "Swell."

Lucas double-parked in front of his brownstone, beside what could only be an unmarked police car. He turned in his seat and looked at Noah doubtfully. "Uh-huh. You in a lot of pain?"

Noah figured lying would be pointless. "Some. It's not as bad as it could be."

Lucas looked him over hard. "Maybe not, but it's bad enough for you to try to turn yourself into the tin man. You feel up to this, Noah?"

"You damn right I'm up to it. I'll be fine. I wanna see the look on Keith's face when I kill his ass." He paused and looked Lucas in the eye. "He's gotta pay for all the stuff he's done, Luke, even if I ain't the one to do it. You hear me talkin' to you?"

Lucas nodded grimly. "Loud and clear. I want to kill his ass as bad as you do."

"Then what are we sittin' here for?"

Lucas started the car and drove into the next block.

******

Keith watched Dom and Mark go up the steps and through the front door of the brownstone. He reached for his ankle holster and removed the gun he'd tucked there. He took his time screwing in the silencer and waited for them to come back. Keith had intended to be done with his next move by the time they returned, but he'd made a stupid mistake. He'd gotten into the back seat. Everyone knew there were no handles in the backseat of a police cruiser. This one was no exception. He was locked in. Oh, well. No worries.

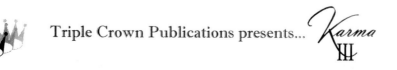

Keith amused himself by searching the block for the plainclothes detail. Except for the four cruisers in front of them, there was only one other car on the block holding passengers. There was a navy blue Impala parked five cars behind him on the left. It held two flatfoots, gabbing and eating, when they should have been keeping an eye out for *him*. Keith hoped their last meal was all it should have been.

Dom and Mark returned and let him out of the back seat. Keith got out and fingered the extra silencer in his shirt pocket, glad he'd brought it with him. He had his gun in his hand, held low and out of the way.

Keith smiled brightly at Giordano and Rigby. "'Scuse me, fellas. I have a stop to make."

Dom eyed the gun. "You need help?"

Keith shrugged good-natured. "Nah. I got this one." He walked to the Impala, still smiling, with his hand behind his back.

Keith tapped on the window and the unsuspecting officer rolled it down, smiling back. "Hey, what's up, buddy?"

"Not much," Keith replied. "You know how it goes."

The driver was shoveling french fries into his mouth. He nodded a greeting as the other one made a face of commiseration. "Tell me about it. This is slow work."

Keith leaned down and peered inside. "How does that *taste*? Is it good?"

They both turned and looked at him strangely. The closer one frowned and looked offended. "*What?*" Hamburger flew out of his mouth and bounced off Keith's pilfered badge.

Keith laughed and stuck his gun in the window. "I hope it was good, 'cause it's the last thing you'll ever stuff in your mouth."

They didn't have time to react. Keith pumped two rounds into each of their chests at point blank range. They were either dead or so close to it. It wouldn't matter. He hadn't shot them in the head because, though he was bold and didn't give a fuck, he didn't want to call immediate attention by leaving a gruesome scene.

Keith opened the door and rolled the window back up. He smiled. That was two consecutive life sentences right there, at the very least. He walked across the street and joined Mark and Dom at Skylar's cruiser. They were engaged in easy conversation about the Yankees.

The windows were already down, so it was easy. Keith walked right up to the driver, stuck the gun in the hollow of his throat and fired twice. He had to get messy with this one — the driver was wearing a vest. Skylar put the windows up and stepped out, joining Keith, Dom and Mark. They all went up the stoop together...

Chapter Eleven

Horror Show

"Food's here," Saul announced when the doorbell rang again. The food may very well have been there, but anyway you cut it — unless they had a grill in the squad car — it was way too soon for anybody to slap an order together that quick. Leah got up and pulled her gun. Nick decided it was the perfect time to have hers in her hand, too. She reached behind the pillow for it and the weight of her service weapon felt like an old friend.

Saul looked at Leah in alarm as he reached out to unlock the door. "Hey! What the fuck's wrong with *you*? It's just the uniforms with the food."

"Don't open the door," Leah said, "It's not the food!"

Saul held up a hand to chill her out and looked through the peephole. He turned back to her, smiling, and Travis looked at her like she was overreacting.

"See, it's just the food. Calm down."

Leah extended her arms and pointed her weapon straight at the door, all the while, yelling at Saul. Nick took cover behind the sofa and put her bead on the door, too. Unless that was Lucas and Noah, she was blasting whoever came through that door. She had the same feeling as Leah. Something damn sure wasn't right here. It stank like an ambush.

"Step away from the fuckin' door, Saul! Don't open the god-damned door!" Leah screamed at him. Saul looked at her like she'd lost her mind and opened it anyway.

"See ..." he said, and fell back instantly, clutching his neck, blood gushing through his fingers.

"Oh shit! Saul!" Travis grabbed at his shoulder holster for his gun and got a bullet in his forehead.

"Shit! Oh shit, Nick!" Leah yelled.

Leah dropped into a crouch as those two uniforms walked into the apartment with their weapons drawn. Leah started shooting and clipped the Italian in the forearm then the shoulder. Nick aimed at the black one and squeezed off a round. He turned his head just as the bullet connected and grabbed his ear. Leah was low and moving toward the door. Nick started firing at the other uniform that stepped in, as Leah shot the black one above his right eye, ending what Nick started. Nick knew, instinctively, to aim high or low — not the body — because it was obvious these assholes were wearing Kevlar.

The Italian was growling like an animal and headed for her. Nick swung her gun in his direction and clicked on an empty chamber. Her heart sank and stuttered in her chest. She backpedaled to get away from him and landed on her ass. Nick had a flashback of Keith standing over her the same way. She did the same thing she did then and went for his balls. Her right foot came up to connect with his crotch, but he grabbed her foot and twisted her ankle like he meant to break it off. Nick screamed in pain and tried to pull her foot away.

"Fuck you, bitch! *Come here!*" He pulled her forward by her foot and Nick swung her empty gun, smashing him in the face with it. That little trick only made him angry. He gave her foot a brutal twist and Nick heard the bone in her ankle snap. She howled.

"Oh no you *don't*, you greasy motherfucker!" Leah came up behind him and grabbed him by the hair. When he turned his head, she socked the muzzle of her gun under his chin and pulled the trigger. Leah grimaced and pushed him away, wearing most of his brains on the sleeve of her light summer blouse. She gave Nick a shaky smile as she wiped her hand on her jeans.

"Jesus Christ! This shit is like killing vampires. You gotta make sure you get 'em in the head." Leah stuck her hand out to help Nick up, but when she reached for her, Nick watched Leah's eyes roll up in her head. She grunted softly and dropped to the floor.

"I agree," Keith said, jovially. He smiled down at Nick and she knew she was going to die. "Hey, baby. Long time, no see." He snatched Nick up by her tee shirt and hit her under the chin. Everything went black.

******

When Lucas drove into the next block, he knew something was wrong. He felt it like a sixth sense, like a rash on his skin.

"Somethin's not right, Luke," Noah said quietly, obviously feeling it, too. Lucas parked the car. There was an unmarked two cars ahead.

"Somethin's not right," Noah repeated.

They got out of the car and surveyed the street. Lucas took two steps toward the unmarked and frowned. Unless the two undercovers were sleeping, or doing something strange ... he looked at them slumped in their seats, their heads almost touching in the middle of the car, and knew they were dead.

"Oh man, Luke ..." Noah said, with a grimace. He took his cell phone out as Lucas walked up on the car. He looked inside and saw both detectives with fatal chest wounds — their lunches all over their laps. Lucas looked at Noah and shook his head. Noah was talking into his phone, but he pointed across the street at the squad car.

They walked over together and looked through the window at the murdered officer with the hole in his throat — a look of surprise in his sightless eyes. Lucas caught the tail end of Noah's conversation.

"Uniform's deceased, too. No ... doesn't seem like he's solo. We're goin' in, Boss."

Noah ended the call and put his phone in his pocket. They looked at each other and took their guns out, displayed their badges and started up the stoop. Lucas looked at Noah. His leg had him moving stiffly, and Lucas knew some of that frown on his face was from the pain in his knee. He also knew that Noah was as tough as they came — that his will and determination were like iron. Knowing that still didn't stop Lucas from worrying about him.

"Noah?" He asked an entire question with one word.

Noah looked back at him and they kept moving. "If I said I was a hundred percent, I'd be lying, Luke — but I'm good. I don't care which one of us gets him. Let's just make sure that bitch don't leave here breathin'." They reached the front door of the brownstone.

"He won't," Lucas said, and he meant it. The only way Keith was leaving was on the inside of a body bag. Guaranteed.

******

When Keith carried the now unconscious Nicole into one of the back bedrooms, he took an impromptu step in his next course of action. Skylar was seriously getting on his nerves. He'd been constantly asking annoying questions, complaining about the flesh wound on his cheek, and generally nipping around his ankles like a high strung puppy. That shit had to stop. He was fucking up his concentration.

Nicky's bed was unassembled. The mattress and box spring leaned against a wall. Keith knocked the mattress over with his foot and dropped Nick on top of it.

"What do you want me to do with her, Keith?"

Keith looked over his shoulder in irritation at this indecisive, pesky, motherfucker. He was carrying Leah over his shoulder. Blood from the head wound she'd gotten from Keith hitting her with his gun dripped on the floor in small red dots.

"Just toss her down next to Nicky."

Skylar did as he was told, then started in with a barrage of questions. "What are you gonna do, Keith? You gotta know Cain and Ramsey will be here any minute, don't you? What's your plan, Keith?"

"Of course I know they're on their way. That's part of the plan."

Skylar's face was filled with consternation. "What are you gonna do, Keith? Why are you doin' this?"

"Revenge."

"Revenge? Fine. Okay. I'm cool with that, but I thought you just wanted to pop Nicky and be gone. I'm good with that, too. Pop her, and let's get the fuck outta here. This waitin' for Cain and Ramsey shit is crazy! What are you gonna do, Keith? Dom is dead. Mark is, too. There's a whole lotta dead cops here, Keith, and I ain't tryin' to be around when Cain and Ramsey to make me one more. Fuck that! When they get here, they won't be lookin' to arrest us. Let's just cap her ass and get the fuck outta the country."

The sound of his voice was like fingernails down a chalkboard. It buzzed in Keith's ears like the drone of an insect. It was driving him crazy. Keith smiled. Well … *crazier*. Keith knew what he wanted to do and he was going to see it through.

He wanted Ramsey and Cain to literally get on their knees and beg him to let them live. He wanted to violate Nicky and kill her right in front of Cain. He wanted him to feel helpless and emasculated. Just as helpless as he was sure Ramsey was feeling right about now. Stupid bastards.

"Keith? What the fuck, man? Where *are* you? I'm standin' here talkin' to you, and you're fuckin' someplace else! We ain't got time for you to be standin' here daydreamin'. I ain't fuckin' with Cain and Ramsey! Make a move, Keith!"

"Okay." Keith extended his arm and pointed his gun at Skylar's forehead.

Skylar stared down the barrel in disbelief. "Come on, Keith! *What the fuck are you doin'?* Come on, Keith!"

"Shut up! Shut up, already!"

Keith pulled the trigger and shot him in the forehead. Skylar grunted, reflexively, and hit the floor. Keith looked down at him in disgust. Sniveling asshole. He picked up his ankles and drug him out of the room, leaving a trail of blood and gray matter.

Keith went back to the bedroom and looked down at the two women lying on the mattress. Leah was out cold. Nicky, not so much. She was turning her head, slowly coming out of it. She frowned as if she were waking from a bad dream. Keith smiled and knelt beside her. She was still beautiful. He tenderly placed his hand on her breast … then closed it into a fist. Nicky gasped in pain and her eyes popped open. She stared up at Keith in horror, still getting her bearings.

He grinned at her. "How've you been, Nicky? Did you miss me?"

******

Nick was repulsed by what she woke up to. Keith was squeezing her breast like a vise, his face so close to her, she could feel his warm, moist, breath on her cheek. Nick shuddered in disgust, curled her hand into a fist and hit him as hard as she could. The blow caught him off guard.

Keith swayed away from her, holding his injured nose. Nick pushed herself away from him and scrambled to her feet, ignoring the pain in her leg and hip, but she somehow forgot her ankle was now virtually useless. It refused to hold her weight and she tumbled backward, over Leah, cursing through her teeth.

Leah! Leah was prone on the mattress, with blood seeping slowly from a head wound. As Keith stood up and came for her, Nick reached out in a panic and shook her.

"Leah! Leah, wake up!" Her hands did a cursory search, skittering over Leah's body, looking for her weapon. Nick came up empty. It would have been too late, anyway. Keith dropped to his knees and grabbed her savagely by the throat with one hand.

"You want to play games, Nicky? You want to punch me in the face, Nicky?" His hand tightened around her throat and the other one slammed into her left eye.

There was a bright flash of pain, but brighter than that was the rage Nick felt swelling up in her. Keith couldn't hold her by the throat, beat her ass, and protect himself at the same time. Nick started punching him with everything she had, not caring where the blows landed, but making sure there was a steady, unrelenting onslaught.

Keith batted and swatted at her hands with his free hand, deflecting most of the damaging blows. When Nick wouldn't let up, he gave her a resounding backhand across the face. He hit her so hard, her teeth rattled and her vision blurred. Both of his hands closed over her throat and he applied pressure. Nick sputtered and gasped as she felt her air supply closing off. She hit him hard with a left, just under his right eyebrow, with a hysteria driven burst of adrenaline. The high setting in her new engagement ring furrowed deeply through his flesh and opened up a large gaping wound.

Keith cursed and punched at her, but Nick turned her head and his fist hit the mattress. Keith grabbed her hands and Nick sucked in air in big gulps. She knew he wasn't playing. He intended to kill her. Keith twisted her left hand and brought it up to his face.

"What the fuck is this, Nicky? You gonna marry that nigga?" he screamed at her. Nick blinked and cringed away from him as he actually roared in anger like some kind of animal. In another situation she may have laughed at him, right now, she just wanted to keep him from killing her.

Nick pushed herself off the mattress and got to one knee. This time she was prepared for the pain in her ankle. Nick grimaced and cried out, but she made it to her feet and hopped her way to the door. Her ankle was broken. She knew it. She was sweating with the pain and effort it took just to get this far. Where was Keith? She thought he'd be on her by now. Nick glanced over her shoulder, risking a look back.

Keith had gotten to his feet. He was wiping the blood out of his eye and smiling at her like a demon. What on earth had happened to him? Had he always been this way? This wasn't the man she'd sworn she'd loved. He couldn't be, standing here smiling at her, so black and malicious. She'd known he'd had a few really bad points, but it seemed somewhere down the line, Keith had turned into a psychopath and she hadn't even noticed.

"Where you limping off to, you slut? Your stupid ankle won't let you get far. I'm gonna catch you, Nicky, and when I do, I'm gonna make sure you die screaming for that sack of shit to come save you!"

Nick ducked out the door. The pain in her ankle and hip was a monster. She was shaking violently and crying. Sweat dripped down her back. She was terrified and immobile. Nick had no weapon. She was totally vulnerable.

Keith was going to murder her! Where the hell was Lucas? She drug herself down the hall as fast as she could, her injured ankle almost blinding her with pain at every step. Keith sprang out of the room behind her and ran at her, snarling. Nick had nowhere to go, but she thought her best bet was to try and stay upright. She pressed herself into the wall and prepared for impact. When Keith collided with her, Nick's head slammed against the wall and she bit the hell out of her tongue.

Her left hand came up like a claw and she dug her fingernails into the gash she'd made with her ring. Her other hand came up and she jammed her thumb into his left eye. Keith bellowed and hit her in the jaw. Nick dropped her head and pressed her thumb in harder. Keith's fist slammed into her ear. He grabbed her hand with both of his and pulled her hand away from his eye. Keith hit her in the side of the head again and Nick went down.

Keith dropped to his knees and started ripping at her clothes. A deep and chilling alarm grew in the pit of Nick's stomach. Her heart trip hammered in her chest as she threw frantic punches, scratched at him, anything to get him off of her. *What did he mean to do?* Her shirt was in tatters. He ripped her bra open with one hand and popped the button off her shorts with the other.

Keith put his forearm across her chest and used his weight to restrain her. He ripped her zipper down and tore at her panties. Nick's eyes transfixed with shock and horror and she let out a sheer cry of desperation, as Keith rudely and violently stuck his fingers where they no longer belonged.

"Nooo! Keith, please! Please! *Don't do this to me!*" Her throat felt raw as she shrieked. Where was Lucas?

Keith hit her again. "Go ahead and scream, Nicky. I'm gonna kill you when I'm done."

******

Lucas was grateful the apartment was on the first floor. Noah was limited as it was; he didn't need a bunch of stairs in his way. They moved cautiously down the hallway — weapons out, safeties off. They reached the door of the apartment and Noah took high, Lucas took low. Lucas put his hand on the doorknob and tested it. The door was unlocked. He looked up at Noah.

Noah raised an eyebrow and nodded, his face set with determination. "Throw it open, Luke," he said, quietly.

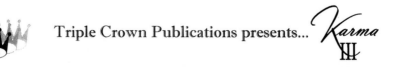

Lucas turned the knob and let the door fly back. He went in low, eyes alert, gun pointed outward. He did a sweep of the room. Noah, standing over him, did the same. Nobody in this room was moving. It was a fucking slaughterhouse.

Lucas counted five dead cops as he stood up to his full height. What the hell was going on? It was more than obvious. Keith had lost his goddamn mind. Noah was standing outside the kitchen. He lifted his gun and leaned into the room with great care. Noah swept the room with his eyes and stepped away, shaking his head.

Lucas put his shoulder to the wall and was about to peer into the hallway when Nicole started screaming, begging Keith to leave her alone. Fury descended over Lucas so sudden, black, and heavy, he felt light headed and his ears popped. He turned into the hall with Noah at his back. The hallway was shaped like an L. There was nothing straight ahead, only a smeary trail of blood. Lucas moved down the hall, Noah as close to him as his own shadow.

"Oh no, Keith! Noooo! Noooo! Pleeaase!" Nick was screeching like he was killing her.

Lucas turned the corner running, his heart pounding with dread. He didn't have time to speculate about what Keith might be doing. Whatever it was that had Nicole screaming like that was about to stop.

Lucas was not prepared for what he saw. It made him stop dead in his tracks and sent his rage into the stratosphere. *What was this motherfucker doing to his woman?*

They were on the floor at the end of the hallway. Keith was on his knees between Nicole's thighs. She was desperately trying to fight him off and Keith seemed just as desperate to have his way with her. Her tee shirt was in shreds. There was torn cloth that vaguely resembled the light blue shorts she'd put on that morning. Lucas could see her body intimately, but he couldn't see clearly if Keith was actually raping her, but it sure looked like he was.

Lucas tucked his gun back in its holster and charged at Keith like a bull. He hit Keith in the middle of his back with his shoulder and Keith went sprawling, turning over and tucking himself back in his pants. Nicole scuttled out of the way and put her back against the wall.

Lucas got to his feet briskly, and looked down at Keith. The tackle had caught him off guard and knocked the wind out of him, but he was reaching for his weapon. Lucas kicked his hand as he pulled it out of the holster and the gun spun away across the hardwood floor. Lucas reached down and pulled him up by the collar. He glanced at Noah. Noah was keeping a serious bead on Keith, his arms extended, looking down the sight of his gun.

Keith clipped Lucas in the jaw with a right. It was a good, solid punch and Lucas felt the blow, but if Keith meant to stop his ass kicking from coming with *that,* he might as well have tried to put out a forest fire with a glass of ice water. Lucas put his fists up and started punching Keith like a boxer.

Lucas hit him twice and broke his nose again. A right hook, and Keith went back into the wall. Lucas was hitting him with every ounce of angry strength he had. A right delivered a blow that would shut his eye. A left and his mouth was a mess. This time Keith decided to fight back. Lucas didn't anticipate the head butt he received.

When Keith's forehead smashed into Lucas's, Lucas wasn't prepared for it. Splintery pain rocked through his skull from his forehead to the nape of his neck. It felt like Keith's skull was made of concrete. Lucas tried to recover quickly, but that fuck had actually hurt him. Lucas staggered back and dropped to one knee against his will. He shook his head to clear it and looked up at Keith. Keith laughed like a maniac and stomped him in the chest, knocking him down.

Nick screamed his name and Noah spoke to her in a sure, quiet, voice. "Hush, Nick. He's good."

His head was clearing. Now Lucas was furious that Keith had gotten the best of him, even if it was only for a second. Lucas didn't have to look at Noah to know he still had a bead on Keith. Lucas rolled and regained his footing. He went back into a fighting stance, with his fists up, and Keith rushed him.

Punching Keith hadn't been part of the plan. When he was close enough, Lucas delivered a neat and potent roundhouse kick that sent Keith reeling past Noah to slam, headfirst, into the wall at the end of the hallway.

"That's what I'm talkin' 'bout! Kick his ass, Luke!" Noah said, enthusiastically.

Lucas was right on his ass. Noah followed, never letting Keith out of his sights. Lucas didn't give him a chance to get his wits. He sideswiped him with another kick to the jaw and felt the bone give way. Lucas kicked him again and Keith lost a few teeth as his blood peppered the wall. Keith fumbled with the utility pocket of his uniform pants as Lucas dragged his sorry ass up. Keith threw a left and got lucky, crashing his fist into Lucas' mouth. Lucas felt his lip split and he tasted blood, but he was too angry to let any real pain settle in. Lucas moved in close and smashed his fists into him — blow after blow after blow.

"He's got a knife in his right hand, Luke," Noah said, calmly, "You want me to take him out, say the word."

Lucas reached for Keith's hand just as Keith's arm came down in an arc. Lucas deflected major damage, but Keith had way too much momentum to stop the blow completely. The knife skipped across Lucas' chest and dug into his shoulder. The pain was hot, deep, and nauseating.

"Son of a bitch!" Lucas cursed through his teeth.

That knife hurt like a bastard. Keith's mouth was a bit slack from his broken jaw, but he looked at Lucas with a cold, steely determination and twisted the knife. Lucas hollered hoarsely and felt the strength drain out of his arm. Nicole screamed his name again.

"Luke?" Noah said, and moved closer.

Warm blood spilled down Lucas' arm and pattered on the floor like rain. Just as quickly as Keith stuck the knife in, he pulled it out.

"Luke, if this motherfucker ain't on the ground in ten seconds, his ass is meetin' Saint Peter, I swear to God. Put him down, Luke," Noah said in that same calm voice.

Lucas ducked the swipe of the knife that was aimed at his face, and hit Keith in his damaged nose with two successive overhand rights. Keith careened backward, holding his nose with his left hand. He fumbled at his side with his right.

You didn't have to be a rocket scientist to know he was going for something. Lucas had his gun in his hand and pointed at Keith just as Keith raised his own weapon: A shiny .22. They leveled their guns at each other and squared off.

"Put your gun down, Keith, or put it to your head. Either way, you ain't gettin' out of this," Lucas said.

Keith stared him down. His eyes were merry and Lucas believed he would have smiled if his jaw wasn't broken. Keith's arm didn't tremble and it didn't waiver. He kept his gun pointed at Lucas' chest and Lucas kept his pointed at Keith's head. There was an audible click from Noah's gun in the silence.

Lucas had enough confidence to turn his head and look back at his old friend. Noah was five feet behind him, turned slightly sideways. His left hand gripped the forearm of his right, which was extended with his weapon pointed straight at Keith. Noah was aiming high, so he had his bead on a head shot. His eyes were like ice and the corners of his mouth were tilted up into a cold, mirthless smile. *He meant to kill him.*

Lucas turned back to Keith in a half-hearted last-ditch effort to save his life. "I think you should put your gun down … unless you feel like dyin' today."

"Fuck you, asshole," Keith replied, his words distorted by his broken mouth.

Lucas shrugged. "A'ight."

"Last chance, bitch. Put your weapon on the floor. I ain't gonna tell you twice." Noah's voice was low and deadly. Lucas knew he meant what he said.

Keith spit blood on the floor. "Fuck you, pretty boy!" he yelled and swung his gun toward Noah.

"Go to hell. Tell Oscar I said, 'Hi!'" Noah said flatly and blasted him. The first bullet tore through his throat. The second took the side of his head off. Keith's gun went off, reflexively, and he hit the floor like the pile of shit he was. Lucas lowered his gun. He turned and looked at Noah. They stared at each other through the gun smoke.

"It was righteous, Noah. He pointed his gun at you and refused to drop it. He didn't leave you much choice."

Noah still held his gun. He lit a Dunhill and looked at Lucas earnestly. "Lucas, I ain't gotta justify nothin' to myself to make me feel like I followed the letter of the law, and neither do you. That's some bullshit. You know it and I know it," he paused and looked at Keith while he smoked his cigarette. Noah pointed at Keith's body with his Dunhill.

"You see that shit right there, Luke? That's what happens when you have the unmitigated gall to start some shit with the wrong fuckin' people. That's what happens when you pick a fight you can't win. You end up stretched out with your brains across the floor. As far as what's justifiable ... he was a dirty cop ◎ a drug dealer, a cop killer." He glanced toward Nick meaningfully, then looked back at Lucas. "A woman beater, a rapist, and unfortunately for him, a killer of pregnant women and a taker of unborn lives. Let's face the facts, Luke. All the things he was, was enough reason to lock his ass up and toss the fuckin' key, but he bought his ticket on the express train to hell when he squeezed the life outta Liz. Liz never hurt anybody in her life, Luke ... and he killed her because of me."

Noah looked at him with hurt and angry eyes that were full of tears that threatened to fall, but didn't. He nodded at him. "I know, Luke. I know how you must have felt to know somebody you loved was killed because of you. *It hurts*. Guilt sucks, Luke."

Lucas put his hand on Noah's shoulder. There was nothing he could really do but be there, and he would. Noah's eyes returned to Keith. "It was righteous. Fucker wouldn't put his gun down. I had to cap him." They looked at each other and they both knew that even though Keith had technically caused his own death; Noah killed Keith and Lucas let him.

"He did it to himself, Noah. You said it yourself. When you live like that, that's how you die."

"Every single time," Noah said. There was a hint of a smile on his face that told Lucas Noah had done all the crying he was willing to do over it.

"All right, then," Lucas said. They gave each other dap and rounded the corner of the hallway.

Nick was just inside. She sat on the floor with her back against the wall, her hurt leg straight out in front of her, and her arms modestly over her chest. Her shirt hung around her in shreds. She looked up at them. Her beautiful face was swollen and bruised. Lucas felt the rage rise back up in him, but he forced it back down because it was useless. Keith was already dead, and it wasn't what she needed.

Nicole looked at him steadily, but he could see trauma right behind her gaze. Oh God.

"Did you kill him? Is he dead?" Her voice sounded hoarse and stripped, like she wounded her vocal cords screaming. Lucas reached down to pull his shirt over his head but his hand came away bloody.

Noah pulled his own shirt off and gave it to her. The scar in his chest still looked very new. "Yeah, sweetie, he's dead. Where's Leah?"

Nicole nodded toward the bedroom. Lucas raised an eyebrow. Nicole was shaking uncontrollably, but when she answered Noah, her voice was calm.

"She's in there. Keith hit her in the head with his gun. Thank you, Noah."

Noah smiled and averted his eyes as she slipped his shirt on. He was smiling, but his eyes were full of concern. "Don't mention it, Nick."

Lucas got on his knees and pulled her into his arms, as Noah went into the bedroom for Leah.

"Are you okay? I know it's a stupid question, baby, but I need an answer," he said and kissed her forehead.

Nicole pulled away from him and avoided the question. "Never mind me. How bad did that bastard hurt you?" She asked, looking at his shoulder, horror touching her eyes. Nicole touched his shoulder lightly, like she wanted to touch him, but didn't necessarily want him touching *her*. Lucas stared at her. Maybe that had been his imagination.

He shrugged painfully. "He did what he could, but I'm still here ... and he's not."

"I'm so sorry, Lucas. I had no idea he was such a monster."

Lucas pushed back his own skepticism. Someone as psychotic as Keith had turned out to be had surely dropped a few hints along the way. Nicole had just chosen to ignore them. In any case, Keith was now the past. It seemed to Lucas they had more pressing issues they had to deal with, but he wasn't too sure on how to go about approaching the subject.

Nicole looked incredibly fragile and traumatized. She watched him staring at her and frowned. She tucked her lips in and turned her face away. "Stop staring at me, Lucas. Don't do that, okay?"

Lucas's heartbeat picked up. He put his hand under her chin and turned her back to face him. Things had happened so fast. He wasn't completely sure of what he'd seen. He'd been so enraged.

"Nicole ... what did he do?"

Nicole looked at him like she was suddenly furious with him. "What did he do? What do you think he did?"

Lucas looked back at her, patiently. "Everything happened very fast, Nicole. I'm not exactly sure of *what* I saw. That's why I'm asking *you*." Lucas didn't like the look she gave him back. She looked at him like she was accusing him of something. She only held that look in her eyes for a couple of seconds, but that didn't change the fact that it had been there. That pretty much told him what he needed to know.

Lucas reached for her. "Nicole. Nicole, baby, I –"

She moved back and looked away. "He ... when you came in he was ... he had his ... he was raping me, Lucas!"

"What? Oh my, God!" Leah said from behind them. She pushed past Lucas and pulled Nick into her arms. "It's okay, Nick. It's okay. We're gonna get you to the hospital."

Nicole dissolved into tears and clung to Leah. Lucas turned and looked at Noah. Noah frowned and spread his hands. Lucas didn't know what to do. He was overwhelmed with about five different emotions. He passed a hand over his beard. That fuck Keith had raped his woman. Lucas felt like killing his dirty ass again.

Since he was at a loss, he instinctively went where he felt most comfortable; given the situation, he probably made the wrong choice. He went into cop mode. Lucas stood up and called Myers on his cell phone. He gave him a brief rundown of the situation and requested an ambulance. He looked at Noah. Noah was looking back at him with his eyebrow up. He tilted his head in Nicole's direction.

This was a horrible situation, and he must have done something to piss her off that he didn't catch, but he didn't care about that. He cared about *her*. He let it go because he knew she'd just gone through something that was both physically and emotionally damaging. He'd deal with his own feelings later. Nicole was the most important thing.

Lucas put his hand on Leah's shoulder, noting the gash in her scalp. "It's okay, Leah. Let me take care of her."

Leah stood up, reluctantly, with Noah holding her arm. She put her hand to her head and grimaced. Noah held her a little tighter. "You okay, sweetie?"

"My head hurts. He *is* dead, right?"

Noah smiled and kissed her somewhere near her ear. "As a door-nail, sugar."

Leah nodded and winced. "*Good.* I never could stand his ass."

Lucas helped Nicole get to her feet. She didn't fight him this time.

"I can't walk, Lucas. One of them broke my ankle."

Lucas pushed his rage back once more and picked her up and held her close, even though the pain in his shoulder was damn near unbearable. He followed Noah, who had his arm around Leah, out of that house of death and corruption.

Chapter Twelve

Little White Lie

The first thing Nadine saw when she woke up was Noah's face. He was watching her intently with those beautiful gray eyes of his. Noah was sitting in the chair next to her hospital bed, low in his seat, twirling his lighter in his hand. His left leg was straight out in front of him, wrapped in what looked like duct tape of all things. There was dry blood on his shirt.

He smiled at her. "Hey, Nadine." She loved him. Noah.

Nadine was groggy, but she was damn glad to be alive. Everything came back at once. The fight in the kitchen; her falling through the glass table.

"Noah … that guy tried to kill me." Her voice was hoarse. It didn't sound like her own. She sounded like she was whispering.

Noah nodded, still looking at her. "Yeah, he sure did. I'm glad he didn't. I'm sorry about this, Nadine. For real."

Nadine frowned. "Who the hell is he? He had on a uniform. Is he a cop? What did he want with *me*?"

Noah shook his head and put his hand over his mouth. He didn't look at her for a long time. Nadine knew him well enough to know he was trying hard not to let his emotions get the best of him. He cleared his throat and looked out the window. Nadine held her frown. This was all some very bad shit. Shit so bad, it had the ever-strong Noah seriously choked up.

"Noah?"

Noah put his face in his hands. Nadine stayed silent, giving him

a minute to get himself together. After a long moment, Noah eased himself out of the chair without putting his weight on his hurt leg and sat on the bed with her. He took her hand in his and kissed it with a tenderness Nadine hadn't seen in a long while.

"I'm so glad that fuck didn't hurt you any worse than he did. I'm sorry he hurt you at all, Nadine. I swear to God, I never saw none of this shit comin'. I swear I didn't." He kissed her hand again, and Nadine was a little surprised to see that her arm was wrapped in a bandage. She blinked twice, realizing that she was actually on some pretty potent pain medication.

"It's okay, Noah."

He shook his head. "Nope. It's *not* okay, Nadine. Keith Childs did some horrible shit before he left this world."

"He's dead?"

Noah nodded. "Yeah, he's dead. I had to put his rabid ass down a little earlier." They sat in silence for a moment.

"What happened, Noah?" Nadine asked quietly, not sure if he was in the mood to talk or not, but feeling like he owed her an explanation. Fortunately, Noah felt the need to oblige.

"It's like this, Nadine, this guy, Keith Childs, me and Luke knew him since the academy. There was bad blood between us, but for simple shit. But all that was a long time ago. We let it go, but apparently this asshole held onto it. Anyway, when we started the Trinidad sting, Lucas started seein' Nick ◎ Nicole — who was Keith's girlfriend until he punched her in the mouth. She's a detective, too, by the way ..." He trailed off, frowning. "It gets real complicated, Nadine."

Nadine felt a stab of jealousy and couldn't help herself from being who she was. "So ... was that Leah chick part of the sting, too? What did you and Lucas do, Noah? Pair off?"

Noah turned his head and looked at her coldly, his eyes dark and stormy. He ran his hand through his dark, curly hair. He was so handsome, Nadine felt like someone was squeezing her heart, but there was a distinct possibility she could lose him forever to that bitch Leah.

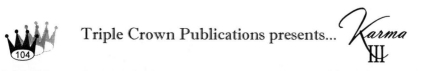

"Stop takin' shots at me, Nadine. I'm tryin' to tell you what happened. You deserve to at least know *why* you're lyin' in the hospital. Don't you think that's right?" Noah chastised her gently, deferring to her condition, but letting her know he wasn't in the mood to take shit off her.

Nadine thought about coming back at him, but she could tell from the look on his face, that wasn't the way to go with Noah today. There were other ways to get to Noah, though. Nadine looked at him serenely and put her hands on her belly. It was low and she knew it, especially given the situation with Liz.

"I'm sorry, Noah. We've got plenty of time to talk about you and Leah, don't we?"

Nadine was shocked at the immediate look of disdain she got from Noah. He looked down at her stomach, then back up at her face. "Don't try to play me, Nadine. This wasn't a good fuckin' day for me, okay? You hear me? If you don't want to hear what I got to say, if you want to lay there and play games with me, I can always get up and limp my ass outta here. I'm done takin' shit for the day."

They stared at each other. Nadine could see that Noah was a heartbeat away from making good on what he'd said. He looked tired, grief-stricken, and very stressed out. Nadine brought her bullshit way down.

"I'm sorry, baby, you're right. You were saying that Lucas is seeing Keith Childs's girlfriend?"

Noah stared at her a moment longer. "Well, now he's engaged to her ... but who knows *how* that's gonna turn out."

Nadine frowned again. "That's a bit pessimistic, Noah. Why would you say that?"

"'Cause Nick was Keith's last stop on his little horror spree. When me and Luke finally got to her at the end of this long ass day, Keith was right in the middle of rapin' her." Nadine didn't know this Nick person, but she instantly felt bad for her.

"Oh, Noah. Wow."

"Yeah, wow. Things are all fucked up. She's fucked up. Luke's fucked up," he looked at her pointedly, "*You're* all fucked up. Damn, Nadine."

Nadine watched Noah's face. She knew she was mean by nature, but dejection was a rare look on Noah's face and it tore at her heart to see it. "What about *you*, Noah? How are you?"

Noah laughed an untickled little laugh and looked away from her. "I'd say I'm pretty fucked up, too, Nadine."

Nadine rubbed his hand. "I'm sorry about Liz, Noah. Did she …"

Noah took his hand away and looked at her hard. "Thanks, but I ain't talkin' to you about Liz, Nadine. You ain't have no love for her when she was alive, don't try to act like you care now that she's not. You're full of shit. I know it and so do you."

If Nadine wasn't wearing a brace on her neck, she was sure it would have snapped back from Noah's attitude. "Well, *excuse me*. I was just trying to give you my condolences. You don't have to take my head off, Noah."

"I'm not. Just don't act like you care when you don't."

"I didn't say I didn't care."

Noah laughed mirthlessly again and stood up. "*I* say you don't. You tried to sabotage her, Nadine."

"I didn't try to —"

"You did! Drop it, Nadine, or I'm walkin' outta here. I'm not playin'. He looked down at her angrily, like Liz being dead was *her* fault. "You'd probably be tap dancin' about it if you could, so just stop."

"That's cold, Noah." Nadine was offended.

"*You're* cold, Nadine," Noah came back at her. "You're so cold and so fuckin' mean, you would rather lay there and get at me about Leah and poor dead Liz, than ask me about our kids — or even tell me how *you* are. Shit! Were you always like this?"

Nadine wanted to say some funky shit to him. She wanted to say 'No. I was cool until you fucked me over,' but because of his current mood, she left it alone and did what he wanted.

"Did your folks get the kids? How are they?"

"Yeah, they got 'em. *They're* all fucked up, too. When I leave here, I'm gonna go get 'em and let 'em stay with me until you're good. Is that okay with you?"

Nadine smiled. Noah was a lot of things, but he loved the hell out of his kids and he took good care of them. "More than okay, Noah. Your folks are great, but they really need to be with their dad right now. I thought you were staying with Lucas. You're going back to your place?"

He nodded. "Yeah. I was goin' anyway. I'm as healed up as I need to be. Besides, Luke and Nick are gonna need their space to get through this shit."

"I agree."

He stared at her for a moment, then sat back down on the bed. Noah took her hand again and smiled at her a little. "Thanks. So ... what's goin' on with you, Nadine? I didn't get a chance to talk to your doctor. I just came right in."

Nadine took a deep breath and let it out. "Well, he says I've got severe muscle strain in my neck — but he didn't say whether or not it came from that guy choking me, or the fall I took through the table. Multiple contusions and lacerations, some deeper than others. I bruised my right kidney and broke three ribs, oh, and I have a slight concussion. Other than that, I guess I'm okay."

Noah smiled and put his hand on her belly. "Okay. What about this guy? The baby still there?"

Nadine stared at him for a second. This was a pivotal point in their relationship, but she didn't have much time to make a decision. Noah was waiting for an answer.

"Almost lost the baby, Noah. But luckily this kid's like his folks. This baby's got strong survival skills. We'll be fine. I've just got to take it easy."

Noah patted her belly and stood up. "All right, then I guess I'll go get our kids. I know they gotta really be freakin' out."

"Okay, Noah. Are you coming back?"

"Not tonight. I'll bring the kids by tomorrow after I'm done with Myers and Internal Affairs."

"Okay."

Noah bent and put his fingers in her hair. He kissed her hard on the mouth. "I'm so fuckin' glad you're all right, Nadine. You scared the shit outta me."

Nadine ran her fingers through his silky curly hair and let him

stand up. "I love you, Noah."

"Love you, too, Nadine." Noah took a Dunhill out of his pack and stuck it in his mouth. "I'll be back tomorrow."

"Okay."

Nadine watched Noah limp his way across the room; his smoke hanging out of his mouth, his badge hanging around his neck, and his gun hanging off his belt. She loved that man. Noah opened the door and waved at her as he went out of it.

Nadine sincerely hoped she'd decided to play this the right way with Noah. Noah was *not* a stupid man — but he was a man all the same. The odds were about ninety percent in her favor that Noah wouldn't question her doctor. He'd most likely take her at her word.

She'd put herself in a precarious position, lying to Noah about the baby. Nadine had lost the baby when Keith tackled her into that glass table. Hopefully, by the time Noah became suspicious, he will have replaced that baby with another one. Nadine wasn't afraid to play her ace in the hole and she wasn't above fighting dirty. *She was keeping Noah.* That bitch, Leah, had told Nadine she was tenacious. Nadine would show that ho tenacity.

There was no way in hell that bitch was walking away with Noah.

Noah belonged to Nadine.

Chapter Thirteen

Hello Stranger

Nick walked out of her rape counselor's office feeling no better than she did when she went in. It had been a month and a half since Keith had done what he'd done to her, but she still felt like she was in a state of shock.

Sure, she couldn't deal with the fact that Keith had ultimately forced himself on her, but it went a little deeper than that. Nick hadn't actually been straight with Butch or Lucas, Leah and Noah, and she hated herself for it. She felt like she was riding on a sea of disaster in a row boat with a hole in it.

Nick stepped into the elevator and twirled her engagement ring around on her finger. Oh God. She wished she'd never met Keith. He was dead and he was still going to ruin her life. He was posthumously going to make her lose her job, her best friend, and the love of her life. All that ruination for something simple and stupid she'd done a long time ago, when she was head over heels in love with Keith and didn't want him to leave her.

Nick had lied about what she knew. She was nervous and on the spot, and in front of her man and their friends. Her partner. Lucas's partner. All damn fine, honest cops. What could she possibly have said? Yes, I knew he was dirty? Yes, I knew about Oscar Tirado? Sure, I let him use my name to hide money in three different banks in the Cayman Islands? Please forgive me for this shit, I was in love with the wrong man and I made a mistake?

A snowball would have stood a better chance of surviving in

hell, than Nick admitting to that. *She couldn't.* Nick had never personally sullied her own badge. It was the things she'd done for Keith that were damning. And it wasn't much more than knowing he was dirty and those bank accounts. There was also a key he'd given her a long time ago. The key was to a public storage in SOHO.

It seemed Keith had forgotten about the key. Hell, so had she. Most likely he hadn't. Keith had always held shit like that over people's heads for insurance. She'd pretty much known where it was until she'd moved in with Lucas. Now she couldn't find it and it was worrying the hell out of her. Everyone knew Keith was dead. Sooner or later, somebody was going to come looking for it. Shit, sooner or later, all this shit was going to come to a head. Then she would lose everything. Then she would lose Lucas.

Nick was in love with Lucas Cain. She'd fallen for him almost immediately, with his dark skin and big chocolate eyes. There was nothing on this earth she wanted more than Lucas … and she was about to lose him over some bullshit.

Nick got in her car and drove home to the brownstone in Carroll Gardens. She hoped Lucas wasn't home yet. He and Noah were due back at work in two weeks and they went to the track everyday and did laps to get back in top form. She hoped they'd stay out for a while. Maybe go to a bar and get a scotch or two. Stay for a while and talk shit to each other. Maybe they'd get drunk and crash at Noah's place.

For once in her life, Nick really didn't want to be around Lucas. Lucas was getting on her nerves. Nick was still very much in love with him and she still wanted to marry him, but right now, Lucas was playing her too close. He was trying a little too hard to be there for her and be all up on her.

When Nick was in Lucas's company, he watched her a little too close with those amazingly dreamy chocolate eyes. Lucas had some serious radar. He could tell when something wasn't right. So could Noah. When he came over, Nick made herself scarce. She may be able to slip by Lucas because she was his woman, but the two of them together would start figuring this shit out. She'd probably give herself away. She felt dirty. She felt guilty.

Nick pulled her car up and breathed a sigh of relief. Lucas wasn't there. Good. She could chill out for a second, gather her thoughts and smooth herself out. By the time she got in the door, she was hyperventilating, having a straight out panic attack.

Nick walked to the sofa on wobbly legs and sat down, breathing with a whistling sound like an asthmatic. She closed her eyes and tried to ride it out, half wishing she'd just die and get it over with. The doorbell rang and Nick jumped. She got up with the same shaky gait. *Who was this?* Maybe it was Leah. She had a habit of just popping by.

"Who is it?" Nick's voice sounded a lot stronger than she felt.

"Candygram," came the smooth velvet voice from the other side. All Nick's hopes and dreams sank and hit the floor, shattering at her feet. She knew that voice without looking out the peephole. Disaster had arrived. It was all downhill from here.

Nick cracked the door open and he pushed it all the way in.

"What are you doing here? You can't be here! You have to leave."

"Damn, baby! You don't look happy to see me. Why is that? I went through a lot of trouble to find you. You could at least smile."

It was Jessie London. Jessie was a vice lieutenant at Midtown South. He was a very old, very close, friend of Oscar and Keith. If Oscar and Keith had been the soil and the seeds of their dirty blue garden, Jessie had been the goddamn fertilizer.

He smiled at her with sparkling white teeth, just as tall and almost as handsome as Lucas. "You look a little faint, but then, I've always been known to make women swoon. You okay, baby?"

Nick was feeling a very real need to throw up. She had to get this Negro the hell up out of Lucas's house immediately. "What are you doing here, Jessie? What do you want?"

He touched her hair and she started to cry. "Now, now, Nicky. Don't act like I'm the big bad wolf. I didn't come here to blow your house down."

Nick backed away from him. "Okay. Okay. Just tell me what you want. I told you, you can't be here."

He laughed. "I ain't scared of Cain."

Nick bristled. "You should be."

Jessie laughed again. "Fuck that nigga. He don't give me the shakes and I ain't in love with him like everybody else. You have somethin' Keith was holdin' for me, Nicky. Give me what I want and I'll leave you alone. Act like you're stupid and I'll cut your throat while I'm fuckin' you in the ass in Cain's bed. What's it gonna be, Nicky? You in the mood to help me out, or you wanna die? Choose right now. I don't have all day," he said, then looked at his watch.

Nick wiped the tears off her face with the back of her hand. "Please, Jessie. Don't screw my life up. Please."

Jessie wrapped his hand in her hair and jerked her head, painfully. "Bitch, I ain't playin' with you! Make a choice. Call it now, or your clothes come off!"

"Okay! Okay … I'll give you what you want, just please, take it and get out of here."

Jessie laughed at her. "You scared of that big-eyed nigga? *Fuck him*. I want to put my papers in. That nigga, Keith, was holdin' some money for me in the Caymans. I want it. Go get it, *right now*." He pushed her away from him. Nick stumbled and almost fell. "Go on. Go get it. I'll make myself at home while I wait."

Jessie went to the bar and poured himself two fingers of The Glenlivet. He unbuttoned his suit jacket and sat on the sofa with his arm across the back.

"Damn, that nigga Cain is livin' almost as large as me up in here. He's got exquisite taste." He looked over his shoulder at Nick. "Don't worry, you can leave me in here alone. I ain't gonna lift nothin'. That nigga ain't got nothin' I wanna steal … except maybe you. Chop, chop, bitch. I told you, I ain't got all day. Don't try nothin' funny either, or I'll kill your ass."

Nick went down the stairs to the basement as quickly as she could on her still healing ankle. This negro had to raise up out of here. The shit would most definitely hit the fan if Lucas caught him here. She rummaged through the boxes of things she'd never unpacked until she found what she was looking for. She took the bankbooks upstairs to the creep on the couch.

"Is this what you want?" she asked, holding them out to him.

Jessie smiled. "Precisely what I was lookin' for. Thanks, Nicky.

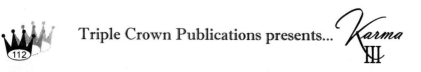

You're a good, obedient, little bitch — but then again, you always were. Now do me a favor and go get the key for the storage down in SOHO. That's mine, too. Do it … I'll be out of your beautiful hair. Don't do it … I'll have to touch you up."

Nick started shaking. She didn't have the fucking key! She had no idea where it was. "Um … about the key, Jessie … I must have misplaced it when I moved out. I can't find it. When I find it, I'll give it to you. I swear to God."

Jessie laughed softly and looked her over. "You know what, Nicky? I ain't a total bastard. I'm gonna be real nice about this 'cause you always turned me on. I'm gonna give you exactly a month to find my fuckin' key. That alright with you?"

Nick nodded quickly. She wanted him gone. "Yeah, Jessie. A month. You got it."

"Good." He walked over to her and pulled her head back. He shoved his tongue so far down her throat, she thought she'd gag. His left hand pinched her ass hard enough to leave a bruise. Jessie broke contact just as quickly as he'd made it.

"Have my fuckin' key, Nicky, or I'm gonna kill your ass when I come back. This time Cain won't save you." He smiled, tucked the bankbooks into his breast pocket, and left.

Nick ran to the kitchen and threw up in the sink. What the hell was she going to do?

Chapter Fourteen

Girlfriend

Noah sat outside Leah's building, in his Escalade, waiting for her to come home. He couldn't say exactly what it was that made him want to see her so bad. Well, maybe he could. He missed her. He lit a Dunhill and stared out the window. Noah liked Leah a hell of a lot more than he was comfortable with and when he didn't see her, it bothered him.

He watched her now as she drove up in her Volkswagen Jetta. She got out of the car, smiling at him. Noah got out of his truck, smiling at *her*. He crossed the street checking her out. She was dressed real simple in a pair of jeans and a white halter, but she looked good. Real good.

"Hey, Noah. You sittin' out here waiting on me?" she asked, smiling at him brightly. She seemed very glad to see him.

Noah tilted his head and smiled at her. "Well, it's a nice day. I went for a drive and ended up here. Imagine that."

Leah's smile got a little brighter. "No you didn't. You missed me and you came to see me. That's a serious compliment coming from you, Noah."

Noah raised his eyebrows and held onto his smile. She had him on that one. Leah walked around and opened her trunk.

"If you're not gonna tell me I'm right, you can at least help me with my bags."

Noah smirked. "Yeah, I can do that."

He helped her up to her sunny apartment and put the bags on

the kitchen counter. Leah started putting her groceries away.

"It's nice to see you, Noah. I haven't seen much of you since we went back to work. What have they got you doing?"

Noah shrugged. "A little of this, a little of that. I don't think the higher ups think Keith was the end of that dirty string of cops."

Leah looked at him over one golden brown shoulder. "I don't think so, either. How's Lucas? I haven't seen much of him, either."

Noah watched her lean over to put something away in a low cabinet. It was a lovely sight to see. "He's good, I guess. Still tryin' to deal with Nick. She's bein' a little difficult, but I guess that's understandable."

Leah kept talking with her back to him. Noah took a step forward. "Yeah, she's being difficult. I was with her earlier. This thing with Keith really shook her up. We had lunch and she kept looking around and acting nervous the whole time. She looked scared to death, like she was expecting Keith to pop out of somewhere and come at her. I tried to remind her that Keith is dead, but she kept acting jumpy. I'm worried about her, Noah."

"I guess we all are, Leah, but she's been through a lot. People don't come outta shit like that real easy. It took Luke a long time to deal with the stuff that went down with Justine. Nick's tough. She'll get through this." He said it lightly, but he was going to make sure to mention that jumpy shit to Lucas.

"You're probably right, but I'm still worried about her."

"Yeah, well, you should be. She's your friend." Leah reached over her head and stuck a box in another cabinet. Enough of this. Noah wanted to put his hands on her. He quietly walked up behind her, glad that springy pain in his knee was virtually gone. He was back to his old self.

"How's Nadine?" Leah asked. Noah didn't want to talk about Nadine. He wanted to take Leah's clothes off. He answered her anyway.

"She's comin' along."

Leah jumped, not realizing he was so close. A surprised little smile crossed her face. "Tell me again why you came here, Noah."

Noah put his hands on her waist and kissed her neck. "You

know what? Why don't you just let me show you instead?"

He went in for a kiss, but Leah put her hand on his chest. "Uh-uh. It's been a minute, Noah. It's given me a second to teach myself not to be so impulsive with you."

Noah sighed in resignation. He'd had a feeling Leah would want to talk to him before she gave him some. He hadn't slept with Leah since before he'd gotten hurt. They'd fooled around a bit, but for once in his life, Noah had to admit to himself that he was a little too hurt to break her down like he wanted to — and Noah didn't believe in half-stepping. So, he'd left her alone, but he let her know he was still interested. Noah wasn't stupid, and he'd been around the block enough times to know that he was setting himself up for this conversation, by not keeping her quiet and dick-whipped.

The thing was, he didn't really mind as much as he thought he would — having this particular conversation, with this particular woman. Noah had never felt this strongly about any other woman in his entire life, except Nadine. In a lot of ways, Leah was starting to make Nadine fade a little.

He kept his hands on her waist and spoke into her hair. "You want to talk to me? Go ahead, Leah. I guarantee you I won't run up outta here."

Leah put her hands on his biceps and looked up at him in pleasant surprise. "For real? You feel all right, Noah?"

He kissed her forehead. "I feel fine, but I think you put somethin' in my drink once or twice."

She hit him playfully and leaned away from him. "That's messed up, Noah. Why don't we finish the conversation we were having in the hospital? Have you changed, Noah?"

He looked at her for a moment before he answered her. "I got the same answer for you, Leah. I don't know."

She looked at him like she was worried. "Same question. Do you want to?"

Noah evaded her question. "I missed you. That's why I'm here. I wanted to see you. I wanted to spend some time with you. Is that okay?"

She blushed. "Yes, it's okay. You must really like me."

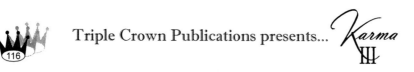

Noah ran his hands up her sides. "Yeah, I like you, Leah. You make me feel better."

She looked at him like he was playing a huge joke on her. A tear slid down her pretty cheek. Noah smiled at her. That was one of the things he really liked about Leah. She was such a fucking girl.

"You better not be playing with me, Noah."

"I'm not playin' with you, Leah."

Noah started kissing her and her arms went around his neck. Noah took his time kissing her. He *really* missed her. Her mouth was soft and sweet. She tasted so good. Her perfume was driving him crazy. Making him dizzy. He wanted her.

Leah was kissing him back like he'd been away too long. Her hands slipped into his hair and she pulled his head down so she could get a little more of his mouth. She was moaning. It was sexy as hell. Leah reached down and started pulling his tee shirt up. Noah let go of her and pulled it over his head. Leah's eyes dropped to the brand new scar in his chest.

She traced it with her finger. Another tear fell. "Oh God, Noah. You almost left me. Don't leave me. I love you so much." He thought so. Actually, he knew it to be true, that it had been for a while.

He wiped her tears with his thumbs and kissed her lips. Leah had the best lips. He could spend a lot of time kissing Leah. She gasped and pushed him back. Noah looked at her and frowned. It wasn't just a lone tear. She was crying.

"Did you hear what I said, Noah? I said I love you, goddamnit!"

Noah's eyebrow went up and he stepped away from her. "I heard you, Leah. What do you want me to say?"

Her mouth dropped open and she looked at him incredulously. "I can't believe you just asked me that! What do you *think* I want you to say, Noah? I don't want to do this shit by myself anymore. I want to know if the only feelings you have for me are in your fucking pants, Noah. You are so frustrating, it's unbelievable! I want to be loved, too!"

"Leah —" Noah started and reached for her. She slapped his hand away and walked out of the room.

"Fuck you, you selfish bastard!"

Noah took a deep breath and followed her into the living room, leaving his shirt lying on the kitchen floor. If it had been anybody else, he would have walked out of there talking shit, but he found he couldn't do that to Leah. He didn't want to. Leah was looking out the window with her arms folded across her chest.

Noah touched her arm. "Hey, Leah —"

She turned her head and cut him off. "If you've got a line of bullshit to feed me, Noah, go get your shirt and get the fuck out of my apartment," she said, quietly.

Noah couldn't stop the chuckle that escaped from his lips. "Come on, Leah. Don't talk to me like that."

She turned her head and looked at him sharply. "You're laughing at me? You think this is funny?"

Noah sighed, still smiling. "Nope. I'm laughin' because, right now, I'm takin' more shit from you than I've taken from *anybody* in a long ass time. Sit down and I'll talk to you, okay?"

Leah stared at him for a moment, then reluctantly sat on the sofa. She stayed perched on the edge with her arms folded defensively over her chest.

Noah sat down next to her and turned her way. "Look, Leah, this ain't high school. I mean, I ain't gonna pass you a note and ask you to be my girlfriend. I shouldn't have to tell you stuff like that, you're a grown-ass woman."

She didn't seem to like how he was saying it, but she seemed to be warming up to what he was saying. She rolled her eyes and tried not to smile at him, but she kept her mouth shut.

Noah leaned a little closer to her and put his hand on her thigh. "You know, Leah, I've always put my cards on the table with you. I know my life is a mess — ain't nobody got to tell me that. I did most of it myself. I can't change all that stuff, Leah, and I don't want to talk about it."

"Then why are you here?"

Noah moved closer until he was right up on her. Leah looked as if she couldn't move away if she tried. "I'm here because I can't leave you alone. I know I should, but I really can't stay away from you. I want to be close to you. You fucked me up, Leah."

His lips brushed hers, but she held him back. "Do you love me, Noah?"

He looked her in the eye and told her what he thought was the truth. "I don't know yet."

She smiled at him and reached behind her, unhooking her halter. "I think you do know, but let's push the envelope and find out." Leah stood up and took her top off. She tossed it over her shoulder like it had been in the way, then she put her hands on the small of her back and stuck her round, perfect breasts out at him. Noah smirked and stood up.

"I'm going to give you what you came here for and let you decide," she said. Leah stepped out of her shoes and unbuttoned her jeans. Noah unzipped them and pushed them down. She shimmied out of them and kicked them away. That left Leah standing there in a tiny pair of gossamer lace panties.

Noah winced like she'd hurt him. "Damn, baby. Did you know I was comin'?"

She looked at him smugly and suggestively, satisfied with his reaction. "I dress like this for you every day, you just never see it."

Noah reached out and ran his thumb over her nipple. Leah shivered and gasped. Noah smiled at her devilishly. "Now you gotta let me see your panties every day. Don't think I'm not gonna ask. I ain't shy, Leah."

"Neither am I," Leah said. She dropped low, pulling his zipper down as she went. She ran her hand along the length of him and kissed him through his jeans. Noah tucked his bottom lip into his mouth. The thought of Leah's lipstick on his jeans was oddly thrilling, but Noah was tired of waiting and tired of playing games. He unbuttoned his jeans and Leah put her mouth on him.

Noah's head went back and he closed his eyes. It was pleasure so potent, it made his mouth drop open. His first instinct was to twine his fingers in her hair and push her head down, but he fought it and pushed his hands through his own hair and locked them behind his head. Leah was doing sinfully crazy things with her mouth. Her warm tongue swirled over him delightfully while her mouth created a sweet and wonderfully hot suction. Noah moaned and pushed his hips forward. Leah's hand slid up his thigh and settled on his ass. She pulled him closer, grasping him firmly and rotating her hand as she teased him with her tongue and lips.

Noah opened his eyes and looked down at her. She popped him out of her mouth and licked him like a lollipop. Noah felt his breath getting short. He plunged his hands into her hair and held her head, trying not to stroke too deep. Leah took this as a suggestion to pick up the pace, which it was, and she did, working him vigorously with her hand while her mouth went into overdrive. Noah couldn't imagine himself being any harder than this, but Leah was succeeding in making it so.

He felt like he was ready to burst, but Noah wasn't done with the sexy Miss Leah yet. He pulled away from her and she stood up. Noah backed her up to the sofa, pulling her skimpy panties down. Leah sat and pulled him down until he was kneeling between her thighs. Noah put his hands on her breasts as Leah guided him to his mark.

Noah inched his way in. Leah had tightened up in his absence. Her breath escaped her in tiny puffs as she worked her hips against his. Noah started his rhythm. She was so hot and so wet it was crazy. He was lunging in; not too fast, not too slow. Leah's eyes rolled up in her head and Noah smiled.

He put his mouth close to her ear and whispered into it, lewdly. "You like this, Leah? Huh?"

"Oh, God. Yes, Noah. Oh yes."

"Tell me again, how much you love me," he said, draping her leg over the crook of his arm. Noah went at her on an angle, pumping hard and fast, trying to make her do her neat little trick. When she started screaming, he knew he had her.

"Oh! Noah! I love you, Noah! Yeah, baby, break me down!" And there she went. She exploded all over him, so wet he could barely stay in. Sucking and pulling at him like he was priming a pump. He gave up and let her pull him in. She was drawing the strength out of him with her luscious femininity. Noah came, drawing himself in as far as he could go and grinding as hard as he could. Leah whimpered and came again. Noah ground into her until they were both trembling and making soft noises. After a long moment, Noah pulled out and pulled Leah to her feet.

He put his arms around her and kissed her lips. "I can't promise you anything, Leah. I got a lousy track record."

She nodded with a resigned smile. "I know, but I really want to see how this turns out."

Noah tilted his head and smiled. He liked Leah a lot. He really did. "Yeah okay Leah, but my name's still Noah Ramsey. I can try, but like I said before, my track record ain't all that."

She smiled at him and took his hand. "At least you're trying." Leah led him to the bedroom and closed the door.

Chapter Fifteen

Just A Few Questions

Jessie London was used to getting his way and he was pretty sure he'd get it this time, too. He still couldn't believe Oscar and that arrogant fuck, Keith, had managed to get themselves killed without him being able to secure all their ill-gotten gains.

Oscar had surrendered all of his shit to him for him to look after while he did his bid. Jessie had been able to muscle and strong arm most of Keith's after his unfortunate demise. He'd even managed to get his bitch to give up that bank account in the Caymans. There was just one thing. Jessie really needed that key to the storage in SoHo.

There was almost 20 million in drugs and cash in there … and with all the major players gone except him, it was his free and clear. After he collected, he was bouncing up out of the NYPD as soon as possible, before I.A. got wind that Keith and Oscar weren't the masterminds. He was.

Fuck those bitches in Internal Affairs, though. Jessie knew he was a cunning, ruthless, bastard. He'd never go out like Oscar and Keith's punk asses did. Jessie was willing to take the heads off a whole bunch of snakes before that shit happened to him. It took him by surprise when he walked out of his office and found Butch Harper standing in front of his door, about to knock.

Butch looked surprised, too, but he recovered quickly. He gave Jessie a bright smile and clapped him on the shoulder like he was glad to see him. "Whoa! Hey, Jessie, it's been a long time." He extended his hand for a shake, that fake-ass bright smile not quite

touching his eyes.

Jessie leaned away from him a little, trying not to narrow his own eyes. He smiled, too, and stuck his hand out, not missing a beat.

"Fat Butch! What's up? Long time, no see."

Butch bristled a bit at the jab and Jessie looked at him slyly, to let him know he'd hurt his little fat feelings on purpose. Shit, he should know by now, everybody called him that shit behind his back. Jessie was just one of the few niggas with balls enough to call him that to his face.

Butch looked him over. "Yeah, Jessie, it has been a long time. Still dressing like a pimp, I see."

Jessie raised an eyebrow and looked down at his sand colored Ferragamo gators and champagne Prada suit. His fucking *tie* cost $150. This little fat fuck was playing himself in his off-the-rack, big boy special from the short and squat shop.

Jessie kept his thoughts to himself because he didn't know what Butch was here for. He smiled his glittery white smile at Butch. "Well, somebody's gotta make you sorry dressin' motherfuckers look good. Might as well be me. Ain't that right, Butch?" he said, and chuckled softly.

Butch laughed, too, and stuck his hands in his pockets. "Guess you're right, London. I gotta tell you, I always admired your fashion sense. Tell me, how much would a clown suit like that run me?"

Jessie laughed. Nice try. "They don't make 'em in your size, Bozo."

Butch laughed with great exaggeration. "You were always pretty funny, too," he said, and patted Jessie's shoulder again.

Jessie looked at his suit when Butch took his hand away. "I ain't laughin' now. No chicken grease on the threads, please."

A very dark look of something very close to hatred welled up in Butch's eyes, but he pushed it back. Jessie smiled. Butch was usually pretty good at hiding his emotions.

"So, who you here to see, Butch?"

Butch looked at him pleasantly. A small twinkle of satisfaction danced in his eyes. "Actually, I'm here to see you, Jessie."

Jessie looked at his watch. He noticed Butch checking out his

Rolex. "I hope it's quick. I got somewhere I need to be."

"Oh, sure. All I need is a couple of minutes."

Jessie swung the door to his office open and made a grand sweeping gesture with his hand. "After you."

Jessie watched Butch as he waddled into his office and perched on one of his chairs like a big fat bird with short-ass arms. Jessie sat at his desk, across from him.

"Hurry up and spill it, Butch. I ain't got all day. I'm a busy man."

Butch took a long look around his office. Jessie grinned. All his "good cop" awards were posted on the walls, and there were quite a few of them. Butch studied these fastidiously, but his eyes lingered on a few other things. The butter soft leather sofa under the window that cost 10 grand. The simple Baccarat crystal paperweight that sat on his desk and the huge painting of a Masai warrior, charging with his spear in his hand. That painting had cost Jessie 30 grand ◎ and he'd gotten it for a song. Jessie knew his office raised eyebrows and set tongues to wagging because it was so ostentatious, but he didn't care.

Butch whistled low. "Who's your decorator, Jessie? The fuckin' Metropolitan Museum of Art?"

"I don't need a museum to set me straight, Butch. I know what I like, and I like nice shit."

"Yeah, Jessie. You'd have to be blind not to see that. That's a really nice painting."

"It's outta your league, Fat Butch, so don't even ask."

Butch leaned forward and looked at him. "Oh, I wasn't tryin' to price it, Jessie. I gotta tell you, I don't think I could afford a beautiful piece like that on an inspector's salary," He paused and smiled at Jessie. "Makes me wonder how you could. If you're moonlightin' you should report it to the Department, you know."

Jessie laughed and crossed his legs, checking the crease in his pants. Fuck this fat motherfucker. "I don't need to moonlight, Butch. I know a lot of people who like me very much. These are gifts."

"From who? Women?"

Jessie laughed again and sat up in his chair. "That's a little personal and none of your motherfuckin' business, Butch."

Butch looked at him with his mouth turned down. "That's just what I like about you, Jessie. You're so fuckin' personable. Enough of the small talk. I'm here for a reason, London."

Jessie didn't get that scared little tingle in the pit of his stomach like some cops did when faced with the prospect of having to deal with Butch Harper and I.A.

"I'm all ears, Butch. Hit me."

Butch reached into his back pocket and pulled out his infamous little brown notebook. He flipped through the pages nonchalantly. "Just gotta ask you a few questions, if you don't mind. Don't worry, we'll be done in a second."

Jessie settled back in his seat. "I told you I'm a busy man. Let's go. I got a lunch date."

Butch refused to be intimidated or rushed. He continued flipping those pages until he found what he was looking for. He looked up at Jessie and his amiable smile was gone.

"I gotta ask you if you can recall your whereabouts on the evening of June 14th?"

Jessie knew exactly where he'd been. That was the day Keith and Oscar went to the Trinidad's home to warn them about Cain and Ramsey. He'd been with them right before the meeting and he'd been with Keith after Oscar lost his head.

He looked at Butch. "June 14th? What the fuck is that? Flag Day?"

Butch was not amused. "I believe so. Yeah, I think it is. What were you doin', London? Do you recall?"

Jessie smiled at the memory. "Yeah, I do recall. On June 14th, I spent the better part of the day fuckin' Shelly Randazzo over in Special Victims as hard as I could. I tried to break my dick off in her." He looked at Butch conspiratorially. "Shelly's got some really good pussy, Butch. You should ask her for some."

Butch nodded his head and looked noncommittal. "Shelly Randazzo, huh? She's a looker. No. Thanks, though. My wife would kill me. Okay … you said that took up the better part of your day. What did you do with the rest of it?"

Jessie laughed. "Shit, I drank some Gatorade and went the fuck to sleep. Why?"

Butch tucked his little notebook into his breast pocket and sighed. He leaned forward with his hands clasped in front of him. "I gotta tell you, Jessie, we've been diggin' pretty deep into this barrel of corrupt cops. You know what they say, Jessie. Where there's smoke, there's always fire — and usually when you see a cockroach or a rat, you can be pretty sure he's got a few friends with him. You get where I'm goin' with this?"

"I might be a lot of things, Butch, but I ain't never been slow a day in my life. Yeah, I know what you're sayin' and I agree. What do you need from me?"

"Just a simple thing, Jessie. I need for you to be straight with me about you whereabouts on the day in question. Could you do that for me? Please?"

Jessie stared at Butch for a second. He'd known Butch Harper for years. They weren't friends, but he'd dealt with Butch long enough to know that Butch wore his unassuming shuck and jive demeanor like a set of disposable clothes — and once he ripped them off to reveal his Internal Affairs superhero outfit, it was on and poppin'. Butch Harper was sharp as a tack and he always got his man. Jessie had to play this motherfucker real smooth, or he'd find himself going to prison instead of doing the bird.

Jessie put his hand under his chin and stared, thoughtfully at the ceiling. "Let me see, Butch. Let me see if I can provide you with a run down. It *was* a couple of months ago, you know."

Butch smiled wryly. "Just do your best, Jessie."

"Okay. I think it went a little somethin' like this. I got up pretty late that day, 'cause I was hangin' out the night before. I had a late breakfast and called Shelly. She came over and like I said, I spent the better part of the day knockin' her off. You can probably get her to corroborate, but be easy. Her husband is a street cop down at the 77th and I don't think he'd appreciate that shit." Jessie smiled at Butch like he didn't mind nurturing Butch's obviously low opinion of him.

Butch smiled coolly. "That's real nice, Jessie. I'll try not to step on anybody's toes when I ask her about it. Keep goin', please."

Jessie held up a hand, but didn't lose his smile. "Alright, be patient. This was a little more than a minute ago. Let's see. After I took my nap, I sent Shelly home to her family. I took another shower and met a chick I know — Rhonda Taylor, her name is, down at the Seaport for dinner. Rhonda's real needy. She's always cryin'. Anyway, I left her and went to Stamps on 4th Street and shot a little pool." Jessie frowned a bit, then his face lit up like he'd had an epiphany. "Oh, yeah! While I was there, I saw Keith Childs. We shot some eight ball and talked a little shit. Had a couple drinks. I'd known Keith for a long time. Nobody could've told me he was dirty like that. I was shocked."

Butch sat back in his chair and gave Jessie one of the sagest looks he'd ever seen. *Butch thought he had him.* "Really? Were you just as shocked about Oscar?"

Jessie looked back at Butch carefully. "Nah. I wasn't shocked about Oscar. Oscar had a snake personality. It was in his bones to be dirty. I'm not gonna try and shit you, Butch. I knew Oscar and Keith. I guess you can say we were friends, but we weren't friends like *that*."

Butch shrugged. "Whatever you say, Jessie. Did you see Oscar that day? Maybe it slipped your mind?"

Jessie looked him in the eye. "If I saw Oscar that day, I really don't recall."

Butch nodded and stood up. "Alright, Jessie. Thanks for the time. Sorry to intrude on your day."

Jessie stood, too. "It's cool, Butch."

If he wasn't speaking on it any further, neither was Jessie. Butch let him know what he had to do just by showing up. Jessie walked him to the door and opened it.

Butch very smoothly pushed it closed. This time Butch looked *him* in the eye. "You know, Jessie, I'm a big fan of old sayings. When I was a lot younger, I thought they were bullshit, but now that I'm older and a lot more seasoned … not so much. I gotta tell you, from where I'm standin', now those old folks make more sense than they ever did. I was thinkin' of two, in particular, just now. Any idea?"

Jessie stared at him. "Nah, man. I ain't a big believer in corny bullshit like that."

Butch smiled a little and put his hand on the knob. "That's okay. I'll tell you anyway. The first one is, 'You reap what you sow,' the second one is, 'Whatever happens in the dark always comes to the light.' Oh, yeah. One more. 'You can run, but you can't hide.'"

"Sorry, Butch. I can't relate. I can't co-sign on some bullshit put out there by a bunch of scared motherfuckers. That ain't me."

Butch nodded. "To each his own. Tell me, Jessie, Rhonda Taylor — she one of your police women?"

Jessie laughed and popped a stick of gum in his mouth. "Nah, Butch. Rhonda's a flight attendant. She might be a little hard to put your finger on."

Butch smiled reluctantly. "You sure keep a lot of women Jessie. It's a wonder you can keep 'em separate."

"Well, Butch, pimpin' ain't easy."

"I heard it wasn't. See you later, Jessie."

"Peace out, Butch." Jessie watched him walk away, his mind working a mile a minute. It pissed him off at first, but he was glad Butch had stopped by. Jessie wasn't willing to play his cards with overconfidence. Sometimes when you did that, you ended throwing out the wrong cards and folding. Butch had given him fair warning. If the fellows in the Ivory Tower *weren't* looking at him, they were about to. Butch had caught an itch to at least check him out and fucking with Butch Harper was dangerous. Even for gangsta-ass Jessie London.

There were ways to get Butch's ass off him, though. They were dire and desperate ways, of course, but fuck it, that little fat bastard needed to fall back some. Jessie was almost gone. He wasn't going out like Oscar and Keith. He planned on enjoying his filthy money, fuck that. He had to find out exactly how hot Butch was for him. He took out his cell phone and made a call.

Chapter Sixteen

Do Me a Favor

Lucas was having some very serious problems dealing with Nicole and he was losing his patience. She was running hot and cold on him. Freezing him out one minute, all up on him the next. Most times she seemed stuck in the middle. Indecisive and indifferent. Lately she seemed like she was just plain terrified of him. Like she didn't want him near her. Didn't want to talk to him. Definitely didn't want him to touch her.

Lucas knew he was looking at giving up. He glanced in the mirror and saw her now, sitting on the bed, watching him dress for work. She was still in her nightgown, her hair loose and flowing, cascading over one shoulder. She was beautiful … and very damaged. Lucas didn't have a clue about what to do to help her. He had no idea what she needed, because she refused to talk to him. He sighed heavily and started to tie his tie.

Nicole got up and stood just behind him. "What are you sighing so hard for, Lucas?"

Lucas ignored her and continued with what he was doing. He didn't need an emotional confrontation this morning. Once again, Butch Harper wanted to see him and Noah in his office at 9:00. Nicole slipped her arms around his waist and put her cheek on his shoulder. She ran her hands over the muscles in his stomach and Lucas didn't feel anything close to arousal. The only thing he felt, was a little annoyed that she was wrinkling his shirt. He turned down his collar.

"Lucas?"

"Hmm?" He picked up a small soft brush and ran it over his beard, which he kept a little darker than a shadow.

"Lucas, I'm sorry."

Lucas didn't stop what he was doing. "I know, baby."

"Lucas … I … never mind."

Their eyes met in the mirror. "Okay, Nicole." He didn't attempt to hold her gaze. He just kept about the business of getting ready for work. He clipped his gun in his belt next to his badge and put his cell phone on the other side. Lucas could feel Nick standing behind him.

"Do you want breakfast?" she asked, turning her engagement ring on her finger. It was a nervous habit she'd picked up. Right now it was grating his nerves.

"No. I'm straight," Lucas said, and slipped into his suit jacket. He still felt her standing there behind him … like a ghost.

"You have to eat something, Lucas."

Lucas put on his watch. "No, I don't. I'm good."

Nicole put her hand on his shoulder and he walked out of the bedroom and away from her. He didn't really want her touching him, either. Especially after last night. He looked at the back of his hand. It was all scratched up. Lucas shook his head and walked into the kitchen.

Lucas had rolled over in his sleep last night and made the mistake of putting his hand on her hip. Nicole had come awake fighting him and shrieking, "Don't you fucking touch me!" Lucas tried to calm her down and she'd scratched him up. His hands, his chest, his arms. That shit still hurt. She'd screamed at him that if he'd been five minutes earlier, Keith never would have raped her. She'd said it was his fault.

Lucas had gotten up and slept in the guest bedroom. His fucking fault, huh? He couldn't believe she'd said that to him. He was hurt and he was angry. She was fucking his head up. Didn't she realize he was damned near as damaged as she was? He was trying his best not to, but Lucas knew he was about to shut down on her.

She followed him into the kitchen. Lucas wanted to leave.

"Lucas, I said I was sorry. Are you still mad at me?"

Lucas took a bottle of water out of the fridge and moved past her. "Yes."

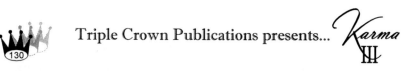

He walked to the door and she kept following him. Now she was mad.

"Fine, then! Don't talk to me! Go on and go to work! And when you get off, you go right on ahead and do me the same fuckin' way you did Justine! I know that's what you want!"

Lucas turned around and punched the wall very close to her head. He very seldom yelled when he got angry. He usually got quieter. Now he was close to screaming.

"You said that shit to me, Nicole! How could you hurt me like that? I'm trying with you! How could you say that to me?"

She looked at him with frosty eyes. "You want to hit me, too, Lucas?"

He backed away from her. "I gotta get out of here. You've lost your fuckin' mind."

"You want me to leave? You want me out of your house?"

Lucas paused in his rage and looked at her. She was beautiful. She'd woke him up after the tragedy of Justine. Now she was putting him back to sleep. She was becoming too much for him to deal with.

"Do whatever you want," he said, and walked out the door.

******

Lucas pulled his S500 into the space next to Noah's truck when he got to One Police Plaza. Noah got out of his Escalade when he saw Lucas pull in. When Lucas didn't get out, Noah walked around to the passenger side and got in.

"What's wrong?" he asked, lighting a cigarette.

Lucas leaned back in his seat and passed a hand over his beard. "I think I'm done, Noah. Nicole's flakin' off the wall like chipped paint. I don't think I can take it anymore. I don't want to."

Noah squinted and blew smoke out the side of his mouth. "You sound damn serious, Luke. You gonna ask for your ring back?"

"Right now, I don't even want it back. She can take it and stick it up her ass for all I care. Give me a smoke, No."

Noah handed him his pack and his lighter. He watched Lucas light a Dunhill and exhale smoke. "Fuck that, Luke. If you callin' it quits, you *gotta* get your ring back. I was with you when you bought it. You could eat for a year with what you paid for that ring."

"I don't care about shit like that, Noah."

"Yeah, well you should. That's an awful lot of money you put on her finger. Get your shit back before she makes a down payment on a condo, Luke."

Lucas looked over at Noah. Noah was dead serious. "Maybe you got a point."

"I know I do. So, what happened?" Noah asked, looking at the scratches on the back of Lucas's hand.

Lucas looked at it, too, and kept smoking. "I put my hand on her while we were sleeping. She turned into a fuckin' mountain lion and started scratching me up."

Noah nodded, thoughtfully. "Oh, I see ... and she's still there, chillin' in your spot, huh?"

Lucas chose to disregard the question. "She said a lot of salty shit to me."

"How salty?"

"She said, if I'd been there five minutes earlier, Keith wouldn't have raped her. She blamed me for that shit, Noah. Said it was my fault. You believe she said that shit to me?"

Noah put the window down a little more and knocked the ash off his smoke. "Yeah, Luke. I believe she said it. Sure, maybe if we'd been a little quicker it wouldn't have happened. But who could help that? We had as much control over that as we had over Keith's ass bein' crazy in the first place. I know that's your woman, and I'm real sorry it happened, but fuck her on that one, Luke. You could just as easily have said, 'You're a cop. You should've fought him off.' "

Noah had his own way of looking at things. Even when he disagreed, Lucas could always see his reasoning. Like he saw it now.

"That's not the only thing she said."

"I'll bet it's not," Noah replied. "Go ahead."

Lucas looked over at Noah. "I froze her out this morning. She tried to apologize for last night, but I wasn't havin' it."

Noah looked back at him. "I don't blame you. So, what did she say, Luke?"

Lucas threw his half-smoked cigarette out the window. "She said for me to go ahead and carry my ass to work, and when I got off, to go ahead and do her like I did Justine."

Noah winced. "Damn, bro. That's some cold ass shit. Damn."

Lucas looked at Noah, seriously. "Noah, I have never in my life come that close to just punchin' a woman in her face. I balled my fuckin' fist up and I aimed for her fuckin' nose. I pulled the punch at the last minute and hit the wall instead."

Noah nodded. "I'd say it's time to take a break, Luke."

"I say so, too … but I don't want to leave her like this."

They were quiet for a moment. Noah threw his own cigarette out the window. "Can I ask you somethin'?" he asked.

"Ask whatever you want, No."

"This question's a little awkward, Luke."

"Go ahead."

"Okay. You sure you love her, or were you just tryin' to recapture some of what you had with Justine? Maybe you were just feelin' a little lonely. Maybe you just wanted to get back that feelin' of bein' in love."

Lucas sighed and ran his hand over his beard. He sat back and gave it some serious thought.

"I mean," Noah continued, "Don't get me wrong, Luke. I'm your best friend. I understand you. You may have some serious feelin's for Nick — genuine, true feelin's — but don't you think you just kinda jumped into this thing with her? I can see her bein' your woman, but I *did* look at you funny when you wanted to wife her. I mean, the first serious woman after Justine — and you want to wife her?"

Lucas hadn't thought about it like that, but again, Noah, in his own way, made a lot of sense. He shrugged. "I don't know, Noah. You said that and now I don't know." He dropped his face into his hands and tried to rub some sense back into himself. Lucas lowered his hands and looked over at Noah, slightly irritated. "If you thought I was fuckin' up, why didn't you say something?"

Noah laughed a little and put his hand on his shoulder. "'Cause I believe lightnin' can strike twice in the same spot. Like I said, Luke, you're the best friend I have in this world. I know the hell you've been through firsthand. I was hopin' you'd be happy, bro. I'm real sorry you and Nick ain't workin' out, man. For real."

"I'll be alright. Thanks, No."

"Don't mention it."

Lucas looked at his watch. "Let's go. We're pushin' it."

They got out of Lucas's car, straightening their ties and turning more than a few heads of their fellow female officers. Noah smiled at a woman in a pretty pink skirt. She smiled back and winked at him.

"So, Luke, you gonna put her ass out or what?"

Lucas smiled in spite himself. A tall caramel honey with a detective's badge thought he was smiling at her. He turned his head appreciatively as she walked by. Funny how this stuff came right back.

"I think she'll leave on her own," he said, returning his attention to Noah.

Noah made a face of severe skepticism. "Fuck *that*, Luke. Give Nick her walkin' papers before she claims squatter's rights. That's some bullshit you're talkin'."

Lucas looked at his old friend as they walked into the building. "I gotta give her time to find somewhere else to stay."

Noah shook his head. "Not your responsibility. Tell her to vacate by 7:00 tonight and please leave the ring on the coffee table."

"That's cold, Noah."

Noah shrugged as they stepped into the elevator. "Maybe, but it's what you need to do."

"Where's she gonna stay? With Leah?"

"Probably not. I'm over there a lot. Nights mostly. We make a lot of noise. I think she's my girlfriend."

Lucas raised an eyebrow. "Yeah? What about Nadine?"

"I'll cross that bridge when I get to it."

Lucas looked at his crazy-ass friend. "Uh-huh," he said, as they stepped out and walked to Butch's office.

"What do you suppose the little plump demon wants, Luke?"

Lucas shrugged. "Don't know. We haven't shot anybody in a minute. Guess we're about to find out." He rapped on Butch's door with his knuckles.

"Come in!" Butch called from the other side. Lucas and Noah walked into Butch's inner sanctum and found him sitting at his desk wearing his reading glasses. There was an unfinished bowl of apple cinnamon oatmeal to his right, along with a banana and a cup of tea. A bottle of vitamins and another of Citrucel were to his left. There were also various books on police procedure strewn across his desk. He had one in his hand.

He looked up at them and smiled. "Hey, fellas. What's the word?"

"We were thinking you could tell us." Lucas said, taking a seat across from him.

Noah lingered at his desk, eyeing Butch's breakfast. Butch put his book down and sat back in his seat, lacing his fingers over his portly belly. He looked at Noah expectantly, like he knew something smart was coming out of his mouth soon.

Noah didn't disappoint. He picked up the Citrucel and looked first at it, then back at Butch with synthetic sympathy.

"Damn, Butch. You got trouble movin' the mail?"

Butch smiled benignly. "Well, Ramsey, I gotta tell you, it doesn't get easier as you get older."

Noah put the bottle down and sat next to Lucas. "Maybe not, but you wouldn't think you'd have to force it out ... or let other people know you have to."

Butch laughed. "You're still a young man, Ramsey. Your time is comin'. You gotta take care of yourself now. When's the last time you had your prostate checked?"

Noah smirked. "I ain't in a hurry to let somebody stick their finger up my ass, Butch. Speakin' of which, why are we here?"

Lucas smothered a laugh. "Yeah, Butch, what's this about? Keith Childs?"

Butch took off his glasses with a sigh and leaned forward. "I'm not sure yet." He took a moment to look them in the eye. His face was worried and full of concern. "I know we haven't always seen eye to eye, but I do know in my heart, you guys are damn fine detectives. We go back a long time, and maybe, for obvious reasons, I've rubbed you guys the wrong way more than once ... but I gotta tell you, no matter how I've gone about my job and played hardball with you, I've always gone about it with great affection and profound respect."

Noah blinked. "You're not dyin', are you?"

Lucas hit him in the arm as Butch chuckled. "Don't listen to him. What's wrong, Butch?"

Butch looked at them fondly. "I need to talk to you guys off the record. Is that okay?"

Lucas settled in his seat. "More than okay. What's on your mind?"

Again, Butch took a moment to look at them before he answered. "What do you guys know about Jessie London?"

Lucas and Noah exchanged a look.

Butch frowned. "What's the look for, fellas?"

"Nothing, I guess. Jessie's a lieutenant in vice. We don't deal with him much," Lucas said with a shrug.

"That's not what I asked you. I asked you what you know about him. Now, what do you know? What's the word on him? I know you've heard somethin'."

"Okay," Noah started, "I can't speak for Lucas, but — I don't know the guy personally — people say he's a pretty gigantic asshole with pimp tendencies. But they also say he gets the job done. I ain't got too much commentary on that, Butch. Hell, they probably say the same thing about me."

Butch laughed. "I only heard a few people call you a pimp, Ramsey. I've heard gigolo and ho more when it comes to you. I *have* heard asshole more than once."

Noah laughed. "Okay. Okay. Fuck you, Butch."

"Don't get mad, No. You earned it," Lucas said with a smile.

Noah gave him a smart aleck frown. "Hey, fuck you, too, Luke. I ain't see you doin' no better."

Butch smiled. "He's right. Until recently, I heard the same things about you, Cain."

They all shared a laugh and Butch seemed satisfied that they were no longer pissed at him for fucking with Nick. They'd fallen back into the same affable relationship they always had when Butch wasn't looking at them for something. It was never personal. Butch had a job to do and so did they. They did their job their way and sometimes they had to butt heads.

"So, Butch, what is it about Jessie London that's got your hackles up?" Noah asked.

Butch raised an eyebrow. "Did I say my hackles were up?"

"You do have that look in your eye. C'mon, Butch, start talking," Lucas said.

"Alright. I've gone this far. You're right, Ramsey. My hackles *are* up. This shit is serious, guys. I gotta tell you. I've rolled it over and over in my head. I made sure I did all my homework three times before I even said it out loud. I haven't even said anything to the guys in the ivory tower about this shit. I had to be sure beyond a shadow of a doubt. I heard Ramsey's opinion of this cocksucker, Cain. What's yours? Do you know him?"

Lucas was a little surprised at the angry tone in Butch's voice, but it made him sit up and answer right away.

"Yeah, I know him. I know that as a person he's a fuckin' slug, but all the awards on his wall say he's much better than a decent cop. What's up, Butch?"

"You care to elaborate on your personal opinion, Cain?"

Lucas stared at him for a moment. Butch seemed to be trying hard to stay even. "It was a long time ago, Butch. Back when we first made detective. We raided a drug house and I saw him pocket some money. I got him to put it back, but I had to put my gun on him to do it."

Noah nodded. "That's right. I forgot about that shit."

"Glad you didn't, Cain. I'm goin' after his ass and I need your help, guys. I think I found the head of the monster."

Lucas frowned. "The head of what monster, Butch? What are you sayin'?"

Noah was frowning, too. "Yeah, Butch. Spit it out. You're soundin' awful serious."

"It is awful serious, Ramsey," Butch said. He took a sip of his tea and went on. "Goddamn Keith Childs and that low life Oscar Tirado ain't have nothin' on this piece of shit."

"What?" That drove Lucas to the edge of his seat.

Butch smiled. "I might talk slow, Cain, but I don't stutter. You heard me right. Tirado and Childs, as bad as they were, were only the tip of the iceberg."

"So you're sayin' Jessie London is the ringleader in all this shit? Do you know what you're insinuating, Butch?" Lucas said.

"I know exactly what I'm insinuating, Cain."

Noah shook his head and raised an eyebrow. "That's some truly deep shit you talkin', Butch. Jessie London is a goddamn vice lieutenant. You gotta come correct if you slingin' arrows at a nigga like that."

"How sure are you?" Lucas asked.

Butch smiled grimly. "I'd bet my shield on it. The three of them stared at each other for a long moment.

"That's some deep shit, too," Noah said. "Must be true."

"You better believe it's true. My shield is sacred to me. I think you already know, but I gotta tell you, fellas, there's nothing — absolutely nothin' — I hate more than a filthy cop."

"This we know, Butch," Lucas said. "What makes you think Jessie's the mastermind?"

Butch chuckled. "Don't look so surprised, Cain. You said yourself, you caught him bein' dirty. I've been following Jessie's career ever since he helped Keith Childs set that rookie, Suarez, up with those three ounces of heroin."

Noah frowned at him. "You knew about that? Why didn't you do somethin'? Suarez lost his fuckin' job, Butch."

Butch leaned forward and looked at Noah intently. "I'm well aware of Suarez losin' his job, Noah. I'm aware of a whole lotta dirty shit that goes down. Being aware of things is not the problem when it comes down to flushing the blue shit out of the toilet. The problem lies in being able to *prove* it. You just can't *accuse* a cop of bein' less than admirable and not be able to prove it beyond a shadow of a doubt, Ramsey. You know that. If you throw it out there and make it stick, you get accolades and commendations. People wanna carry you around on their shoulders. But if you throw it out there and it doesn't stick — if it slides down the fuckin' wall and hits the ground instead ... well you know what happens then. You get ostracized as a traitor. Might as well turn in your badge."

"And shoot yourself in the head," Lucas said. If Butch had gone this far, he was more than sure. He was certain. "Okay, Butch. We believe you. Now tell us why we're here. Why'd you feel the need to share your speculations with us?"

Butch smiled and there was a twinkle in his eye. "It ain't speculation, Lucas, it's a fact. I'm gonna prove it. Hopefully with the help of the two best first grade narcotics detectives in New York City."

Noah looked skeptical. "Thanks for the compliments, Butch, but why us? I had the feelin' you thought we were fuck-ups. You're always after us."

Butch's eyes held the twinkle. "I gotta tell you, Noah, I really don't think you're half the asshole you wish I'd believe you are. Maybe you are in your personal life, but I happen to know for a fact that you and Cain are exemplary cops. You guys made detective damn near straight outta the academy. Second grade six years later. Shining stars in an elite narcotics unit. Then that goddamn Nine bust. *Bam!* A lot of trouble and a river of pain, but *Bam!* Detectives first grade. What do you assholes have, like twelve years on the job? That shit's unheard of! You're fuckin' incredible! The goddamn go-to guys. First Grade Detectives usually stay behind the scenes and don't work the field. That's the first place they put you because they know whoever they send you after is goin' the fuck down. Nobody gets away from you two guys. You may get hurt, but you get right back up and go right back out there, because you know it's where you belong. Do you think I don't know how highly regarded you are by your own peers, even if they talk shit about you behind your backs? Do you know how impressed *I am* with you? Every time I had to investigate an incident with you guys, I did it hiding a smile behind my hand and with a huge amount of pride. Don't you think I know you're the *Rock Stars*? That's why I need your help. If I put you guys after Jessie London's greasy ass, he won't slide away. He's goin' to prison or the graveyard, and I don't give a shit which one. So what do you say, fellas? Will you help me nail this fuck?"

Though he knew they weren't truly adversaries, Lucas had no idea Butch felt that way about them. He was sure Noah didn't either. It would probably never stop Noah from getting at Butch, but Lucas knew Noah well enough to know that Butch's speech would change the way he felt about him for the better. The same way he'd just changed for Lucas.

Lucas looked at Noah. Noah smirked and checked the shine on his shoes, giving him the okay.

"Alright, Butch," Lucas said, "Tell us what you want us to do."

Chapter Seventeen

Busted

Noah was late and Nadine was getting pissed off … and a little nervous. Noah was rarely late. The last two times he'd promised he'd drop by, he'd stood her up. That was out of character, too. Usually, when Noah made plans to show up, he did. Now he was quickly becoming MIA. Nadine was starting to worry that he was on to her.

Nadine looked in the mirror. She'd just gotten her hair and nails done and she wore a pretty, smocky, little print dress. She should have looked beautiful, but she still had a ways to go. The concussion was gone and her ribs were okay. It was a relief that her kidney was back to normal. The bruises had faded, but her neck still bothered her.

The worst part was the scars. That Keith Childs bastard had fucked her up when he tackled her through that glass table. She had random scars all over her. The lightest ones were healing nicely and starting to fade a little, but the deepest ones had needed stitches. There were eleven of them altogether. She'd counted them. They were scattered all over her legs and arms mostly, but there was one on her neck and another one high on her right cheek, that were seriously fucking with her self-esteem.

When the doorbell rang, it caught her off guard. He'd decided to show up after all.

"Mom! Daddy's here!" Noah Jr. called out, brightly.

Nadine looked in the mirror again. She thought about putting more makeup on her face, but decided against it. Instead, she smoothed her dress down and looked at her reflection. Nadine stuck her stomach out as far as it would go. She sucked her teeth. Noah was a whole lot smarter than she wanted to give him credit for. She walked out of the room wondering how she was going to pull off giving him some, without him knowing she wasn't pregnant anymore.

Noah was standing in the kitchen with Noah Jr. and Raine when she walked in. As usual, Nadine got that little flutter in her chest that she always got when she saw Noah. He was gorgeous in a suit just as gray as his eyes. His skin was a creamy and beautiful café au lait. Noah's scars had healed damn near to perfection, Nadine noted with a tad of jealousy. His hair was dark and lushly curly. She wanted to push her fingers through it in the worst way.

Noah smiled at her with his pretty teeth. "Hey, Nadine. You're lookin' much better. Feelin' okay?"

Nadine pursed her lips. 'Lookin' much better?' What was that supposed to mean? She threw it right back at him with a big ass smile. "Feeling great, considering. You're looking much better, too."

Noah smirked at her. "You know me, Nadine. I never stay down long. I always bounce back like a rubber band."

Nadine looked at him knowingly. "Fine as ever, right?"

He gave her a real smile. "That's right."

Just like that she wanted him. All jokes, schemes, and plots aside. It was time to send the kids away. Nadine put her hand in her son's hair — so much like his father's.

"Noah, baby, why don't you take your sister to the library. She has a book report tomorrow."

Their son frowned. "Aw, Mom! Come on! I don't wanna go to the library."

Noah looked down at him like he'd just sprouted a pair of horns. His frown was a lot worse than his son's. "Who you talkin' to, Noah? You don't talk to your mother like that. You lost your mind?"

He dropped his head and mumbled. "I'm sorry, Daddy."

"Don't say you're sorry to me. Apologize to your mother, then take your sister to the library like she said."

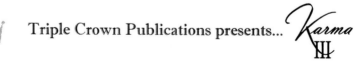

Noah Jr. looked back at his father like he'd been wronged. "But Daddy —"

"But nothin'. Do like I said. Don't make me have to fold you up, son." Nadine wondered if Noah knew how much he sounded like his own father. "You must think you're grown or somethin'."

"He always acts like that, Daddy. I'm glad you checked him." Raine said, putting on her backpack.

Noah raised an amused eyebrow at her. "*Checked him?* They teach you that in school, little girl? Mind your business and listen to your brother. I'll see you guys later," he said, and kissed the top of her head.

Noah Jr. grabbed his bag and headed for the door with the same wronged look on his face. Noah stepped in his way and pulled out his wallet.

"Here, son. Take your sister to McDonald's and stop bein' disrespectful." He handed him a twenty with a smirk.

Noah smiled and hugged him. "Thanks, Daddy. Will you be here when we get back?"

Noah smiled. "Doubt it. See you Saturday." He kissed the top of his head, too, and watched them leave. Noah stuck a cigarette in his mouth and eyed Nadine.

"When did those kids get so fresh? If I talked to my mother like that, she woulda knocked my ass out."

"Well, you see they don't talk like that to you."

Noah took out his lighter. "That's because they know I'll put my foot in their asses."

Nadine smiled. "I hope you don't plan on smoking that cigarette, Noah."

His eyes dropped to her belly. "Sorry, Nadine. I forgot myself." He put the cigarette back in the pack and pocketed his lighter. He looked her over and frowned slightly.

"How've you really been doin', Nadine? You feelin' okay?"

Nadine hesitated. "Yeah, Noah. I'm okay."

He moved closer to her. "You sure? You look a little weak around the eyes."

Nadine put her hands on his chest to keep him back a little, but

she let them fall and ran them over the muscles in his stomach to let him know she still wanted him.

Nadine looked at him suggestively. "I'm fine, baby, but I've missed you. Why have you stayed away so long?" She looked up at him and he looked at the scar on her cheek.

"I'm sorry for what he did to you," Noah said plainly.

Nadine's heart sank a little. She'd accepted his apology long ago. She didn't want to talk about it anymore. Nadine went back to her conversation.

"I said I missed you, Noah. Didn't you miss me?" She kissed his neck and got a murmur of pleasure from him, but he didn't put his arms around her. Noah put his hands in his pockets instead.

He spoke into her hair. "You eatin' okay, Nadine? You look like you're carryin' a little small this time."

Nadine dropped her hands completely and stepped away from him. She looked up at him and there was a hint of his trademark smirk on his face, but his eyes weren't smiling. Noah was angry. She took another step away from him because she wasn't exactly sure why. *Shit!* Had he figured out she was lying to him already?

Time to go another way with this. It was time to drop real low and play the sympathy card. Nadine pulled up the tears and gingerly put her hand over the scar on her cheek.

"What's the matter, Noah? Don't you think I'm pretty anymore?"

Noah lost his smirk and shook his head. His eyes were dark and stormy. "Gimme a break, Nadine. That scar don't bother me."

"Then what's wrong, Noah? Are you mad at me?" Nadine hadn't seen the look he gave her since he'd found out she was pregnant and flipped on her in that restaurant. Oh, God. He knew.

"Yeah, Nadine. I'm mad as hell at you."

Nadine wasn't copping to anything. She was going to ride in this car until the wheels fell off. She spread her hands innocently.

"But why, Noah? What did I do?"

"You know, Nadine ... a whole lot of stuff has gone down the last couple of months. A lot of *foul* shit. Shit you did. Shit you said. I tried, but I just can't seem to get past most of it."

She had no idea where he was going with this. "What are you

talking about, Noah? Why are you so mad?"

Noah advanced on her. "You want to know why I'm mad at you? Well, brace yourself, Nadine, 'cause I'm gonna fuckin' tell you." Nadine backed away from him. Noah was almost screaming at her.

"Do you know what you did, Nadine? *Do you? Huh?*" Nadine was backing away from him, but Noah kept advancing until he had her up against the wall.

"What's the matter with you, Noah?" she asked, pushing at him, and trying to move back. Noah wasn't having it, though. He was on her and he wouldn't let her get away.

He grabbed her by the arms. "I'm tired of you stickin' your foot out and tryin' to trip me up, Nadine. I've been watchin' you, Nadine: scheming, conniving, manipulatin' me. You've been doin' it for a while, too. I didn't even notice 'cause I was tryin' to be easy with you because of Noah and Raine. Tryin' to keep you smoothed out, 'cause I knew since the day I married you how crazy you can get. And 'cause I loved you and I didn't want you to hate me anymore than I already thought you did. You've been fuckin' me in the ass since you divorced me, Nadine. Hell, you divorced me to fuck me in the ass. To punish me, right? I got a fuckin' news flash for you, Nadine. Fuck you and your goddamn punishment! I ain't been on punishment since I was 15 years old."

Nadine wasn't really shocked that he'd latched onto that. She'd known the moment she'd told him she divorced him to punish him, that it would stick in his mind like peanut butter sticks to the roof of your mouth.

"Noah —"

"No, Nadine, be quiet! You wanted to know why I'm mad, so I'm tellin' you. You threw me away. Cast me the fuck out. And you were a bitch to me every day until you found out Liz was pregnant. All of a sudden you wanted me back and I played right into your little plottin' hands. You destroyed my relationship with Liz and she was carryin' my baby. She *died* carryin' my baby, Nadine."

Nadine narrowed her eyes at him and wriggled out of his grasp. "Noah, I know you're not trying to blame me for what happened to Liz."

Noah looked at her like he thought about what he said before he said it, but he still said it. "All I'm sayin' is, if I hadn't chased her away, she would have been safe with me."

Nadine wasn't happy about what happened to Liz, but hey, she was one less chick she had to worry about. She folded her arms across her chest and looked him in the eye.

"I am not responsible for the death of your whore, Noah."

Noah withdrew from her like she'd struck him. He gave her the darkest look she'd ever seen on his face. "I could put your goddamn lights out for that shit, Nadine. You better be damn fuckin' glad I'm a gentleman, 'cause you ain't bein' too much of a lady right now."

Nadine smiled, knowing she was pushing her luck with Noah, but almost certain she could still make him bend. "You want to put my lights out because I said something funky about your bitch, Noah? Go right ahead, but remember *I'm* carrying your baby now. You're mad at me because I love you and I want my husband back? Then be mad, Noah. You'll get over it. Come home, already! Stop acting stupid and reaching for reasons not to."

Nadine started to put her arms around his waist, but Noah stepped away from her. He was frowning at her hard.

"Don't say anything else about Liz, Nadine. She's gone. Don't talk about her like that."

Nadine laughed. "Oh, now she's some kind of angel to you. Do you have her on a pedestal now, 'cause you sure didn't think enough of her when she was alive, not to fuck around on her — even if it was with me! Don't make her a saint, Noah. She was what she was. A pretty little skeezer with a fucking agenda, who couldn't keep her weak-ass spot in your heart."

Noah smirked and his eyes glittered dangerously. "You need to stop talkin' *right now*, Nadine. You crossed the line with me on a whole lot of levels. Quit while you're ahead." He turned and started for the door.

Nadine was furious with him. Noah had balls being angry with her for anything, after all he'd put her through. And who the hell did he think he was to leave in the middle of this conversation? How dare he insinuate she was responsible for that heifer's death? Where was he going, now? To screw that bitch, Leah? More than that, Nadine was furious that he was trashing her plans. By now she should have been well on her way to replacing their lost baby. She hated that she couldn't read him like she wanted to. She went after him.

"Don't you walk away from me, Noah Ramsey!" She grabbed his arm and Noah snatched it away.

"Don't touch me, Nadine! Just let me go, okay?" He pulled the door open and she slipped in front of him and pushed it closed.

She looked into his stormy eyes. "*Come home, Noah.*"

He stared back at her. "No way. Move and let me go."

Nadine realized with a jolt maybe she *had* crossed the line with him. She knew she was blowing it, but her mouth seemed to have a will of its own.

"Where are you going? Are you going to your other fucking whore, Leah?"

Nadine was shocked when Noah picked her up and moved her out of the way. She ran at him and he pushed her back. Nadine reached out and slapped him in frustration. Noah's reaction was so comical, Nadine almost laughed. His eyes widened, his mouth dropped open and he put his hand to his cheek like that kid from Home Alone. It didn't stay funny for long.

Noah reached out and grabbed her. He turned her around so quick, Nadine didn't even have time to put up a fight. He held her tightly against his body with her back against his chest.

"Want to know the other reason I'm mad at you, Nadine?" She didn't, but Noah was determined to tell her. Noah grabbed the hem of her short dress and pulled it up to her breasts. He ran his hands over her flat stomach and laughed in her ear before he pushed her away. Nadine stumbled back and felt tears spring to her eyes.

Noah smirked at her. He lit his cigarette before he opened the door. His eyes were cold and knowing.

"I told you before. *I get paid to notice shit, Nadine*. Your ass better start showin' real soon." He stepped out the door and smoothly swung it shut behind him.

Nadine put her face in her hands and started crying for real. She'd just lost her leverage.

Chapter Eighteen

Disturbing Behavior

Leah had been having a great day until now. Noah had shown up out of the blue late yesterday evening looking gorgeous with some upscale takeout and a great bottle of Moscato. You could have knocked her over with a feather when he handed her a bouquet of really nice flowers. Not roses, mind you, but not those bullshit deli flowers, either. They obviously came from a florist, which meant he'd put some thought into it. It meant he cared.

Leah lit some candles and put on some music and they'd had a nice, romantic dinner. She'd even managed to convince Noah to watch a movie with her. He'd agreed, but he'd tried to get at her the whole time. When that was over, he'd taken her to bed and made love to her like he was never going to see her again. Off and on for hours. They hadn't fallen asleep until the very wee hours of the morning.

Noah had a hard time letting her out of the bed that morning, but he'd finally taken her to brunch and they'd had a meal that was just as romantic as last night's dinner. They'd parted company after that. Noah hadn't told her he loved her or anything, but he'd treated her like she was his girlfriend, not a jump off.

Leah had gotten a call from Nick a little later in the afternoon. She'd asked to meet her downtown at a club called Shelter for drinks. Leah was a little surprised. Nick was not a club person by nature, and neither was she — but here she was sitting at the bar, waiting for Nick to show up. Her whole mood changed when Nick walked through the door.

Nick looked like she hadn't slept in days. She had dark circles under her eyes and she looked like she'd been crying. Hell, she looked like she was *still* crying. Leah stood up. She couldn't ever remember seeing Nick look quite like this. Not even after the rape. She looked nervous and shaky and terrified.

"Nick, what's wrong?"

Nick wouldn't answer her at first. She sat down and ordered a double Hennessy and knocked it back. Then she looked at her.

"I'm leaving Lucas, Leah."

Leah's mouth dropped open. She put one hand on her chest and clutched Nick's hand with the other. "Nick, what the fuck are you talking about?" Leah sat back a little, frowning. "What's the matter? What did he do?"

Nick smiled sadly and it looked horrible on her still beautiful face. Leah frowned deeper. *Nick looked horrible*. She looked drawn and like she'd lost fifteen pounds she didn't need to lose. Even her hair had lost its luster.

"Lucas didn't do anything, Leah. He's been as wonderful to me as he's always been." She signaled to the bartender for another drink. Leah ordered one of the same. They didn't speak until they were drinking again. Nick drank half of hers. Leah noticed her hand had a serious tremble to it. Leah put her arm around her and Nick burst into tears. She put her arms around Leah's neck and cried harsh, sobbing tears. She cried like someone had died. People gave them passing concerned glances. There was a boyishly handsome guy at the end of the bar with a clipboard in front of him. He was watching them with more than a little interest.

Leah didn't give a shit who was watching. Her very dear friend needed her. She rubbed Nick's back and spoke soothing words in her ear. After a couple of minutes, Nick pulled herself together. She looked woefully down at her ring and drank the rest of her drink.

"I … I really wanted to marry Lucas, Leah, but it's not gonna happen."

Leah put her hand on her shoulder. "Nick, what's wrong?"

Nick wiped at her face." Nothing, Leah. I just changed my mind, I guess," she trailed off and signaled to the bartender again. He looked at her warily, but he brought her another drink. "Lucas has been through a lot, Leah. He doesn't need or deserve to deal with the shit I'm bringing to the table. It's just not fair. I won't do that to him. I love him too much to torture him."

This shit didn't make any sense to Leah. "Changed your mind? Didn't you tell me once that trying not to have feelings for Lucas was like trying to stand up in an avalanche? Hell, Nick, you asked Lucas to marry you. What the hell has changed in your relationship to make you want to leave him? You changed your mind? Sorry, honey, but I don't buy that. What's really going on with you, Nick? Is it the rape? Are you guys having a hard time dealing with that?"

Nick's face crumpled and fresh tears fell. She drank her third drink in three big gulps. Leah couldn't keep the frown off her face. This shit was not like Nick — guzzling booze like this. She signaled the bartender again. He was at the other end of the bar, talking to the guy with clipboard. They exchanged a few words and the guy with the clipboard looked at Nick, nodded, and walked away. The bartender brought her another double.

Leah watched her friend take another huge gulp of liquor and she was scared for her.

"Honey, if you keep drinking like that, you're gonna get alcohol poisoning or something. Stop and talk to me. Something's obviously killing you. *Tell me*. I'm your best friend. I'll do anything in my power to help you."

Leah was stunned when Nick laughed. It was a dry, brittle, tuneless laugh — and she didn't smile when she did it. It was creepy.

"Thanks, Leah, but you can't help me. Lucas can't help me … Noah can't help me, either. I'm in a whole lot of trouble that I can't even talk to you about. Dying of alcohol poisoning is the least of my worries. I hope I fall off this barstool and hit the floor with no pulse. I'd rather be dead than deal with the shit in front of me. Oh God, Leah. Oh God." Nick finished her drink and pushed the glass away. "Maybe I should go home and run a nice hot bath and slit my fucking wrists. That's how they do it, right?" She was slurring now and wavering a bit on the stool. She'd just had four doubles in less than 30 minutes. She was talking about killing herself. Nick was in trouble.

"Does Lucas know —" Leah started, but Nick cut her off with that scary laughter.

"Lucas doesn't know shit! I stay *the fuck away* from Lucas, because he'll look at me and he'll know, Leah! He'll fuckin' *know*!"

Leah looked around quickly. Nick was getting those curious stares again. Leah tried to smooth her out. "Know what, Nick? Nothing can be that bad after the shit we went through."

"Sure it can and it can get fuckin' worse, too."

Nick's cell phone rang and she jumped like someone had shot at her, but she answered it. Leah leaned in close to hear her one-sided conversation, as Nick turned away and stuck a finger in her other ear. She was agitated at once.

"H-Hello? Aw, God! Please stop this. Stop calling me! I said I would, okay? You're driving me crazy! You're *what*? Oh no ..." Nick trailed off and put her phone away like she was scared to death.

"Oh, shit! Look who it is! Fine-ass Leah Wheeler. The goddamn girl of my dreams!" Someone was speaking right over Leah's shoulder. She turned around in annoyance and looked into Jessie London's handsome face.

She mustered a smile. "Hey, Jessie. Been a long time."

Jessie looked past her at Nick, still smiling his pretty smile. "Damn! Is that you, Nicky? You look like you lost your shine. Havin' a bad night?"

Nick wouldn't even look at him. She kept her head down and her face turned away. It didn't seem to affect Jessie at all.

"Well, I saw you two lovely ladies over here and thought I'd buy you a drink, but Nick here looks like she'd reached her limit and seems antisocial ... so I'm gonna bounce. Nice to see you, beautiful," He said, and kissed Leah's cheek. Jessie put a hand on Nick's shoulder. "You look like you're goin' through some shit, girl. Haunted, you know? Keep your chin up and work it out. Night, ladies," he said, and walked away, leaving them with the scent of his alluring cologne.

Nick got the shakes and started crying again. Leah put her arm around her and was about to say something when the boyishly handsome guy with the clipboard spoke to her from behind the bar.

"How you ladies doin' tonight?" he asked, with a charming smile. He was really cute, with an old thin scar along his jaw line.

Leah smiled back. "We've had better."

He nodded in commiseration. "Your friend alright?"

Leah rubbed Nick's back. "She will be."

He set another drink in front of Nick. "This one's on me, if she needs it. I took the liberty of callin' you ladies a cab. It's waitin' outside when you're ready."

"Thanks, but you didn't have to. Sorry about this."

He smiled. "I'm used to stuff like this. It's my pleasure. You ladies get home safe and have a good night." He walked away, still smiling.

Leah watched Nick drink her drink and walked out of the club holding her up, grateful for the cab. She wondered what in the fuck was really going on with her

Chapter Nineteen

Speculation

Myers had put a tail on Jessie's ass at Butch's request. Lucas and Noah followed him to a trendy little club called Shelter in Chelsea. They sat outside now, in an ice blue Maxima Butch had rented with his own money. Jessie arrived about 45 minutes earlier with Darryl Gilford. Darryl was 280 pounds of muscle in a 6'5" frame. Notoriously nasty and not afraid to lay hands on you. Darryl was an infamous narcotics detective everyone called "The Brute."

Jessie hadn't rolled up with Darryl like they were two buddies hangin' out. Darryl had shadowed Jessie like he was his personal bodyguard or something. They met yet another unsavory narc, Merlin Nash. Just about every move Merle made seemed like it was done with raised eyebrows and a hand over his mouth. Everyone had their suspicions about Merle, and I.A. had looked at him hard more than once, but it was like Butch said, "If you pointed a finger and couldn't prove it, you would probably come out the other end of it smelling a lot less like a rose than the person you pointed at."

Noah reviewed the pictures they'd snapped of London, Gilford and Nash with the digital Myers provided them with. Shit, it left no doubt they all knew each other well. They had one shot of Nash and London actually hugging. Noah put the camera down and looked over at his boy.

Lucas was looking out the window, seemingly at the club, but that might not be the case. Noah knew he had other things on his mind. Noah decided to see where his head was at.

"What do you suppose they're talkin' about in there?" he asked, turning his head Lucas' way.

Lucas glanced at him and laughed a little. "They probably ain't talkin' at all, No. This place is a club. They're probably dancing."

Noah snickered. "Yeah, right! Probably doin' the crooked cop boogie as we speak."

Lucas smiled. "Uh-huh. Butch was right."

Noah nodded. "Yes he was. Right as rain. I get the feelin' those are some pretty shifty bastards in there."

"I got the same feelin', No. I know for a fact, London's shiesty. I'm surprised you don't know him."

Noah shrugged. "Never had the pleasure. From what I can see, I ain't miss nothin'."

"Damn sure didn't. What about the other two? Nash and Gilford?"

Noah smiled. "Well, hell, we both knew who they were when we saw 'em, right? It would be safe to say their reputations precede 'em and the shit we been hearin' ain't good."

"Sounds like we're on the same page, No."

Noah grinned. "Shit, we *stay* on the same page, Luke. That's why you my boy."

Lucas held out his fist and Noah dapped him. Lucas turned his head back to the window and the smile fell off his face. "Look at this shit, Noah."

Noah followed Lucas' gaze out the window and was surprised to see Leah and Nick coming out of the club. Leah seemed like she was okay, but Nick looked very unsteady. They paused at a cab parked out front and exchanged a few words. Leah seemed to be holding Nick up. Noah had definitely seen Nick look a whole lot better. Leah was obviously trying to get Nick to get in the cab and Nick was obviously putting up a fight.

"Damn, No. I should go over there," Lucas said, sounding like he really didn't want to.

Noah frowned. "What do you think they're doin' here, Luke?"

Lucas laughed without humor. "Drinkin' would be my guess."

Noah looked at Lucas. "What's goin' on with Nick, Luke? She

ain't lookin' too good."

"I really don't know," Lucas said, shrugging. "Whatever it is, she's not talkin' to me. Shit, maybe it is me."

Noah shook his head, still looking across the street. "I don't think that's the truth, Luke. Look at her. She may be a little drunk, but she also looks like she's got an awful lot on her mind. What do you suppose she's thinkin' about?"

It was Lucas's turn to shrug. "I really don't fuckin' know. Like I said, maybe it's me."

Noah looked at Lucas wryly. "I think, right about now, you might be flatterin' yourself, bro. Stop and *look* at her for a second. What's got her shook so hard, Luke? I've known you a long time. That *can't* be about you, bro."

Lucas looked across the street at her like he was seeing her for the first time.

"That's it," Noah urged, "Take yourself out of the shit y'all got goin' on and really look at your woman, Luke. I mean, *what is that shit about?* That ain't the Nick I know." Noah watched Lucas watching Nick through narrowed eyes.

"Oh, shit," he said quietly, "You're right, No. That's not anger. She's scared."

Noah smiled. "I'll say. That looks a lot like terror to me. Maybe you should think real hard about what the source of that terror could be."

They sat in silence and watched Leah practically force Nick into the cab. She got in after her and the cab sped off.

Noah watched Lucas stare out the window after the cab. He let him sit and stew for a minute. Let him marinate. After a few silent moments, Noah prodded him. "Remember what I said, Luke. Stop bein' her boyfriend for a minute. Be a cop. What's wrong with this fuckin' picture?"

Lucas passed a hand over his beard, then turned and looked at Noah. "You don't have to keep pressing me, No. I pretty much got it when you did."

Noah looked at him patiently. "Got what, Luke? Milk?"

"That shit wasn't half as funny as you thought it would be."

Noah lit a Dunhill. "Sorry, bro." He put his lighter away and blew smoke out the side of his mouth. "So what did you get?"

Lucas looked like he wasn't feeling this conversation at all and Noah wished they didn't have to have it, but the shit was there. It was important and they couldn't ignore it, no matter whose feelings got hurt in the long run.

Noah looked over at him again, feeling bad for riding him so hard, but forging ahead anyway. "Come on, Luke. Let's get it over with. Put it out there."

Lucas stared at him hard. "Alright. I'm feeling like it's no coincidence that we saw Nicole and Jessie London at the same place, at the same time."

Noah shrugged magnanimously. "Yeah, but it could be, right?"

Lucas got angry, but it was okay, because Noah expected it. "Fuck you, Noah. This ain't your world gettin' blown apart."

"Sure it is. I'm your best friend."

Lucas didn't hold on to his anger. "Damn, No."

"I know, Luke." Noah said, nodding in genuine commiseration. "I know."

They were quiet for a time, then Lucas sighed in resignation. "Maybe it is a coincidence, Noah, but I got that fucked up nagging feeling that's tellin' me it's not. It's not, is it?"

Noah shook his head. "Nah, bro. I don't think it is. We got what we always get. We *both* smell somethin' fucked up."

"Nicole and Jessie are tied by something."

"I don't know what it is, Luke. Somethin's just tellin' me that this wasn't no coincidence. But don't worry. We'll get to the bottom of it soon enough. I'm gonna pop by Leah's tonight and see if anything jumped off. I'm sorry, Luke, but I don't think I'll get good news."

"I don't think you will, either. Here we fuckin' go again, No."

"It'll be alright, Luke." Noah said it with a surety he didn't feel and hoped Lucas overlooked it. Of course, he didn't.

Lucas repeated his sigh of resignation. "Okay, Noah. For the record ... I don't think it'll be alright, either."

They fell back into silence and continued to watch for Jessie.

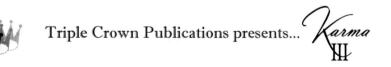

Chapter Twenty

So Hard to Say Goodbye

Nick woke up the next day well past noon. The heat from the sun on her face pulled her out of her dreams. She sat up in the bed, disoriented, because this wasn't the room she'd grown used to sleeping in. This was the room she'd slept in *before* she and Lucas had become lovers. This was the guest bedroom.

Nick got out of bed and took a long shower. She tried her damndest to wash away the tainted feeling she'd picked up recently. As hard as she scrubbed, it wouldn't go away. It was on her skin like a film. She frowned as she stepped under the water. That bastard Jessie was trying to ruin her life. She was in serious peril of losing Lucas. If she lost his love, the game would change dramatically.

Nick toweled off and got dressed, thinking she might have made a mistake in seeing Leah, but she'd felt like she really needed someone to talk to at the time. She'd always felt like she could talk to Leah about anything, so she could really appreciate the irony that Leah was one of the last people she could talk to about this.

It was very hard to put one over on Leah. She picked up on virtually everything. Nick had no way of knowing Jessie would be at Shelter. She'd picked the club randomly, herself, because she wanted to be somewhere where there were a lot of people — in case he did show up. That had become a habit of his lately. A method of intimidation. Nick wasn't stupid. She knew he'd put a tail on her to scare her and make her find his key quicker. If Leah thought about it for a moment, she'd put two and two together.

Nick went downstairs and poured herself a glass of orange juice, wishing she'd never met Jessie London's ass. Fuck him and his goddamned key. She couldn't believe Jessie had manipulated himself back into her life like this. Contrary to popular belief, she and Jessie went back a long way. Jessie had been her sergeant when she came out of the academy. He'd been brash, handsome, and a damn good cop. Nick had fallen for him like a brick.

Jessie was a bad boy and a bit of a rogue. Nick had been thoroughly impressed with him, and had gotten involved with him against her better judgment. Jessie had been married at the time, so they'd kept their relationship under the radar. Nick was never in love with Jessie, and she seriously doubted he'd ever felt anything more than something physical for her. Back then she would have told you she was in love with him, but in retrospect, she knew it had been nothing more than infatuation.

She couldn't speak for Jessie. Nick couldn't say what he'd felt. All she knew for sure about Jessie London was, once you ripped off all his handsome trappings, the only thing left was a festering degenerate, who truly didn't give a shit about anyone or anything in this world except Jessie London.

Nick's relationship with Jessie didn't last very long. About a year. Jessie didn't treat her like she was someone special. He pimped her from the beginning, even telling her point blank not to get too comfortable. He told her he could easily put another pretty bitch in her spot whenever he felt like it.

Nick's first taste of violence hadn't come from something she'd had to deal with on the streets. It had come from Jessie London. Jessie was very free with his hands. If she said something he didn't like, he popped her in the mouth. He hit her anytime the mood hit him. He'd hit her while he was having sex with her. No slap on the ass to make her call him Daddy. More like an actual fist in the face. Still, she came back for more. Of course by then she came back mostly because she was afraid of him.

Jessie might be a highly decorated lieutenant, now — and it still bewildered Nick how he made it this far — but she'd seen him do some pretty horrible shit with her own eyes, and heard about even more. Nick came from a family of cops and she wasn't trying to sully her badge for anybody. Jessie London included. But ... she seen him take and confiscate narcotics. She'd seen him shake people down ... she'd even put herself in the awful position of having to hold things for him. The bolder he'd gotten, the more distance Nick tried to put between them. Then she'd gotten pregnant.

She didn't think Jessie would be happy about it, but she didn't think he'd do what he did either. He didn't even give her a chance to tell him she didn't think having his baby was the best idea in the world. Nick didn't plan on having the baby, but she really didn't plan on Jessie putting her in the hospital for a week. She also didn't plan on the doctors telling her she'd been brutally attacked, and not only had lost her baby, but had been beaten within an inch of her life.

Of course Jessie didn't do this odd little piece of work himself. All she remembered about it was two guys coming at her after she'd parked her car after work. She hadn't even attributed it to Jessie until he showed up at the hospital talking shit to her. Well, actually one line of shit. It was the last thing he'd said to her until recently. Jessie had looked into her eyes and smiled when he said it. "I don't let bitches run *me,* Nicky. I run *bitches*. Get well soon." He'd dropped a red rose in her lap and walked out of her life.

When Nick went back to work, it didn't take her long to get into the narcotics unit. She'd partnered up with Leah and they'd made third grade. Four years later, they made second grade and Nick met Keith Childs. The only difference in Nick's relationship with Keith as opposed to the one she had with Jessie was that Nick really did love Keith at one point and Keith didn't put his hands on her until the very end. Other than that, it was more of the same. She'd known Keith was dirty, too. Just not to the extent that he was.

It didn't matter anyway. The shit was about to hit the fan once again. She twirled her ring around on her finger and thought of Lucas. The thought of him tore at her heart. Lucas didn't deserve to go through a bunch of bullshit with her. He'd gone through enough with Justine. She'd been awake when he came home last night. Nick heard him come up the stairs and turn the light on in the hallway.

She'd pretended to be asleep, but she knew he'd stood there, leaning in the doorframe watching her. He watched her for a long time, then he disappeared as quietly as he'd come without saying a single word to her. Only watching. Like he was waiting for this house of cards to collapse.

Nick was sure it would. It was only a matter of time. She frowned, washed her glass and put it away. She thought about eating, but she wasn't hungry. She had too much on her mind. Her heart was about to break. It was breaking already. *Lucas*.

Her cell phone rang. It didn't startle her. Nick looked down at it expectantly. It was that bastard, Jessie London. Nick let it go to voicemail and sat back in her seat, trying to decide how she wanted this to play out. She smiled to herself. She'd found his fucking key *days* ago … she wanted Jessie to suffer for fucking her life up. For intruding. All this shit should have died with Keith.

The front door opened suddenly and Lucas walked in, dressed like he'd been doing a buy and bust. Jeans and a tee shirt. Nick watched him shuffle through his mail and put it on the mahogany table by the door. He hadn't noticed her sitting there. Nick watched him run his hand over his beard and check his cell phone. He looked very sad. Sad enough to make Nick cry.

Nick brushed her tears away and smiled for him. "Hey, honey-bunch. Why so sad?"

Lucas looked at her sharply and tucked his lips in. He was staring at her like he was trying to decide how he felt about her. Nick hated that look. She got up and crossed the room. She stood as close to him as she could without actually touching him.

Lucas was looking down at her with those big and incredible chocolate eyes. Nick knew she was being scrutinized. He looked so sad, yet so very handsome. Nick wanted him, badly. She wondered if there was any part of him that still belonged to her. Or had she totally pushed him away?

"Lucas?"

"We need to talk, Nicole."

"Okay."

"I need to know what's really going on with you. I need for you to tell me the truth, Nicole. No lies, no omissions, just the facts … after that … I think we need to talk about this engagement."

Nick raised an eyebrow, though she wasn't surprised. "So you *do* want your ring back."

Lucas's eyes shot her a warning. "Don't play with me, Nicole. That look's no good on you, right now."

Nick took a step back. "I'm sorry. I thought —"

Lucas cut her off. "Don't, Nicole. What do you know about Jessie London?"

Nick took a step back. Oh shit. "*Who?*"

Lucas started advancing on her and Nick started backing up for real. Lucas was furious.

"Jessie London! I said, Jessie London! Tell me what the fuck you know about him. Tell me right now, Nicole!" He had her backed up against the island in the kitchen. Nick's eyes filled with tears and she opened her mouth to say something, but nothing came out.

"Answer me, goddamn it!" Lucas thundered at her.

Nick flinched away from him and put her hands up defensively. Getting hit was nothing new to her and right now, Lucas seemed more than capable. They stared at each other. Lucas looked at her hands and stepped away. He ran his hand over his beard and looked away from her.

"I'm sorry I came at you like that, Nicole, but you really need to talk to me."

Nick knew she had to answer him and she knew she couldn't afford to hesitate. She had to make a decision right now. Lie or tell the truth. She didn't want to hurt Lucas by catching him up in her bullshit.

"Jessie London?"

Lucas stared at her. "Yes. Jessie London."

"Jessie's a lieutenant over in vice. Yeah, Lucas. I know Jessie. What about him?"

"*How* do you know him, Nicole?" Lucas was looking at her like he was expecting her to lie to him.

She swallowed hard and told him the truth on a small scale. "I used to… I used to see him when I first got out of the academy. It was a long time ago."

Lucas winced and shook his head. "Yeah? Why'd you stop seeing him?"

Nicole kept with the truth. "He got a little free with his hands."

Lucas nodded and looked at her like he needed convincing. "That's a real good reason to get pushed to the curb. Anything else?" He sounded a lot more like a cop than he did her man.

"Are you interrogating me, Lucas?"

"Call it what you want, Nicole. I need answers."

She stared at him in disbelief and he stared back like she better fucking well answer him. Nick didn't know where Lucas had caught the scent of Jessie London, or how he'd managed to associate him with her, but there was certain shit he didn't need to know if there was a snowball's chance in hell of saving this relationship. Nick was pretty much sure it was a wrap if Lucas was coming at her like this, but there was a tiny ray of hope that things could swing the other way. The last thing in the world she wanted was to lose Lucas.

"Why are you asking me about Jessie London? What could he possibly have to do with anything? I *told you,* Lucas. I told you the truth." A tear ran down her cheek. Nick brushed it away, thinking she'd been crying an awful lot, lately. Maybe her tears were just starting in earnest.

Lucas tilted his head and peered into her eyes. "Why are you crying? What does that mean?"

He was starting to make her angry, which she knew was his intent. He wanted her to get emotional so she'd slip up or blurt something out. If Nick had her way, that wasn't going to happen. She figured pushing him even further away was most likely her best bet. It was becoming clearer by the second that Lucas was already gone from her.

"It means I'm tired of being bullied. I thought you were the absolute last person that would get on me like this."

Lucas looked at her like she was crazy. Then he completely lost it. Lucas, by nature, was not an incredibly vocal man, much less a screamer, but he was screaming at her now, at the top of his voice. He started screaming so suddenly and so loudly, Nick cringed away from him with her fingers in her ears.

"You're tired, Nicole? I'll tell you who's fuckin' tired! That would be me, Nicole! I've fuckin' tried with you! I understood about that asshole, Keith, and I was fuckin' there for you! *There*! Do you hear me? I fuckin' let you live in my house because I was already more than a little in love with you!"

Nick didn't need a rehash. She knew he'd been there and she loved him for it, but she had no desire to hear how much she was hurting him, because that would kill her.

"I'm not gonna listen to this, Lucas!" she yelled back, hiding behind a façade of indignation and trying to force her way past him. Lucas grabbed her wrist and wouldn't let her go.

"No, you don't! You're gonna stay here and listen to me! You must think I'm real fuckin' stupid, don't you? Maybe I was at first. I thought that rape changed you. Hell, maybe it did, but I didn't make first grade by not being able to tell when something is not right. You're hiding behind this goddamn rape thing, Nicole, and I know it."

Nick tried to wrench her arm out of his grasp, but Lucas tightened up on her, determined not to let her go.

"Let me go!"

Lucas pulled her back, violently. "I won't! You fuckin' answer me, Nicole! Why are you pushing me away? Do you want me not so close, so I won't find out you're a fuckin' liar? What are you lying about? What are you hiding? Who is this Jessie motherfucker to you? Why were you at the same place last night? Why do you have all these incoming calls from a private caller on your cell? Why, Nicole?"

Nick's heart started pounding in her chest. How did he know about last night? Leah, most likely. Had Lucas actually checked her phone? She narrowed her eyes at him.

"You've been checking up on me, Lucas?"

Lucas smiled a very dark smile at her. He was fucking gorgeous. "You bet your sweet ass I checked up on you."

Nick's mouth dropped open. "Are you serious?"

Lucas jerked her wrist and pulled her to him. "Do I look like I'm fucking playing games with you, Nicole?"

Nick's resolve to make Lucas think whatever he wanted, so he'd stay off her, and her quest to try and save his feelings started to crumble. She looked up at him. He was furious, but he was hurt. He was hurt anyway. Nick stopped fighting him and couldn't stop her tears.

"Lucas … I love you. I'm sorry. So sorry."

Lucas loosened his grip, but he didn't let her go. "Sorry for what, Nicole? Tell me."

"I can't!" she sobbed. "I don't know how." Nick was crying so hard, she couldn't see him through her tears.

Lucas let go of her. Nick half-expected him to put his arms around her, but he didn't. Instead, he took a step away. "Sure, you do. Just tell me."

This was the exact moment she'd been dreading. To tell him or not to tell him. She wiped her tears away and looked at Lucas. He had his cop face on and he was looking at her like she was highly suspect. There was no way in hell she could come totally clean with him, as much as she wanted to. She twisted her ring around on her finger. Lucas frowned and watched her do it.

"I can't, Lucas. Everything is complicated. It makes me not look so great." She took his ring off and held it out to him.

Lucas stared at the ring and folded his arms across his chest. "We're not talking about that right now."

Nick smiled at him sadly. "Can you still love me through this, Lucas?"

Lucas's frown deepened. "What kind of question is that, Nicole? How bad is this? What have you done?"

She shrugged, still holding his ring in her outstretched hand, not discarding her sad smile. "Who says I *did* anything?"

Lucas stared at her hard. "Why won't you talk to me, Nicole?"

"Because you're in cop mode right now, Lucas. I really don't think it would be wise to talk to you at the moment without a lawyer. It's plain to see you don't trust me anymore, even though I really haven't given you a reason not to. You know what they say, Lucas. Once trust is out the window, the relationship goes down the drain." She held his ring out to him again. Lucas tucked his lips in and moved away from her. "Take your ring back, sweetheart. Things are all fucked up, but I love you and I don't want to hurt you. You've been hurt enough." She meant to say the last part stoically, but she couldn't really seem to stop crying.

"Nicole …"

Her hand was shaking, but she held it out. "Take it, Lucas."

Lucas sighed and dropped his hands. "That's not what I want. I want you to tell me what's going on, Nicole. I want to help you. Let me help you."

Nick shook her head. "You can only make it worse, honeybunch. You're not even in it, and you're too involved because of who you are to me. I just told you I don't want you hurt because of me. Let it go and take your ring. Please, baby."

He shook his head. "No, Nicole."

Nicole took his hand and folded the ring into his palm. "Yes! I love you, Lucas. Please take it back. It's the only thing we can do. Let me walk away from you now, honey, before …"

Lucas cut her off, anger returning to his face. He held the ring in his fingers; it caught a bit of the sun and glittered brightly. "*Take it back?* I don't want it! What do I need it for? To remind me of you? If you don't love me, if you don't want me — if you want to run the fuck off and be whatever the fuck you are to Jessie London, fine! Do it, but take the fuckin' ring, okay? I've got enough reminders of bad shit layin' around this place. If you're going, take the ring and get the fuck outta my house right now! I don't fucking need you! Go!" He threw the ring at her. It bounced off her shoulder and landed near the sink.

Nick's mouth dropped open. She couldn't think of anything he could have done that would have hurt her worse. "Oh, Lucas. I'm sorry, baby."

He looked at her like he hated her. "*You're* sorry? Okay, that's great, Nicole. I'll be needing my key."

Nick felt like she couldn't breathe. Oh God. It couldn't end like this. She wanted to scream. He acted like he didn't want her anymore. That just couldn't be! She threw her arms around his neck and pressed her body into his. He tried to push her away, but she held onto him.

"Lucas, no! Please, I don't want us to end like this. Please, Lucas. Wait a minute!"

"Wait for what? For you to twist the knife? You've got the wrong guy, Nicole." He pulled down on her arms to free himself, but Nick tightened her grip and pulled his head down. She put her mouth on his and drew his bottom lip in. Lucas grunted softly and slipped his tongue in her mouth. Her knees went weak, but it didn't matter because Lucas put his hands under her ass and lifted her up. Nick's legs went around him, instinctively, as Lucas backed her up and sat her on the island.

Lucas unbuttoned her blouse and pushed it off her shoulders, urgently unhooking her bra with one hand, as he kissed her like she'd had some damn nerve keeping her lips away from him. He moved her bra like it was in his way and put his hands on her breasts, cupping them and using his thumbs.

Nick arched her back and moaned when he put his mouth on her nipple. She'd missed Lucas's touch. She held his head as he changed sides and smiled when she heard him unbuckling his belt.

Lucas started kissing her again. He worked the band out of her hair and plunged his fingers into it. Nick kissed him back, hungry for the taste of him. She unbuttoned his jeans and pulled down the zipper, as Lucas pushed her skirt up and pulled her forward. Nick pushed his jeans down and he sprang free. Lucas was in such a rush to get into her, he didn't even pull her panties down, he just moved them to the side.

Lucas took his time sliding into her, like he always did, savoring the snuggly wet feel of her. Nick shut her eyes and bit her bottom lip-savoring the hard and hotly thick feel of *him*. Lucas moaned and pulled her to the edge of the counter as Nick pushed herself up on her elbows. Lucas put his hands under her knees and pushed her legs back. He slid in as far as he could go and turned his head like it hurt. Nick put her hands on his ass and pulled him in. Lucas looked down at her and almost smiled, but then he seemed to remember how angry he was with her.

He frowned instead and kissed her intensely. He put his hands on her hips and started hammering her with a short sweet stroke. Nick tightened up on him and exploded almost instantly. Her toes curled and she locked her legs around his waist, throwing her head back and screaming his name.

Lucas followed her face with his own, chasing her lips. He started kissing her again, teasing her with his tongue as the force of his thrust started to push her back. Lucas was relentless. He pulled her into his arms and Nick wrapped her legs around him. Lucas carried her to the sofa, still maintaining the bounce of that sweet short stroke. He laid her down and drove himself into her, slow and deep, at that fantastic angle he always found. Nicole was screaming in less than a minute, shaking and trembling, trying to catch her breath. She ran her fingers through his hair and arched her back.

"Oh, Lucas! I love you, I love you, I —"

Lucas kissed her again and found his way to heaven with a deep, slow grind. It seemed to go on forever and Nick wished with all her heart he'd left a part of himself with her. That way, she'd always have him with her. Lucas wrapped his arms around her and they held each other for a long time, not speaking. Just kissing and holding on to each other. Nick knew in her heart, this wasn't the fixer. She knew they were probably in the last sweet moments. This felt like goodbye.

She knew Lucas well enough to know there were some things he absolutely would not tolerate; first and foremost was a dirty cop. She might not want to admit it to herself, she'd denied it to herself for years, but there were things she'd seen, things she'd tolerated, and things she'd been coerced into doing herself, that made her less than pure. If she'd seen another cop in the same situation, she would have looked at them with great disdain and pulled her cuffs out. Guilt, even if it was mostly by association, was guilt all the same. Lucas and Noah and Leah were cops other cops looked up to, especially Lucas and Noah. She would not tarnish them.

Nick couldn't be sure, but she knew from the way Lucas came at her about Jessie that more than likely something was up. Someone somewhere was looking at her, Jessie, or both of them for something foul. She couldn't believe her life had come to such hard choices to be made from silly shit and truly bad decisions she'd made years ago. The old saying, 'The past always comes back to haunt you,' weighed heavily on her mind.

She sat up and Lucas sat up with her. Nick touched his face and he sighed and took her hand away.

"What are we gonna do, Nicole?" he asked, quietly, "Why won't you talk to me?"

"I told you, baby. It's complicated."

Lucas nodded resolutely and stood up, putting his clothes back on. Nick watched him, memorizing him. She stood up, too, and fixed her clothes.

"Is that how it's got to be, Nicole?" he asked, slipping his tee shirt over his head. Lucas stared at her. Nick didn't like the look in his eye.

"I think so."

Lucas went to the door and picked up his car key. "Okay. You called it. I need you to know, I'm always here if you need me, but if this is the way it's gotta be. I'm done."

Nick knew this was where they were headed, but knowing it didn't make it hurt any less to actually hear him say it. She blinked back tears.

"Done?"

Lucas looked at her coldly. "Yeah. I'm done. You don't trust me enough to talk to me, and I don't trust you. I don't know exactly what it is that's going on with you, but I'll tell you one thing, though. If I find out you've got dirty ties to Jessie London ... if I find out you pulled the wool over my eyes, Nicole, I'm gonna fuckin' lock you up myself."

Nick couldn't keep the shock off her face. "Lucas ..."

He held up his hand. "Unless you're ready to talk to me, don't say anything else. Just take your ring, leave my key on the coffee table and go. I'll give you 'til the end of the week to get your stuff. Be gone when I get back," he said, and walked out the door.

Chapter Twenty-one

Pointing the Finger

Butch Harper must think he was awfully fucking funny, either that, or he had balls of steel. Jessie parked his car and looked around. He knew somebody was following him. He wasn't stupid and his cop skills were exceptional. Nissan must have kicked up production on ice blue Maximas or he had a fucking tail on him. It wasn't always there, but it was there enough to get him spooked. And whoever was doing it was damn good at it. If he wasn't the cop he was, he never would have noticed it was there. He wondered who the fuck it was.

Jessie went into the Starbucks across the street from the precinct and got his morning cup. Merlin Nash was at the register. Jessie shook off the last of his annoyance and walked over to him with a smile.

"Hey, Merle! What's good, baby?"

Merlin greeted him with dap and a smile as bright as his own. "You know how we do, Jess. It's all good, all the time."

Jessie looked at him seriously. "That's right, Merle. It's our world. All the rest of these motherfuckers are just squirrels tryin' to get nuts. Let's walk." They got their coffees and walked out into the sunshine, away from the precinct.

Jessie took a sip of his coffee and looked over at Merlin. "I think I've got a pretty serious problem."

Merlin sipped his own coffee. "Yeah? What's that, Jessie?"

"I think Butch Harper put a tail on me … little fat bastard."

Merlin whistled low and raised his eyebrows. "Damn, Jessie. Are you sure?"

"Either that, or I'm seein' things, and I ain't dropped acid in a long time. If Butch thought I was important enough to put a tail on me, that means he's lookin' at me *real* hard. It means he's tryin' to gather information on me to bring me down. It means I'm gonna have to get out sooner than I planned, or find a way to get Butch off me."

Merlin stopped walking and smiled slow. "Well, Jess, you know there's always a way to deal with Butch if he don't pull his claws in. Fuck that nosy motherfucker."

Jessie stared at Merlin for a second before he smiled. That had been just what he'd hoped he'd say. Jessie and Merlin had done some pretty greasy shit together. Wet work was a small thing for both of them. Neither one of them minded blowing somebody's candle out.

"What are we talkin', Merle?" Jessie asked.

Merlin shrugged. "I usually charge at least 25 grand to come down hard on somebody, Jess, you know that." He paused and lit a cigarette. "But we been down with each other a long time. I'm also takin' into account that Butch Harper has been a major thorn in my fuckin' side more than once. Takin' care of Butch would be my pleasure. Tell you what, Jessie. I'm gonna give you the ultimate discount. I'll do it for free."

Jessie grinned and put his hand on Merlin's shoulder. "No shit, Merle? You'd do that for me?"

Merlin smiled back. "Yeah, I would, but like I said — it's not just for you, Jess. I've been dyin' to erase Butch's ass for a long time. I almost did when Oscar got sent up, but it would have been way too obvious."

Jessie nodded. He really could give a shit less about Merlin's musings about his reasons for wanting to pop Butch. All Jessie cared about was getting him off his back. "I heard that, Merle. What do you say we meet at Stamps later? We can set the wheels in motion over some cold ones."

"Sounds good to me. Any idea who your tail is? You can't expect for this shit to just go away when Butch is out of the picture."

"That's true. We can figure that out, too," Jessie looked at his watch. "I'm late. See you around six?"

Merlin nodded. "Six is good. See you then."

"Cool." Jessie said, and gave him dap. Jessie finished his coffee as he watched Merlin Nash walk back toward the precinct. Butch had one fuck of a nerve putting a tail on him. He wouldn't be putting a fucking tail on anybody else.

Jessie looked at his watch again. Time to call that bitch, Nicky, about his key. She was giving him some song and dance about Cain putting her out. Jessie couldn't see what the fuck that had to do with his key. Time was running out. Once Merle got rid of Butch, Jessie would have to get gone ASAP. He didn't have time to pussyfoot with her. Nicky was about to make him hurt her. He needed that key. He needed what was in that storage facility. Jessie wondered what Cain had put her ass out for. Oh, well. It was none of his concern.

Jessie walked back to the precinct and rode up in the elevator to his office. He wasn't real surprised to find Butch standing outside his door. Jessie swallowed down his irritation and put his hands in his pockets.

"Hey, Butch," he said, grinning broadly. "What brings you back so soon?"

Butch had his little notebook in his hand. He'd been jotting something down when Jessie walked up. He looked over his reading glasses and smiled benignly. The smile never touched his eyes. Jessie wasn't feeling that look. Butch looked like he thought he had him by the balls.

"Just stopped by to shoot the breeze. You got a second, Jessie? I promise, this won't take long."

To say no would have been backing himself into a corner and admitting guilt, at least superficially.

Jessie opened the door and waved Butch inside. "Just came by to admire my artwork, huh, Butch?"

Butch put his glasses away and sat down. "Mostly, but there are some things I wanted to ask you about."

Jessie sat behind his desk, unbuttoning his suit jacket. He tried, but couldn't hide his annoyance. "What now, Butch?"

Butch didn't even bother to crack open his little snitch book. "Be easy, Jessie. I just wanna clear some things up."

Jessie looked at him directly. "Things like what?"

Butch leaned forward a little. He dropped his smile and looked at Jessie with his wise eyes. He reminded Jessie of a cat who catches a mouse, but just wants to bat him around a bit with his paw before he eats his ass up.

"I did a little pokin' around — you know me. I was lookin' to talk to Shelly Randazzo and Rhonda Taylor. You know the cop and the stewardess?" He paused and rubbed his chin. "I gotta tell you, Jessie, I ran into some pretty odd, coincidental shit."

Jessie chuckled. Why wouldn't this fat bastard just spit it out? He already knew what he was going to say.

"There's really no reason to laugh, Jessie," Butch said, admonishingly. "Maybe you didn't hear what happened, and this was just since the last time I talked to you."

Jessie smiled. "Can't say that I was checkin' that hard for those hoes. Hit me with the news, Butch."

Butch frowned like he didn't appreciate Jessie's blatant disrespect for women. "That's bad, Jessie. Even for you."

Jessie shrugged. "I never said I was no nice fuckin' guy, Butch."

Butch stared at him a second longer before he went on. "No, you never did. I gotta say, I really believe that you're not. I was sorry to find out Shelley Randazzo met with an unfortunate accident. A *freak* accident, you might say. It was so bizarre, I'm kinda surprised you didn't hear about it. It was in the paper for a few days. Seems she was in her garage after she parked her car and she slipped on some oil. Oil of all things! When she fell her service weapon discharged and the bullet severed her femoral artery. Poor Shelley bled out in her own garage. Isn't that a strange story, Jessie?"

Jessie stared back at Butch. "Wow. How weird is that?"

"That's the same thing I thought. That street cop husband of hers — Vinnie you said his name was — is holed up somewhere in Nevada on a leave of absence. I *think* he's in Vegas. Nothin' like slot machines and a bunch of showgirls to get you through your grief, huh?"

Jessie shrugged again and looked bored. "Whatever gets you through the night, Butch."

Butch nodded and looked contemplative. "I guess … you know what else, Jessie?"

"Nah. What else, Butch?"

"I tried to put my finger on your stewardess friend and she seems to be stayin' abroad. Hasn't been home in a month. Imagine that."

"I believe you, Butch," Jessie said, with a melodramatic sigh. "I always had to track that ass down before I could tap it."

"Yeah … maybe she's stayin' away on purpose."

They stared at each other for a prolonged moment. Jessie knew Butch was going for his balls. He was just going about it in his relentlessly meandering way, and Butch knew he knew.

"So, Jessie, how close are you to Merlin Nash and Darryl Gilford? You guys best pals or drinkin' buddies?"

Jessie felt something like lead drop into the pit of his stomach. The jig was obviously up. Jessie had just gotten conformation about the tail. Jessie just stared at Butch and tried not to let hostility creep into his eyes.

Butch looked back at him patiently. "I'm waitin' on an answer, Jessie."

If they had been sitting anywhere else but in that precinct, Butch would no longer have been a problem, because Jessie would have shot him right where he sat. "You put a tail on me, Butch?"

Butch chuckled and his eyes twinkled, merrily. "Who me? Not personally, Jessie, no. At least now you know I'm not the only one givin' you more than a passin' glance."

Jessie frowned and stood up. "What the fuck is that supposed to mean?"

Butch stood, too, and looked at him hard. "It means I know how you operate, Jessie. I didn't just start watchin' you, you know. I've had my eye on you since Oscar Tirado. Actually, I had my eye on you first. Merlin Nash, too. Maybe a few others. I gotta tell you, if somethin' happens to me for snoopin', they're instantly lookin' at you. Do you understand?"

"Who the fuck is *they*?" Jessie asked, narrowing his eyes.

Butch gave him a cold hard stare. "Don't worry about who the fuck *'they'* are. Your glory days are over, Jessie."

"Fuck you, Butch. You don't know shit about me."

Butch smiled. "I beg to differ, Jessie. I know just about everything about you. All I need to know, anyway."

"You don't know shit. Prove it."

"I got no problem provin' anything I say you're responsible for. Don't forget, Jessie. I write everything down and I make copies."

"What are you sayin' I'm responsible for?"

"Bribes, extortion, the sale of narcotics, racketeering, money laundering, assault, murder in several degrees — some against police officers. *You're a dirty cop, Jessie.* Fuckin' Oscar Tirado ◎ even Keith Childs, with all the last-ditch mayhem he caused, had nothin' on you. You're the head of that particular snake. I know it and I can prove it. Your pals are tellin' on you, Jessie. Like rats deserting a sinkin' ship. They're makin' deals and leavin' town."

"Get outta my office, you fat fuck!"

Butch smiled. "I gotta tell you, I'd rather be a fat fuck, than a filthy cop. Next time I see you, I'll be lockin' your ass up. That's a promise. Have a nice day, Jessie," Butch said, and walked out the door. Jessie smiled slow. That was bullshit. The next time Jessie saw Butch would be at Butch's funeral.

Chapter Twenty-two

Is She or Isn't She

"You alright, Luke?" Noah asked from his shotgun seat in the Maxima.

Lucas nodded and lied. "Yeah, Noah. I'm good." They'd followed Jessie to a small café on Jane Street. He was sitting outside at a table, now sipping an espresso and thumbing through the paper like he thought he was the goddamn black Godfather.

"I don't believe you, but I'm not fuckin' with you, Luke. You look like you need a break."

"Thanks, No. I could use one." They sat in silence and watched Jessie sip his espresso. Lucas had filled Noah in about Nicole earlier, and he didn't feel like talking about it anymore. He thought he would have been a bit more broken up about it than he actually was. His own reaction had him second-guessing his feelings for Nicole. Did he really love her enough to marry her? *Did he?* Or did he just miss Justine so much, he was trying to replace her? He'd asked himself the same question more than once. He knew he cared for Nicole a lot, but right now, his anger was clouding everything. Lucas was furious with her. He knew Nicole loved him, but whatever it was that was going on had her shaken to the point of throwing their relationship away. He was furious that she wouldn't let him help her. What did this nigga, Jessie, have to do with anything? What was his hold on her? Was Nicole dirty? Lucas looked at Jessie sipping his espresso like he was king of the world. He wanted very badly to put a bullet in his forehead. Who knew? Maybe he'd get his chance.

In the meantime, he looked over at his boy. "What's going on with you and Leah? Y'all seem pretty chummy, lately."

Noah smiled around his Dunhill and blew smoke out the window. He didn't answer him right away. He finished his cigarette first. When he was done, he looked over at Lucas and smiled brightly.

"What?" he asked, like he hadn't heard the question.

Lucas frowned at him. "Noah, what the fuck's wrong with you?"

Noah actually laughed. He turned his head and looked out the window. "Nothin'."

Lucas's eyebrows went up with real surprise. "Oh shit!" He reached over and pushed him. Lucas couldn't help but laugh. "Get the fuck outta here, No! When did this shit happen?"

Noah smiled, but he wouldn't look at him. "When did what happen? Everything's cool, Luke. Stop lookin' at me like that. For real."

Lucas was looking at him in amused disbelief. "Damn, No. You feelin' Leah like *that?*"

Noah winced, but he didn't lose his smile. "I like Leah *a lot,* Luke. Yeah, I do."

"How much? You love her?" Lucas could not believe he was sitting here having this conversation with Noah. He couldn't believe Noah had let Leah get close enough to him to turn his head like this.

Noah finally looked over at him. "You know what, Luke? If you were anybody else, I'd really try to bullshit you and act like I don't know what you're talkin' about."

Lucas smiled. "But I'm your boy and you know you can't hold out on me. Besides, I know you need somebody to talk to about this shit. It's gotta be fuckin' your head up."

Noah lost all but a trace of his smile. "Yeah, it is. I'm gonna be real honest with you, Luke. This is one of the reasons I didn't sleep with Leah right away. I knew she had the potential to do this shit to me. I liked her the minute I saw her."

Lucas smiled. "I know the feeling." He'd felt that way about Justine. She'd given him butterflies like he was in high school.

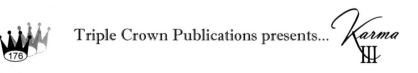

"I know you do, bro. I *tried* not to sleep with her, Luke. I mean, I really did. But it was like I *had to, 'cause* I liked her. Then when I finally did, Luke, I knew she was gonna fuck me up. The second time, I really knew she wasn't just some piece of ass," He paused and looked at Lucas seriously. "The only other woman that ever made me feel like that was Nadine. Remember when me and you first started hangin' out? Remember I told you fuckin' was the way to go; makin' love was for pussies?"

Lucas nodded and smiled. "Yeah, No. I remember that."

"You know," Noah said, looking thoughtful, "I only made love to two women in my whole life."

"Nadine and Leah?"

"Yeah, that's right, Luke."

"So you do love her," Lucas said with a smile.

"Against my better judgment. I don't want to, but I'd be in serious denial if I said I didn't."

Lucas looked at his friend. "Why don't you want to?"

Noah shrugged. "'Cause I suck at love, Luke. This is me. Noah don't change. Sooner or later I'm gonna fuck around. Besides, looks like lovin' me is hazardous to your health. Look what happened to Liz. I'll feel terrible about that shit 'til the day I die, Luke. And then there's Nadine. Lovin' me must've drove her crazy or somethin'."

Lucas frowned. "Why do you say that?"

Noah smirked and gave him a very dark look. "Nadine's walkin' around actin' like she's still pregnant. Her fuckin' doctor told me she lost the baby when she fell through that glass table. She must think I'm stupid, tryin' to get me to replant the seed so she'll get pregnant again. What the fuck is wrong with her, Luke? That shit turned me totally off. That, and the fact that she divorced me to punish me, like I'm some little fuckin' kid. I'm done with Nadine, Luke. I never should have gone back there. It was nothin' but heartache for everybody."

Lucas looked at Noah and tried to keep his skepticism out of his face. He didn't quite believe Noah was done with Nadine. He very well may be, but Lucas had been his friend long enough to know that Nadine Ramsey would be Leah's fiercest competitor for Noah's heart. It seemed no matter how hard they fought or how long they went without speaking; those two loved each other way down deep where it really counted.

"That's crazy, the way Nadine's tryin' to play you like that, No."

Noah lit a cigarette. "I let her ass know I'm on to her. I," Noah looked past Lucas. He frowned hard. "Ah, shit Luke."

Lucas turned his head to look back at Jessie London. He wasn't all that surprised to see Nicole sit down across from him and swing her hair over her shoulder, but he still felt like someone punched him in the stomach. His natural instinct had him reach for the door handle. Noah reached across his body and knocked his hand away. Lucas was surprised when Noah grabbed him by the collar and pulled him over to his side of the car.

"You listen to me, Lucas. You stay the fuck in this car and you let this shit play out. Don't you get the fuck outta this car. Calm your ass down."

Lucas grabbed Noah's hand and wrestled it off his collar he leaned toward the door and went for the handle again. Noah snatched him back, bodily, with both hands. Lucas grabbed Noah's shirt and pushed him back.

"Don't make me knock your ass out in this car, Lucas! Get your shit together, bro! Cut it out!" They stared at each other. Noah had both hands in his collar like he wasn't above choking the shit out of him, or knocking his ass out, to keep him in the car. Lucas pushed against him and Noah pushed back.

"I ain't playin', Luke. I *will* hit you to keep you here. Don't try me."

Lucas had absolutely no desire to be hit by Noah. Noah hit just as hard as he did, and that was pretty fucking hard. Lucas let go of Noah. Noah looked at Lucas very warily and reluctantly took his hands off him.

"You good, Luke?"

Lucas nodded. "Yeah. Sorry, No."

"This is me, Luke. I understand."

Lucas looked out the window. They seemed to be arguing. Nicole was sitting back in her chair with her arms folded across her chest. Her head was swiveling on her neck like she was really giving him the business. Jessie leaned forward and tapped the table with his finger several times. Nicole pushed away from the table, angrily, like she was about to stand up, but Jessie grabbed her wrist. She tried to pull away from him, but Jessie smoothly stood and pulled her close, still gripping her wrist. He put his cheek against hers and appeared to be whispering sweet nothings in her ear. Lucas tried, but he couldn't stop his top lip from creeping up. His trigger finger itched like crazy.

"It's not what it looks like, Luke. See it for what it is. He's hiding the fact that he's bein' abusive," Noah said over his shoulder.

Lucas didn't acknowledge the statement. He sat in silence and watched this piece of shit fuck his woman over. Sure, he might have asked for his key back and told her it was over, but he still had feelings for her. This was fucked up. He couldn't even do anything about it.

Nick tried to walk away, but Jessie moved with her. To the untrained eye, this may have seemed like a lover's spat. Maybe Jessie was whispering in her ear, begging for forgiveness for some wrong he'd done, while Nick was being hurt and resistant. To Lucas and Noah, however, it was what it was. She was trying to get away from him and he wouldn't let her go.

"If he hurts her, I'm kickin' his ass, Noah." Lucas said quietly.

"I don't blame you, Luke," Noah replied.

Nicole pushed away from him. They could hear her shouting, but couldn't make out what she was saying. Lucas let his window down a little, just as Jessie tried to pull her back. Nick slapped him and walked away. Jessie let her go, rubbing his face and smiling blackly.

"Just make sure you do what the fuck I told you, bitch!" he yelled back at her, unconcerned with the general public. He stared after her for a moment, then he turned suddenly and looked their way. He kept that dark smile and started walking in their direction.

"Damn, No, look at this shit," Lucas said, putting the car in gear.

"Let's peel outta here, Luke. He sees us."

"No shit?" Lucas said. He screeched into a broken u-turn and went back up the block hauling ass.

"Wonder how he knew about the tail," Noah said, once they

were far enough away from him to be easy.

"He may be dirty, but he's a really good cop, Noah. Shit, you'd probably know if you had a tail on you, too."

Noah lit a smoke. "I guess you're right. Speakin' of bein' dirty, Luke, what do you suppose it is that Jessie wants Nick to do?"

Lucas frowned. "I really don't know. It's lookin' like she's dirty, too, isn't it?"

Noah blew smoke out the side of his mouth and looked over at him. "You said it, I didn't. Let's go see Butch."

Chapter Twenty-three

Boyfriend

Leah wasn't shocked when Noah rang her doorbell unannounced at 11:30 at night. It had become a habit of his, to pop up like that, and Leah secretly loved it. It made her feel like she was really his girlfriend. She was glad to see him, but she didn't like the look on his face when she opened the door. He looked worried.

"Noah, what's the matter?" she asked, frowning up instantly.

Noah looked down at her grimly, as he stepped inside and closed the door behind him. "We got problems, baby. I need to talk to you."

Leah's heart skipped at beat in alarm. Oh, God. What now? Problems with who? Nick or Nadine, most likely since he'd said 'we.' She followed Noah to the sofa and sat down next to him.

"Talk to me, Noah," she said, turning to face him.

Noah leaned forward and put his hand on her thigh. He looked into her eyes like he was searching for something. "Listen, Leah, as fucked up as I am, I've always been straight with you, right?"

She frowned a little more. Where was he going with this? "Yeah, Noah, I guess you have."

"Okay. I need for you to be real honest with me right now, okay? It's real important, Leah."

"Ask me the question, Noah. I'll tell you the truth. I promise."

He stared at her hard. "Alright. Is Nick dirty?"

Leah's mouth dropped open and she knew her eyes were huge. "What, Noah? *What?*" She popped off the sofa like she'd gotten a jolt of electricity. Leah put her hand to her forehead and took a deep breath. She knew Nick had been weird, lately, but *Nick?* A dirty cop?

Noah stood up. "Leah, sweetie —"

Leah put her other hand on his arm to silence him. "No, Noah … wait. Wait a minute." Her mind was clicking back in reverse. Nick had been Leah's partner for a long time. Leah closed her eyes. There were snatches of things that hadn't seemed right, pushed to the back burner because she was her partner. Not enough to seriously raise an eyebrow. Just odd shit. Keith had been dirty as hell … oh God. Oh, no.

Leah opened her eyes and looked at Noah. "Oh God, Noah. You … I don't know. I don't want to think it, but shit, Noah. It makes sense. All types of sense. Oh shit. Oh hell." Noah folded her into his arms and Leah buried her face into her hands and put her head against his chest. Tears came. Tears of shock and betrayal, but they seemed outweighed by the ones she shed out of grief and loss. Nick wasn't just her partner, she was also her best friend. If she was dirty, that was gone. Nick was gone.

Noah rubbed her back. He was surprisingly strong, calm, and soothing. "I'm sorry, Leah. Maybe it's not true. We'll get to the bottom of it. Don't cry."

Leah pulled back and wiped her tears. "Sorry. I didn't mean to just burst into tears like that."

Noah smiled down at her. "It's alright. You can wet up my shirt anytime you want to." They looked at each other for a moment and something very nice seemed to pass between them. Noah gave her a squeeze and let her go. "We saw Nick with Jessie London today. Do you know who he is?"

Leah nodded. "Yeah, Noah. I know Jessie. Not well, but I know him. How does he fit into this? What's going on?"

Noah sighed like he was tired and ran his hand through his curly hair. He might have been tired, but his sparkling gray eyes fell over her body with more than a little interest. "Were you waiting up for me?"

Leah smiled, conscious of the pink baby tee and boy shorts she was wearing and was honest with him. "I was hoping you'd stop by. Glad you did."

Noah gave her his trademark sexy smirk. "I'm glad I did, too. Back to the matter at hand. Let me ask you another question — and please don't get offended by it, because it's something I gotta know."

Leah looked him in the eye. "I'm not dirty, Noah. I've walked the straight and narrow all my life. I'm not lying. I promise you that."

Noah gave her that same searching look he'd given her earlier. He finally nodded. "Okay. Alright."

"You didn't answer my question, Noah. What does Jessie London have to do with all this?"

"Butch thinks Jessie was the brains behind Oscar and Keith."

Leah blinked and tucked her lips in. Oh shit. Noah saw the look on her face and frowned.

"What's the matter?" he asked, touching her arm.

"Nick told me once … she told me she used to go out with Jessie a long time ago." Leah looked at Noah. "She was Keith's girlfriend, too. I really don't want to believe that about Nick, but damn, just the fact that she was involved with both of them doesn't make her look too good."

"You got that right," Noah said quietly.

Leah shook her head. "I don't believe this shit."

"Me neither," Noah spoke in that same quiet voice.

Leah frowned. This was fucked up. This was terrible for everyone involved. "Noah … how's Lucas?"

"Not good. He tried to get her to talk to him about this shit. Nick declined, so Luke gave her the old walkin' papers and told her she could keep the ring."

Leah was tremendously sad for both of them. "Man, Noah. I'm sorry about that. I really wanted them to have a happy ending."

"Yeah, me too, but I gotta be honest. I'm glad he found out now, before they got married. Luke's a little fucked up now, but I don't wanna think about how hard he woulda tripped if he'd found out after the fact."

Damn. In Noah's mind, it sounded like he *believed* she was dirty. They still had to prove it.

"You know, Noah, everyone is innocent until they're proven guilty."

Noah stared at her for a moment before he answered. "That ain't really the way my mind works, sweetie. You gotta prove to me that you're *innocent*. In Nick's case, the old sayin' applies. If it walks like a duck and talks like a duck, it's a fuckin' duck, Leah."

Leah put her hands on her hips. Noah's shoot first, ask questions later attitude was rubbing her the wrong way. Nick was still Nick to her. They hadn't proven anything. She didn't want to throw her under the bus.

"That's character assassination, Noah," she said, unable to keep the swivel out of her neck. "I know you were never crazy about her, but don't do that. Give her the benefit of the doubt."

Noah checked out her posture and smirked. "That ain't character assassination, Leah. Nick's makin' *herself* look guilty. If she were innocent, she'd talk to Lucas and we could all help her out with this. Instead, she's keepin' her mouth shut and havin' coffee with Jessie London. Come on, Leah. What am I supposed to think?"

Leah could see his point, but she still felt a certain loyalty to Nick. She was her friend. She also knew that Noah and Lucas' loyalty to each other was like steel. She looked up at him. She didn't want to fight with Noah.

"You're right, but she's still my friend, Noah."

Noah raised an eyebrow. "Yeah, for the time bein' but Lucas is my friend, and he's been through a lot. He didn't deserve this shit. So if it seems like I don't like Nick, I really don't care, Leah. Her shit is about to hit the fan and she's gonna splatter my boy with it. *For that*, no, I don't give a shit about her."

"Noah ... " She hadn't really seen it before, but she saw it now. Noah was very pissed off. She attempted to smooth him out. Leah touched his face. "Don't worry, baby. All this stuff's gonna work itself out."

Noah took her hand down and laughed dangerously. "I ain't worried. Nick's ass better be worried 'cause, if she's dirty, she's goin' directly to jail. She ain't passin' go, and her ass ain't collectin' $200.00. I *guarantee* that shit."

Leah stepped away from him, very aware of the fact that he'd taken her hand away. "Okay, Noah."

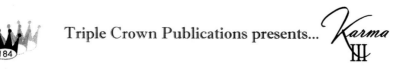

Noah looked at her. Most of the fire left his eyes and he lost his smirk. "I ain't mad at you for lovin' your friend, Leah, but you gotta understand that I'm way past pissed for what she's doin' to Lucas."

"I understand, Noah."

"Good." He put his hands on her waist and moved in close. Leah got goose bumps. "I don't want to talk about Lucas and Nick anymore," he said and kissed her forehead.

"Okay, Noah," Leah answered him, slipping her arms around his neck. Noah kissed her lips, lightly, and slid his hands under the waistband of her panties.

"You sleepy, Leah? Hmm?" he asked, kissing her mouth again, with a bit more intent. Noah ran his hands over her bottom, amorously, easing her panties down at the same time.

"No. Are you?" Leah could feel her body revving up for him. She *always* wanted Noah, which was cool, because it seemed he *always* wanted her. He had her boy shorts pushed down until they were almost off her hips.

"Nope. Take these off, Leah."

She smiled at him. "Say please."

Noah smiled back. "Please," he whispered in her ear. Leah pushed them down and stepped out of them.

Noah looked down at her with a very naughty twinkle in his eye. "Damn, Leah. I don't think I've ever met anybody that made me feel quite the way you do."

Leah wanted to ask, 'Not even Nadine?' but she knew better than to let that fall out of her mouth at a moment like this. She smiled at him seductively. "And what way is that?"

Noah tilted his head and smiled at her. "I think you just might have changed the game."

Leah's eyebrows went up in genuine surprise. "Wow, Noah, what does that mean?"

His gaze didn't waver. He looked her in the eye. "It means a whole lot of stuff."

Leah rolled up on *him*. She pulled him forward by his belt and stood on her toes to get to his lips. She kissed him teasingly. Noah had the best lips in the world. His tongue was heaven. She tasted it now and tried not to melt in his arms.

"Hey Noah?"

"Yeah?"

"Why don't you take me into the bedroom and tell me how you really feel about me?"

"You got it," Noah replied, and scooped her up without warning. He carried her into the bedroom and put her down on the bed. Noah took his shirt off and smiled at her, as she leaned back into the pillows. As always, Leah was impressed with his six-pack and a little startled by that damned scar in his chest. It wasn't huge, but it was serious. It looked like it had been made to save his life. She got a sudden flashback of Noah falling to the ground with all those holes in him, of him crashing right before their eyes. She thought he was going to die.

Leah got to her knees, suddenly, and put her arms around him. She hugged him fiercely, grateful he was okay.

Noah hugged her back. "Hey, Leah ... you okay, baby?"

She put her fingers in his hair. "I'm great. I almost lost you Noah, and even if you never say it back, I *love* you." Leah held his face in her hands and kissed him tenderly. Noah put his hands low on her hips and pulled her to him. They kept kissing with that same tenderness, their tongues doing a sweet, long, slow dance. She dropped her hands and ran her fingernails lightly over his body. Noah's breath caught and he moaned a little. Leah moved back a bit and let him get out of his jeans.

Leah could barely stand being this close to Noah without having him very deep inside of her. Her hand was on him immediately. Noah was hot and hard. She wanted to put her mouth on him, but Noah didn't seem to be done kissing her yet. She held him tightly in her hand and ran it up and down the length of him in a circular motion.

Noah broke the kiss and looked down at what she was doing. When he looked back up at her, his face was very serious. He moved his body against hers and forced her back. He followed her, on his knees until he had her back in her starting position, against the pillows.

"Turn around for me."

It was a command and Leah let go of him and did as she was told. She thought he was going to bend her over, but Noah put his chest against her back and started rubbing her nipples between his thumbs and first two fingers. Leah threw her head back and gasped. Noah kissed her cheek and started moving against her.

"Oh!" She pushed her breasts against his hands in delight, enjoying the sweet friction.

"Yeah, baby ... " Noah said in her ear, and dipped his fingers into her expertly. His middle finger glided over her erotically, making her wet and slippery in seconds. Leah's thighs parted and she leaned forward on the pillows, reflexively, working herself against his hand.

Noah entered her slow. Leah knew he was watching himself go in. He moaned like it was the best feeling in the world. "Ahh. Ahh, Leah ... you feel so good."

Leah closed her eyes and grabbed the headboard. Noah leaned into her and put his free hand over hers, still working on her with his other hand. He kissed her neck and started pumping slow. Grinding and hitting corners. Leah felt herself barreling towards an orgasm so strong, her legs got weak, but Noah had her. He pulled her back against him and held her across her body, while his other hand kept up its relentless stroke. Noah abruptly changed gears and started hitting her fast and quick. Leah threw her head back to scream, as her body started to throb, but nothing came out. All she could do was make noises like she was crying.

Noah let up a little and pushed her back on the pillows. He put his hands on her ass and pushed up. Then Noah did the thing that always drove her crazy. He went all the way in and retreated almost to the point of pulling out. Leah sighed and frowned. He was making her take it all and it felt marvelous. Noah was moaning randomly. Leah wondered if this felt as good to him as it felt to her.

Noah patted her hip and pulled out. "Turn over, baby."

She did and Noah went back in. He was killing her with a luscious long stroke. He twined his fingers in hers and held her hands down. Noah started kissing her. A sweet and beautiful kiss. He was working her back to another thundering climax. She felt her toes start to curl.

"Leah?"

She opened her eyes and Noah was looking at her with his startlingly gorgeous gray eyes.

"Huh?" That was all she could get out before her climax took her over and sent her through the stratosphere. Her hips left the bed of their own volition and she felt herself close up around him and pull him in. Her body was pulsating, wetting him up.

Noah dropped his head and started pumping fast and hard. He kissed her lips and spoke into her ear. "You see? I told you I couldn't leave you alone. You want me to tell you how I feel? I *like* you, Leah." He kissed her hard and went in all the way. Noah took his lips off hers and started coming hard. This was where Noah usually talked shit to her, but not tonight.

"Oh God, Leah ... you make me not want anybody else. Ah, Jesus Christ! I love you ... I love you ... Leah ..." He trailed off, kissing her and filling her up, then slowing down to a grind.

Leah couldn't believe what she'd just heard. She put her fingers in his hair and kissed him back. She couldn't stop herself from crying. "I love you, too, Noah. I love you so much."

"Alright ... good." He kissed her again and took his weight off her. "Alright." Noah did something else he didn't usually do. He held her. Leah was in heaven.

She put her head on his shoulder and snuggled into him. "When did you decide that?" she asked.

"Decide what?"

She smiled. "That you loved me."

Noah looked thoughtful. "Probably right before we brought Draco down."

Leah ran her hand across his chest. "And you're just telling me now?"

"Well, Leah, I *did* have a lot goin' on. Liz and Nadine were both pregnant ... then I got shot."

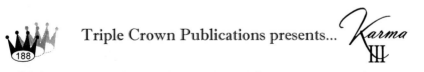

Leah was surprised to hear him mention Liz's name. Noah didn't talk about Liz at all. "What do you think Nadine's going to say about this? She *is* carrying your child and hoping you'll come home."

"Nadine's not pregnant anymore and that ain't been my home in years." He sat up and Leah sat up with him. Noah took her hand and looked into her eyes. "Listen to me, Leah. I ain't the world's greatest guy. I really stink at bein' in a relationship, but I can't help the way I feel about you. I got my doubts, but like I said before, I'm really gonna try for you, okay?"

Leah grinned at him, happily. "Okay. So do I have girlfriend status now?'

Noah smiled at her and his eyes sparkled. "Leah, you had girlfriend status months ago. You knew that."

Leah raised an eyebrow. "I didn't know anything until you decided to tell me, Noah. I've never been the type of woman to just assume my position. That's how you make a fool of yourself, in case you didn't know."

Noah's smile turned into a smirk, but his eyes didn't lose their sparkle. "You gettin' smart with me, Leah?"

Leah shrugged noncommittally. "Not really. Just saying you could have let me know sooner."

"Let you know sooner? Come here, Leah." Noah pulled her to him. She laughed and straddled his hips.

"You tryin' to bully me, Noah?"

He laughed, too. "Nah. I was just tryin' to get back in." He put one hand on her bottom and guided himself back in with the other. "Ah, that's much better. Now play your position, honey. Take care of your man," he said it with a cocky smile.

Leah tilted her head and started moving. "You my man, Noah?"

He looked at her with his pretty gray eyes. "Shit, I'm tryin' to be."

That was all Leah needed to hear. Everything else didn't matter. Noah had finally given her reciprocity and she was elated. She'd been shocked to hear that Nadine wasn't pregnant anymore. Leah wasn't evilly happy about it, but she was glad all the same. It had probably given her that last edge she'd needed with Noah. Leah smiled to herself and played her position well, She made sure she pleased her man.

Chapter Twenty-four

War Games

Noah followed Lucas out of the precinct and down the steps. They'd just left Myers' office. Myers had pulled them in from the field, where they'd been backing up a buy and bust. When they got to his office, he'd told them he wanted them posted at Butch's house ASAP.

Butch mentioned his conversation with Jessie to Myers. He told Myers that he had an almost certain feeling that Jessie was going to move on him. Butch, he said, hadn't seemed particularly worried, but Myers was worried about him. He'd decided on his own to put him and Lucas in an unmarked in front of Butch's house.

They'd just reached the bottom of the steps when someone bumped into Lucas hard enough to knock him into Noah. Lucas recovered quickly and they both turned around and looked into the face of Jessie London.

Jessie smiled at them and checked his French cuffs. "Whoops! Sorry, fellas. I must've made a misstep. Hey, Cain! I see you all the time, but I never get a chance to talk to you. Funny … bumpin' into you like this. How you been?"

One glance at Lucas told Noah he was one step from kicking Jessie's ass. Noah stood a little closer to him to keep him from wildin' out if that was the path he chose, but he was more than a little interested to see where this was going.

"I'm fantastic, Jessie," Lucas said, Noah noted he'd clenched his fists. Noah had his back. He lit a cigarette. "You're right. It is funny bumpin' into you. Did you try to knock me down, or were you in a hurry?"

Jessie grinned and bit the tip off a cigar that looked very much like a Cuban. He looked at Noah. "Got a light?"

Noah didn't like this motherfucker, either. He stuck his cigarette in the corner of his mouth and put his lighter back in his pocket. "Sorry. Ran outta butane."

Jessie gave Noah an oily look and turned his attention back to Lucas. "So, how you been, man? Word on the street has you shackin' up with Nicky Hardaway. You pick her up before or after you killed Keith Childs?"

"What?" Lucas advanced on Jessie so quickly, Noah almost lost his opportunity to step between them.

Noah stepped in front of Lucas and pushed him back. "Chill, Luke. It's cool." He turned to Jessie. "I killed Keith, bro. You want some?"

Jessie laughed and lit his cigar. "I ain't fuckin' with y'all hair-trigger niggas. Y'all wanna kick my ass for askin' a question. Fuckin' high-strung ass first grades."

Lucas reached over Noah's shoulder and grabbed Jessie by his tie and pulled him forward. His other hand reached for his collar. Noah found himself sandwiched between them with Jessie laughing in his face.

"Why you so *hostile*, man? You got a problem with me?" Jessie taunted. People were starting to stare.

"Let him go, Luke," Noah said with a slight feeling of déjà vu. Lucas had said the same thing to him not so long ago.

"I'll kill you," Lucas said very quietly and very distinctly. Noah grabbed Lucas' wrists and physically pulled Lucas off of Jessie. Lucas went without much of a fight because his common sense probably started kicking in. They couldn't stand here fucking around with Jessie. He probably knew they were on to him.

Jessie fixed his tie and straightened his collar. "Looks like you're the same uppity motherfucker you always was, but it seems talkin' about that skank, Nicky, gets under your skin. Have a nice day, ladies." He walked away whistling.

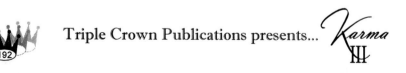

They turned and watched him go. Lucas passed a hand over his beard and looked at Noah. "When this shit goes down, his ass is mine."

"I got no problem with that, Luke." They watched him walk to his silver Audi and peel out of the lot. "Wonder where he's goin' in the middle of the fuckin' workday, Luke," Noah said and tossed his smoke.

"Wherever it is, I'm sure it ain't good, No. Let's get to Butch."

"Right behind you, Luke."

******

It had been dark for an hour before they saw any activity at Butch's house. They'd spent the better part of the day watching his place, and other than the mailman, there had been nothing. Noah was so bored, he wanted to start screaming. They'd been cooped up in this car all day and Lucas hadn't been in a particularly talkative mood thanks to Jessie London. Noah left him alone after he couldn't draw him out. Sometimes a man just needed to be with his own thoughts.

A midnight blue BMW X5 pulled into Butch's driveway and they both sat up a little. Butch got out of the driver's side and did a cursory inspection of his surroundings.

"Look at Butch, ballin' in an X5!" Noah said, with a snicker.

"Everybody's gotta drive somethin'," Lucas replied, absently, staring out the window. Noah wanted to point out the fact that everybody didn't drive, but he wasn't fucking with Lucas in his current state of mind.

They watched in silence as Butch walked around to the passenger side and opened the door. A woman got out. She appeared to be somewhere in her late thirties. Her hair was cut into a bob and she was wearing a clingy little dress appropriate for late summer. She was curvy in all the right places. She was beautiful. Butch planted a kiss on her and led her to the house.

"Look at this shit!" Noah said, laughing, "Butch's wife is bangin'. Who woulda thought that shit?" Noah looked over at Lucas. He was finally smiling.

"I gotta admit, I didn't see that comin', No."

"She's a lot finer than I thought old Butch was capable of."

"He's probably good to her," Lucas said with a quiet smile.

"Probably so. No wonder he had that bottle of laxatives on his desk. He must've been too shy to show his Viagra." Noah laughed.

Lucas laughed, too. "That's fucked up, Noah."

"Maybe, but I bet it's true."

"Uh-huh." Their laughter trailed off and their silence was finally comfortable. They watched them enter the house and turn the lights on.

"That's nice for Butch," Lucas said in that same quiet voice.

Noah looked over at him and felt for him. "You really want that, don't you, Luke?"

Lucas smiled, but his smile looked sad. "I think it would be nice."

"Be careful what you wish for. I had it and it wasn't that great."

Lucas laughed and looked at him. "Come on, No. This is me. You made it not so great."

"Yeah, I did. I ruined it. I'm probably about to ruin some more shit."

Lucas raised an eyebrow. "Leah?"

Noah nodded. "Yeah. I told her I love her."

Lucas laughed out loud and hit the steering wheel with his hand. "Get the fuck outta here! You're lyin'. I really don't believe you."

Noah looked at him in bogus disbelief, trying to be indignant, and trying not to laugh at the same time. "Fuck you, Luke, I *did* tell her."

Lucas kept laughing. "You're a fucking liar, Noah. Fuck you back."

Noah was about to come back at him, but that was when everything went left. A black souped up Oldsmobile Cutlass Supreme rolled soundlessly to a stop in front of Butch's house. They both stopped talking and reached for their weapons. Three men got out, dressed in black from head to toe, moving fast. One went around one side of the house, another to the other side, and one to the front door.

"Let's go, Noah! Move! Move!" They bolted from the car at top speed. Noah had a fleeting thought that they hadn't had time to call for backup and he was sure Lucas was thinking the same thing. Everything jumped off at once.

Butch lived in a large and lovely Tudor house in Jamaica Estates. Like most upscale houses, Butch didn't have a storm door because it would have distracted from the beauty of the entryway. Right now, a very large man was having great success kicking his front door in.

Lucas pointed at the front door and disappeared around the side of the house. Noah screeched to a stop and leveled his gun. "Police! On your knees, hands behind your head!"

The big guy turned around grinning. It was Darryl Gilford. Noah was aware of glass breaking and shots being fired as he lined Darryl's forehead up in his sights.

Darryl's hand came up, holding his own gun. "Police!" he screamed back, and brought his weapon up. "Fuck you!"

Noah tucked his lips in and took the side of Darryl's head off with no hesitation. Darryl fell to the ground, a giant, bloody mess. Noah stepped over him and shouldered the door open. He went in low, swinging his gun in a wide arc. There were sirens in the distance and commotion toward the back of the house. Butch was yelling and so was someone else: another male.

Sudden movement in the kitchen caught Noah's attention and he swung his gun in that direction. It was Lucas. He was standing flush against the kitchen wall with a body at his feet. He waved his gun to get Noah's attention. Noah crossed the room quickly and joined him.

"Fuck you, you son of a bitch! Kill me, then!" Butch yelled. They ran down the hall to the exchange of gunfire. They stopped at the door and went in cautiously. Butch whirled around and pointed his gun at them.

"Whoa, Butch! Be easy. It's us," Noah said, lowering his own gun.

Lucas stepped into the room. "You okay, Butch? Are you hit?"

Butch brought his gun down and turned to face them. His left arm was dripping blood. "What are you guys doin' here? Myers send you?"

"Yeah. Myers said Jessie might move on you," Lucas said,

looking down at Merlin Nash. He had a hole in his shoulder, another in his stomach and one in his thigh. He was writhing in pain, grunting low and spewing curses. "Looks like he was right."

Butch was winded and breathing hard. "Those bastards shot my wife," he said, moving to the other side of the bed. Butch dropped to his knees. "Oh God, Debra ..." She was prone and breathless, shot low in the torso. Noah requested an ambulance as Lucas put cuffs on the struggling Merlin Nash and read him his rights. Butch did his best to console his wife and keep her calm.

"Ambulance should be here soon, Butch," Noah said, and turned to Lucas. "I gave Darryl Gilford a head shot by the front door. Who'd you get?"

Lucas looked at him grimly and Noah was a bit shocked by his answer. "Would you believe Victor Calderon?"

Noah shook his head and looked disgusted. Vic had a pretty decent role in the Draco sting. He'd wired their club, Façade. "Get outta here, Luke. How deep does this go?" Vic had been a bit of an asshole, but Noah would have never pegged him for dirty.

Butch got up suddenly and walked over to Nash with his gun drawn. "Why don't we ask this motherfucker here?" He smiled a deadly little smile at him. "I ain't gotta tell you, you're gonna wish I'd shot you in the fuckin' head, Nash. Start talkin'! Where the fuck is Jessie and what's he up to?"

The sirens stopped and Lucas and Noah moved to the door with their badges displayed prominently, both of them very interested in Butch's line of questioning.

"Fuck you, you fat bitch! I ain't tellin' you shit!" Nash spat at him.

"I think you will," Butch said blackly. He put his gun down and did some of the strangest shit Noah ever saw. Nash couldn't even try and stop him because Lucas had cuffed him. Butch unfastened Nash's pants and rudely shoved his hand in his underwear. All of a sudden, Nash was screaming like someone had set him on fire. Noah felt sympathetic horror creep into his eyes, but he couldn't seem to look away. Noah glanced at Lucas. He was wearing his poker face.

"You cocksucker! You'll talk or I'll rip 'em off. I swear to God!"

Butch yelled at him.

Two cops entered the room with their guns drawn. Lucas and Noah automatically held their guns and badges up. Butch was still twisting Nash's nuts and Nash was still screaming like he was ablaze.

"What the fuck's goin' on?" the first cop asked. He was a rookie with no hair on his face. He didn't seem to want to lower his weapon.

Lucas nodded toward Butch. "That's Inspector Butch Harper from Internal Affairs. The perp on the floor is Detective Merlin Nash, narcotics, Midtown South. He's a dirty cop just like the two bodies you stepped over to get in here."

The other cop was a woman. She had her gun on Noah. She looked him over, her eyes lingering on his badge. "Who the hell are you?"

"Detective Noah Ramsey, First Grade. Narcotics, Midtown South."

She looked at Noah dubiously, then turned to Lucas. "And who are you?" Lucas identified himself as Nash broke.

"Jesus! Jesus! Okay! He's gonna meet that chick, Nicky at City Storage in SoHo! She's got his key. Please! Let me go, Butch! Please!" he shrieked.

EMS entered the bedroom as Butch got clumsily to his feet. His right hand was covered in blood to the wrist. Nash was still howling. Noah looked at Lucas with raised eyebrows. Lucas had finally lost his poker face. He was looking at Nash with his lips tucked in. Blood was starting to seep through Nash's pants. Butch directed the EMS to his wife as Lucas placed a call to Myers, who said he was on his way with the Commissioner. A senior officer from the rookie cop's precinct had been dispatched to secure the scene and discourage the media. They didn't want this leaking to the news just yet.

When Butch was satisfied that his wife was in good care, he went into the bathroom and washed his hands. He returned to the bedroom and put his suit jacket on. "Let's get goin', guys, and see what's down at City Storage."

Chapter Twenty-five

Who's That Lady

Nick was just stepping out of the shower when someone knocked on her door. It startled her because no one was supposed to know where she was. She'd been holed up in her room at the Chelsea Hotel since Lucas had thrown her ass out. Even though she knew why, she still couldn't quite believe Lucas had shown her the door like that. She knew any animosity for him for it was illogical, but she couldn't help feeling that way anyway. A part of her was angry at him for forsaking her and opting out of their relationship so quickly.

Nick wrapped her hair in a towel and put on her robe. When she got to the door and looked out the peephole, she saw that the hall was empty. Nick frowned and opened the door, not even thinking about the obvious.

Jessie stepped in and grabbed her neck with his right hand. "Hey, baby! It took me a minute to find your ass. You weren't tryin' to leave town on me, were you?" He had her neck in a vise grip. He laughed and pushed her back into the room, as Nick grabbed his hand with both of hers. She tried to pry his fingers loose to no avail.

Jessie snatched Nick's service weapon off the dresser as they passed it and threw Nick across the bed. "I doubt you'll be needin' this," he said, tucking her gun into his waistband. "Get dressed, Nicky. We gotta make a run."

Nick sat up rubbing her neck, furious at Jessie's intrusion. "I'm not going anywhere with you. Give me my gun back, you son of a bitch."

Jessie slapped her so hard, tears flew out of her eyes. "Bitch, don't make me kill you now instead of later. Get your ass up and get dressed."

Nick slid off the bed, trembling and wiping at her tears. "You're gonna kill me, Jessie?"

Jessie opened the mini-bar and removed two bottles of Absolute. "I'm still thinkin' about it, Nicky. I'm kind of leanin' toward yes. You know how I hate loose ends." He broke the seal on one of the bottles and tossed it back. "Why? You interested in tryin' to change my mind?"

Nick turned to go into the bathroom, but Jessie grabbed her wrist. "No, Nicky. No bathrooms with closed doors. You get dressed right here where I can see you."

Nick looked at Jessie and bit her bottom lip. She was in a situation she couldn't possibly win and Jessie had her gun. Jessie sat on the bed. He took off the jacket to his suit and removed her gun from his waistband. Jessie looked at her rudely and laid the gun on his crotch, while he lounged back on one elbow and cracked the seal on the second bottle.

"Come on, Nicky. Take it off. Let a nigga take a walk down Memory Lane," he said, and tossed the second bottle back. Nick went to the dresser and took a pair of panties out of the drawer. She could feel Jessie's eyes on her. When she attempted to step into them, Jessie sat up and ripped them out of her hand. "No, uh-uh. I said take it off. That means *disrobe*, Nicky." He smiled at her. "What's the matter? Am I humiliating you?"

"Jessie … please don't —"

"'Cause if you think that's humiliating, you ain't seen nothin' yet. This party just started, baby."

Nick looked down at him and he was honestly almost as fine as Lucas, with his velvety chocolate skin and his pretty brown eyes — but Lucas, he wasn't. He was making the bile rise up in her throat. She didn't want him to touch her, but she knew he was probably going to. She started to cry.

Jessie stood up with her gun in his hand. He stood so close to her, she could smell his cologne. "Cryin' ain't gonna help you, boo. I like that shit. It only makes my dick harder."

Nick shook her head and started crying in earnest. "Oh, God. Please don't, Jessie. You don't have to do this to me. I'll do what you say. Please don't do this to me."

"It ain't nothin' you never done before. Why you so uptight?" He reached out and took the towel off her head. "Look at you. You're still a fine motherfucker, Nicky. That's my word." He reached for the belt on her robe and it reminded her of that first night with Lucas. Nick couldn't stand that he'd made her associate something so sweet with what his violating ass was about to do to her.

Nick made a fist and hit him from the shoulder with everything she had. Her fist connected satisfyingly with his eye and Jessie stumbled back in surprise. Nick threw another punch with her other fist and hit him in the mouth. She had the edge of surprise and she used it to her advantage. She threw punches unrelentingly, like a prize fighter, hoping he'd drop her gun. Just when she thought she'd gotten the upper hand, Jessie hit her in the face with her gun and she fell across the bed. It hurt so bad; she couldn't move at first. She could only lie there holding her face.

"You wanna fight me like a man, bitch? Get up and fight!" he yelled at her. Nick was scared to move. She'd lost her chance and she knew Jessie was mean and crazy. When she felt Jessie's weight on the bed, Nick rolled off of it and made a mad dash for the bathroom. Jessie was right behind her, so close, she couldn't shut the door because he was in the frame.

Nick started screaming, "No, Jessie, no!"

Jessie brought the gun up and put it to her temple. "Stop screamin' or I'm gonna blow your beautiful brains out." Nick's mouth clamped shut and she started trembling uncontrollably as Jessie put his hand under her robe. Nick screamed in protest and Jessie laughed.

"I don't know why you're actin' like this, boo. I ain't a stranger. Bend over." He pushed her head down with his gun hand and bent her over the sink. She heard his zipper come down and closed her eyes, steeling herself against the invasion, hoping he'd hurry up, that it would be over soon. Unfortunately, Jessie took his time. Nick grimaced and tried to block this shit out of her mind. She couldn't

believe this was happening to her again. When Jessie was done, he slapped her on the ass and kissed her cheek.

"Let's go, Nicky. I told you, we gotta make a run. You do have my key, right?"

Nick felt like a whore as she silently stepped back into the shower. She thought about Lucas. If he hadn't thrown her out, this would never have happened. It only lasted a second, but she felt a pang of dislike for Lucas that was so strong, it took her breath away.

Nick washed Jessie off of her, not quite believing her life had come to this ... and feeling like it was about to get a lot worse. The worst part was she couldn't seem to stop her tears. She wiped at them now and then went back into the room and got dressed quickly.

Jessie watched her silently, with his hands in the trouser pockets of his perfectly cut Brooks Brothers suit. "Don't cry, Nicky. It was about control. That's it. You'll do what I say, or I'll do whatever the fuck I want to you. I'm the dictator in this shit, you understand?"

Nick nodded but kept her eyes on the floor as she buttoned her blouse. "Whatever you say, Jessie."

He smiled at her. "Good. Hurry up. You got my key?"

"Yeah, I got it," Nick said, tonelessly, stepping into her jeans.

Jessie rolled up on her. "Let me see it."

Nick glanced at him. He was holding her gun on her as she pulled the drawer out in the nightstand. She'd taped Jessie's key to the bottom. Nick ripped it off and threw it at him. It hit his tie and fell to the floor.

"Shit like that can get you shot for bad behavior. Pick it up and hand it to me like a fuckin' lady," Jessie said, taunting her with his eyes, still pointing her own gun at her. Nick picked the key up and gave it to him. Jessie laughed, "You seem pissed, Nicky. What did I do?" He was jeering at her. Nick wished he'd die.

"You know what you did. How dare you ask me? You did the same thing your buddy Keith did before Noah killed his ass."

Jessie smiled at her. "Really? Damn, then it looks like you got fucked twice. Put a little makeup on, boo. You look like somebody's been beating your ass with a gun." He couldn't keep the snicker out of his voice.

"I hate you, Jessie," Nick said, rolling her eyes at him.

Jessie laughed. "I hate you, too. Now put your face on and let's go, before I make you eat some lead."

******

Lucas sat in the backseat of Butch's X5 and listened to Butch and Noah's exchange about Nash's groin injury. Lucas smiled and tried not to laugh. He knew Noah very well. He knew that shit Butch did to Nash had horrified Noah. Noah was not a fan of bloody crotches and dick jokes.

"Yeah, Butch, but what did you actually *do*?" Noah asked, all frowned up, like he could actually feel the pain himself.

Butch lifted his hand, made a fist and twisted it in the air. "I twisted, pulled, and used my thumbnail to open him up."

Noah's mouth dropped open in outrage, and he looked at Butch's hand like he better not get any ideas. "What the fuck's wrong with you, Butch? Where'd you learn some shit like that?"

"Oh, in the Gulf War. There's all types of things you can do to get a man to talk. Torture it is, but I gotta tell you, torture has its benefits, Ramsey. And stop lookin' at me like I'm some kinda monster. His ass talked, didn't he?" Butch said nonchalantly.

The only thing about Noah's expression that changed, was the fact that he closed his mouth. "You're a sick fuck, ain't you, Butch? I'd rather get waterboarded."

Lucas laughed a little and looked out the window. They were parked across the street from City Storage on Spring Street, waiting for Jessie to make an appearance. Lucas thought the shit with Noah was comical, but he felt the weight of some serious shit about to go down and it cut his laughter short.

Lucas ran his hand over his beard and couldn't accept the fact that Nicole had obviously played him. Five years ago, this shit would never have happened to him. Not Lucas Cain. After Justine, everything had gone downhill, even when it seemed to getting better, and maybe there was a chance life could still be sweet. He felt like Justine had taken his luck when it came to women.

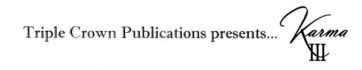

As Noah would say, it was time to pop his collar. After what he'd been through with Justine and Nicole, he wasn't trying to be in love anymore. Love was bullshit. Love was a sham. Love came with too many strings attached. The hurt love could cause was devastating and it was too hard to recover. Lucas believed he'd had enough. Maybe he'd feel different later, but right now he'd had his fill. Fuck love.

Lucas raised an eyebrow as a silver Audi pulled up three spaces from the entrance to City Storage. He sat up and pulled his gun out of his holster. Jessie London got out of the driver's seat and walked around to the passenger side of the car.

"Jessie's here," Lucas stated, leaning forward. "How do you want to do this, Butch?" Noah looked over at him and saw that Lucas had unsecured his weapon. Noah did the same and looked at Butch expectantly. He was ready, but then, Noah was always ready. Noah never cowered away from anything.

Butch watched Jessie open the door on the passenger side, rubbing his chin, thoughtfully. Nicole got out and Lucas wasn't surprised to see her. Disappointed, but not surprised. "Aha," Butch said a bit smugly. "What have we here? Cain, you still pissed at me about questionin' Nick at the hospital? I gotta tell you, it looks like it was the right way to go."

Lucas leaned forward. "That's not cool, Butch. I got eyes and I can see. How do you want to proceed?"

Jessie turned to walk to City Storage, but Nicole didn't budge. Jessie came back to get her, smoothly twisting her arm behind her back and walking away with her.

"Sorry, Cain. Don't get pissed. We'll wait for them to go inside, then we'll go in after them. Neither one of them is gettin' away." He turned in his seat and looked at Lucas. "Think you can deal with this, Cain? I mean, at the very least, we gotta take her in for questionin' — you alright with that?"

"He's fuckin' peachy, Butch, and if he ain't, I got his back. You don't need to worry about that. What you need to be worried about is the fact that there's most likely gonna be shots fired. I don't wanna see you fuckin' with us about it later on. This is your baby, Butch. Jessie's bitch ass is leavin' the buildin' in cuffs or a body bag — we guarantee it — but I swear to God, Butch, I don't wanna hear boo from you about some bullshit. You got me?"

Butch put his hand on Noah's shoulder. "Fair enough, Ramsey. You got it."

Noah looked at Butch's hand. "Ain't that the same hand you tried to sever dude's balls with?"

Lucas had to crack a smile. "Radio in, Butch. If we ain't out in fifteen minutes call for back up. You stay here in case somebody else shows up. Come on, Noah. Let's go get Jessie's ass."

******

Jessie had made up his mind. He was going to kill Nicky. She was a pain in the ass and she didn't want to follow directions. He couldn't think of a single reason why he should let her ass live. If he did let her live, he knew sooner or later she was going to open her mouth and start dropping dime. He'd brought her with him because if Nicky was selling him a wolf ticket and this wasn't his magic key, he was going to torture her ass until she coughed up the real one. Then he was going to kill her and dump her body in Putnam County for trying to put one over on him. Jessie smiled as he moved Nicky along. Who was he kidding? Even if it was the right key, her ass was going to be at the bottom of Lake Mahopac by sunrise.

"Stop pushing me. I'm walking as fast as I can!" Nick complained.

Jessie twisted her arm and she yelped. "Shut up, before I stick this gun in your mouth and blow your brains out. Be quiet and don't make any trouble when we get inside." He pulled the door to City Storage open and ushered Nicky inside, walking very close to her. "Not a sound, Nicky."

The clerk looked up from the desk, and what started as a cheerful look of welcome, quickly turned into a look of alarmed concern. "Miss, are you okay?"

Nick sniffed loudly and Jessie sucked his teeth. *This bitch was crying*. "Her mother died," Jessie lied with a straight face. "She has to get some papers out of storage."

The clerk instantly looked sympathetic. He was a young white guy with red hair and blue eyes. "Oh. I'm sorry. Do you have your card? And I'll also need to see a valid photo ID."

Jessie smiled. Keith had rented the storage space and his ass was dead. The card had totally slipped his mind. He knew the unit number and he had the key, but he'd forgotten about this one little detail until now. "Damn. I must've left my card at home," Jessie said, not even bothering to pretend to look for it.

The clerk frowned. "I'm afraid you're going to have to go get it. Or you can get a new one, but it's going to take a little longer to get to your belongings."

"It's a long drive. Where's your manager?"

"The manager goes home at 6, sir. If you need to speak to him, you can come back in the morning. He'll be here."

"There's nobody else I can speak to?"

"No, sir. I'm the only one here and I'm afraid the card is policy."

Jessie smiled again and the clerk smiled back, thinking he'd diffused the situation. He didn't know that Jessie was smiling because he'd been trying to find out if the clerk was alone.

"I'm afraid this gun is policy," Jessie said. He shot him in the forehead with Nicky's gun. The clerk looked at him in surprise, then fell to the floor. Nicky started squealing and Jessie went back to twisting her arm. "Shut up and start walkin', bitch. You can still get some, you know." He forced her ahead, toward his unit on the third floor.

******

Lucas hadn't even gotten his foot on the pavement before he heard the pop of a gunshot. "Shit, Butch! Shots fired!"

He didn't even have to look at Noah. When he got out, Noah was there with his gun out and his badge still around his neck. They looked at each other, briefly. The light had just changed and traffic was flowing. Lucas took his badge off his neck and held it up as they crossed the wide avenue, running straight through traffic. They dodged and weaved and made it to the other side in one piece. When they got to City Storage, Lucas went to the right of the door and Noah went to the left.

"I'll go low," Lucas said and threw the door open. They swept the room and saw no movement. Lucas and Noah entered the storage facility with extreme caution, their weapons raised and ready to fire.

"There," Noah said in a low voice, pointing to the blood on the counter. They both edged over and looked over the counter, sideways. The clerk was down, a hole in his forehead, and a growing puddle of blood forming around him. They glanced at each other with regret. Damn.

There was a sudden purr of hydraulics. The elevator. They tilted their heads, listening hard. It sounded close. Down the hall. They froze, listening.

When it ground to a stop, Noah looked at Lucas. "What floor would you say that was, bro?"

Lucas looked back at him. "Second or third. I'm thinkin' third."

Noah nodded. "Me, too. Let's go." They started up the stairs, moving fast.

******

Jessie had Nick's arm pushed so far up her back, she thought it would pop out of the socket, or snap in half any second. The pain was making her breathless.

"Jessie, please," she panted. "You don't have to hurt me like this. Please! You're breaking my fucking arm."

"Sweetheart, I really don't give a fuck about you or your fuckin' arm." He paused and looked around. So did Nick. Her mind was going a mile a minute, trying to whip up a way to get away from him. They were at the mouth of the hallway. It veered off to the left and right, and there was another corridor straight ahead. It seemed all three sections had storage spaces on both sides. They all looked like dead ends to Nick.

"Hmm … 3-4721 … let's go this way." Jessie said, and pulled her to the left. Nick pulled back, even though it felt like her arm was about to snap.

Jessie turned around and yelled at her. "Stop raisin' up! What's wrong with you?" He pulled up on her wrist, and Nick felt something in her arm go terribly wrong. She shrieked, and Jessie hit her in the head with the gun. "One more noise outta you, and you're dyin' in this warehouse, Nicky. Do not fuck around with me." His voice was low and devoid of emotion. It was black like death. He dragged her down the hall.

******

When they got to the third floor, Lucas stopped before he threw the door open. He turned and looked at Noah. Down at his leg, and then back to his face with the question in his eyes.

Noah smirked at him. "I'm good, Luke. No zings, no pings, no pain. Let's go get his ass."

Lucas checked for him. Noah wasn't even breathing that hard.

"Stop worrying about me, Luke. I'm tellin' you, I'm good."

Lucas stared at him a moment longer. "I'll go low."

Noah looked back at him like he was annoyed with him. "Good. I'll go high."

Lucas crouched and threw the door open. They swept the vicinity. Nothing. Three corridors.

"Choose, Luke," Noah said. Lucas did. He started down the corridor in the middle. They'd just passed the fourth set of storage cells when they heard Nicole scream. The sound echoed and bounced off the walls. They couldn't discern exactly where it was coming from. They frowned at each other.

"Where?" Lucas asked.

Noah shrugged and pointed left. "There?"

Lucas shook his head. "No. No. Up the middle." Lucas led the way and Noah had his back. Up the middle they went until they got to the end. They found themselves in front of the elevator.

Noah popped Lucas in the arm and pointed down. "Look." There were fresh drops of blood on the floor. Noah pointed his gun at the trail of droplets. They went left.

"What are we waitin' for?" Lucas said quietly. They went left.

******

Nick was staring at Jessie hard, or trying to anyway. He'd hit her in the head hard enough to knock a hole in her scalp. Blood was oozing down the side of her face and hitting the floor in bright red drops. Her vision was blurring. This fucker had given her a concussion.

Jessie stopped in front of 3-4721 and smiled at her. "It's the moment of truth, Nicky. This key better work or I'm gonna empty this gun in you." Jessie stuck the key in the lock and it turned like it was supposed to. He pushed her inside and turned on the light.

Nick held her breath and waited for his reaction. Jessie let her go and pushed her away from him in his haste to start opening the storage bins. The first three bins were full of stolen bricks of cocaine. Jessie was grinning gleefully. Nick backed up and smiled herself. Men were so stupid, especially this arrogant man in front of her. Didn't he realize that he'd pushed her into a corner? Ruined her life and left her with nothing to lose? Did he have an inkling of what he'd done to her? He'd made her lose everything. Lucas, her job ... her father was a retired Captain. How would he feel about this shit? Jessie hadn't left her with a lot of choices.

Jessie was starting to frown. Nick was starting to smile a little brighter. For the first time in a long while, she didn't feel like crying. She felt like laughing her ass off.

"What the fuck?" Jessie said, incredulously. He put the gun down absently, and opened another bin. More coke. He walked behind the stack of bins and reached for another one. There was nothing in it. There was nothing in the next one or the third. Jessie took a deep breath. "Where the fuck is my goddamned money?"

Nick was eyeing the gun. It was between them. She edged toward it. "What money, Jessie?"

"My fuckin' money!" He turned and looked at her murderously. "You take my money, bitch?"

Moving closer to Jessie meant moving closer to the gun. Nick took two steps toward him and braced herself. This was the end. Everything was about to jump off now. She had nothing to lose.

She lifted her head defiantly. "Yeah, I took it. What's the worse you can do? Kill me?"

Jessie's face contorted with rage. "What did you say?"

Nick smiled. "I said fuck your black ass, Jessie London." She took another step forward and spit in his eye. Nick went for the gun.

Jessie's hand went, reflexively, to his eye, wiping at it frantically. He reached for Nick with his other hand. Nick ducked, but he grabbed her by the hair and wound his fingers in it. Jessie snatched her backward and put her in a headlock. Nick felt cold steel against her temple.

"You goin' for the gun? Bitch, I'll kill you!" Jessie screamed at her.

"No, you won't. Put the gun down, London." Relief washed over Nick when she heard Lucas's voice. She stopped fighting Jessie so hard and waited for Lucas to take him out.

"Aw, shit!" Jessie said in disgust.

"That's about right, Jessie," Noah said. Nick could hear the smile in his voice. "You heard the man. Put your gun down. Don't make us hurt you."

"I don't believe this shit!" Jessie said. He turned with Nick until they were facing Lucas and Noah. Both Lucas and Noah had serious beads on Jessie.

Lucas looked Nick in the eye, then looked back at Jessie. "Let her go," he said, flatly.

Jessie laughed at him. "Nigga, is you crazy? Let her go? Fuck no! I got myself a hostage, don't I?"

Lucas brought his gun up a little higher. "No, you don't. Let her go."

Noah looked from Lucas to Jessie. "I'd do it. I think he means to kill you."

Butch Harper chose that moment to appear in the doorway. He had his own gun drawn and there were two officers behind him. Butch held his hand up to the other officers and walked into the room, looking quite smug.

Jessie smiled at him in reluctant admiration. "You fat, sneaky, bastard."

Butch smiled back. "I told you I was comin' for you, Jessie. You ain't gettin' away, so drop the weapon, let go of Hardaway and assume the position."

Jessie barked laughter. "I ain't assumin' shit, Butch. If you gonna take me, take me. I ain't goin' to jail. Guess that means I'm gonna die and Cain, here, will probably do the honors since I fucked his woman." He paused and winked at Lucas. Nick saw Lucas' finger tighten on the trigger as Jessie continued to taunt him. "Bet you didn't know she was dirty, did you, Cain? This bitch just stole $10 million in drug money from me. After you kill me, you need to put her ass in jail for conspiracy, intent to sell, and aiding and abetting. You need to —"

Nick had enough. She was already in trouble. *Time to go, Jessie.* She smashed the back of her head into his nose as she slammed her foot into his shin. Jessie let go of her and she spun away from him. When Jessie turned his gun on her to shoot her, Lucas lit his ass up like a Christmas tree. He shot the gun out of his hand first, then he gave him four shots to the body.

Jessie hit the floor screaming and squirming. Lucas advanced on him, still aiming his gun at him, and kicked his gun away. Lucas was so angry he was shaking. Nick glanced at Noah, who was looking at her like he didn't like her anymore.

"Go ahead and finish what you started, Cain!" Jessie yelled.

Noah put his hand on Lucas' forearm and spoke in a low voice. "Don't do it, Luke."

Lucas stepped away from Jessie, like he'd been holding his breath. He lowered his gun and ran his hand over his beard.

Jessie laughed and spit blood out of his mouth. "You're a pussy, Cain."

Lucas whirled around with his bottom lip tucked in and shot Jessie in his kneecap. Jessie screamed. "Fuck you, London. I didn't shoot you in the head 'cause I want you to serve your sentence, you piece of shit." He shot him in the elbow and was about to shoot him again when Noah put his hand on Lucas' gun and pushed it down. Nick knew Noah was the only person in the world who could have gotten away with that.

"Chill, Luke. Damn, Butch is right there," Noah said, in that same low voice.

Butch shrugged. "I didn't see shit, Ramsey. I gotta tell you, Cain, you're about to get real upset with me, so put your gun down." Butch walked over to Nick and smiled at her sadly. "You know how I feel about dirty cops, Hardaway. I think you lied to me about your involvement. I feel bad about this all around, but I gotta take you into custody."

Nick knew this was coming, but that didn't keep away the panic that descended over her. She started backing up. "No! Wait a minute, Butch. It's not what you think. Lucas, please … tell him it's not what it looks like!"

Lucas looked at her with his incredible chocolate eyes and Nick couldn't believe how cold they were. "I can't tell him anything, Nicole. You wouldn't talk to me." He turned his back and walked away without another word. Nick opened her mouth to say something, but she closed it when she saw Noah staring at her with that dark dislike in his eyes. Noah smirked and followed Lucas out of the room. Nick had a feeling she'd remember this moment for the rest of her life. Her life shattering. Lucas walking away from her like he didn't care, and Noah smiling about it.

She wasn't as guilty as everybody thought she was. The things she'd done weren't that bad, even though they were against the law. She didn't think she'd earned this horrible treatment from Lucas, or Noah looking at her like she was garbage. She didn't think she'd done anything to warrant Jessie forcing himself on her and putting his hands on her. She looked at Butch and felt like she was dreaming and he was moving in slow motion.

Butch removed the cuffs from his belt. He reached for her and put his hand on her wrist, turning her around so that her back was to him. He put the cuffs on as Nick stared out the doorway at Lucas. He'd stopped and he was staring back at her. Nick wondered why he hadn't done something to keep this from happening to her. *Anything*.

Noah put his hand on Lucas shoulder and turned him around. Lucas dropped his head and kept walking. *So cold*. Nick straightened her back and blinked back tears that she refused to let fall. If jail was in her future, there was nothing she could do about that, but her time would most likely be short.

"You have the right to remain silent. Anything you say can, and will, be used against you in a court of law. You have a right to an attorney. If you cannot afford one …" Nick didn't need to listen to Butch read her rights to her. She knew them by heart. Hell, she'd said the same thing many times, herself. Nick felt something go cold in her. Fine. She'd do her time, but when she got out, she had Jessie's 10 million to fall back on. She'd start over and live well on that cash, but

one of the first things she'd do would be to let Lucas know exactly how much he'd hurt her when he washed his hands of her.

Nick smiled as Butch escorted her out of the room.

Chapter Twenty-six

State of Shock

Lucas sat in a cop bar on Smith Street with Noah, sipping his second drink. It had been five months since Nicole had pulled the wool over his eyes. She'd been indicted on conspiracy and money laundering charges. She was currently somewhere on Riker's Island, he supposed, in protective custody because she used to be a cop. Her trial was in two months.

Lucas tried to pretend it wasn't having a profound effect on him, but that wasn't so. He wasn't dealing with this very well and he knew it. Lucas decided this, on top of Justine, was enough to make him swear off love and throw himself back into his hardcore player ways. He knew it wasn't the best decision to make, but it was what he needed right now. It kept his mind off being hurt and wondering if there was something wrong with him, why, it seemed, he attracted tragedy and disaster the way he did. It was like he was a fucking magnet for that shit.

He was actually a lot angrier than he was hurt. The catastrophic climax he'd had with Justine had hurt him. This thing with he'd just gone through with Nicole had left him reeling with a myriad of emotions. He felt like she'd perpetrated a fraud. He felt duped and betrayed. Not to mention used. Lucas felt like she'd put a huge one over on him, and he didn't appreciate it.

He was angry at her for misrepresenting herself to him and taking advantage of him when she knew he was still shell shocked from Justine. He was angry with her because her misrepresentation had made him rush Justine's memory away. Lucas would always love Justine, but he'd pretty much changed the way he felt about Nicole when Butch took her away. He was too angry at her to love her anymore.

He was probably angriest at himself. He couldn't believe he'd been that weak; that bad a judge of character. He couldn't believe he'd been played like that. He wasn't trying to let it happen again. Fuck love. He'd been down that road twice. It was time to cruise for a while. He was done searching for love because ultimately he had issues with his mother abandoning him when he was a kid. Fuck her, too. Fuck Delilah. This shit was all her fault. Like Noah said, it was time to pop his collar, keep it movin', and remember who he was. It was time to stop being soft and time to stop letting women fuck his head up.

Noah had gone outside to have a smoke. He returned to his seat on Lucas' left, still talking into his cell phone. "No, Nadine. I won't and you can't make me. I'm a grown-ass man." He paused, and sipped his drink, then he gave Lucas the 'this bitch is crazy' look. Lucas chuckled into his own glass and took a sip, convinced most women were on some level.

"No, Nadine. I'm only comin' over there when my kids are home. You ain't settin' my ass up again, fuck that. No! Stop beggin'." Noah hung up on her and put his phone on the bar. He looked at Lucas in exasperation. "What the fuck's wrong with her, Luke? I told her, she straight up blew whatever shot she had with me when she lied about the baby. She's tryin' to get me over there so I can have a weak moment and give her another one. She must think I'm stupid, Luke, for real."

"I think they all think we're stupid, No," Lucas said. He was talking to Noah, but his eyes were on the bartender. She'd been flirting with him outrageously since he'd sat down. Talking suggestively and doing little things to make him look at her. Lucas didn't mind flirting back, but he wasn't harboring any serious thoughts of getting with her. Some women were cop groupies. That's probably why she worked here.

She made her way back over to their side or the bar, with two more buttons undone on her shirt, swinging her ass from side to side. "You guys good over here, or do you need me to get you something?"

Noah looked at Lucas and he nodded. "One more time, sweetie."

She smiled and winked. "No problem, sugar. This round's free."

Lucas laughed. "It's been a long time since somebody sent us a free round. Whose it from? *You?*"

She put her elbows on the bar and leaned forward, giving them both a nice view of her cleavage. "If I bought you two guys drinks … what would you be willing to do for me?"

Lucas sat back and smiled. He looked at his boy. Noah grinned charmingly and raised an eyebrow. "You askin' for a threesome, honey?" He asked, leaning forward, too, and checking out her breasts, devilishly.

She blushed and stood her ground. "Sounds like a pretty good idea."

Whore, Lucas thought and wondered for a second if he'd said it out loud. He held onto his smile and let Noah do the talking.

"Thanks for the offer, sweetie, but we're gonna have to pass. See, I got no desire to see my boy here naked, and I'm sure he feels the same. Besides, he just became a card carryin' member of the He-Man Woman Hater's Club."

She smiled gamely, but her disappointment seemed real. "Some other time?'

Lucas and Noah both kept smiling, but they looked at each other as if to ask, *'Is she serious?'* Lucas spoke first. "I don't think we'll be changin' our minds, love … but thanks for the offer."

She smirked. "Your loss, fellas." She pointed down the length of the bar. "The guy in the dark blue T-shirt sent your drinks. Let me know if you need me," she said and walked away with a final smile.

"What's somebody sendin' us drinks for? And a dude, at that," Noah asked, sipping his new drink.

Lucas watched the bartender make her way back to the guy. He shrugged, indifferently. "Who knows? Probably a rookie. You know how they are." It might have sounded conceited, but it was a true statement. Rookies usually acted like star struck teenagers around them.

Noah sighed. "Oh, God. He's comin' over here. Look at him grinnin'."

Lucas laughed and hit him in the arm. "Shut up, Noah. Be nice."

Noah grumbled something Lucas didn't catch. He was too busy watching this guy make his way around the crowded bar to where they were sitting. He stopped a couple of times to say hello to some people. Something about him seemed vaguely familiar to Lucas. He was a nice looking guy — so much so it made him stand out.

He was tall — somewhere around Lucas's own height; his skin, a smooth and even chestnut brown. He wasn't a muscle bound guy, but he looked like he put in his time at the gym. He was dressed in that plain T-shirt and a faded, but stylish, pair of Seven jeans. He smiled and shook someone's hand and Lucas stood up, frowning.

Noah stood, too, looking at Lucas like he was ready if some shit jumped off. "What's the matter, Luke? Somethin' not cool about this guy?"

Lucas was glad to know Noah always had his back, but he didn't think it was that type of party. He didn't detect any bad vibes and this man was obviously a cop. He didn't seem to be approaching them sideways, like he had a beef. It was something else. Lucas had excellent radar and he felt like it was in overdrive.

"Nah, Noah," he said, shaking his head. "I feel like I know this guy. I just can't remember where I know him from."

Noah sipped his drink and nodded toward him. "Well, shit, ask him. Here he is."

This kid was grinning an enormously big grin as he walked up to them. He had a light moustache and goatee, like hair had only recently started growing there thick enough to keep it. His smile was white and perfect ... and he had dimples. He stuck his hand out to Lucas like he could barely contain himself.

"He's a newbie. Be careful, I think he's gonna piss his pants," Noah said quietly, with a smile in his voice.

"Wow!" he exclaimed. Lucas shook his hand and noticed his grip was strong, but a little shaky, like he was very nervous. "I can't believe it's really fuckin' *you*."

"Oh, Christ!" Noah snickered, behind him.

"I guess so," Lucas said. "Thanks for the drink."

He smiled and let go of Lucas's hand. "Thanks for acceptin.'" He looked around Lucas at Noah and reached for his hand. "Hey. Hey, Noah. Wow."

"Hey, how you doin'," Noah said it facetiously, as he shook his hand. Again, Lucas didn't really hear what Noah said. He was too busy looking at this kid. There was something about him. Something about his eyes.

"Good. I'm good." He was talking to Noah, but he was looking at Lucas. "I can't believe it's you." He touched Lucas's arm like he was trying to make sure he was real.

Lucas stepped back out of his reach. He was frowning, but not in anger. He was frowning because this guy's familiarity was, naggingly, just out of his grasp. Like something on the tip of his tongue.

"I heard about you my whole life," he continued.

Noah nudged Lucas and whispered, "This dude is weird. Let's find out what he wants and send him on his way."

"Nah, it's cool," Lucas said over his shoulder. He turned his attention back to the man in front of him. "Your whole life? What are you? 26?"

He nodded, still smiling. Yeah, Lucas. I'm 26."

"Oh shit, Luke," Noah said in quiet shock. He got it just before Lucas did, but it hit him all at once. Those eyes. Holy shit. They looked familiar to him because they were very much like his own. Big chocolate eyes with long ass eyelashes. Delilah's eyes. Oh shit.

Lucas's mouth dropped open. He never thought this would happen. "Myles?"

"Yeah, it's me, Lucas. Your brother, Myles."

"I'll be damned," Noah said, and tossed back the rest of his drink.